BETH LINCOLN

THE SWIFTS

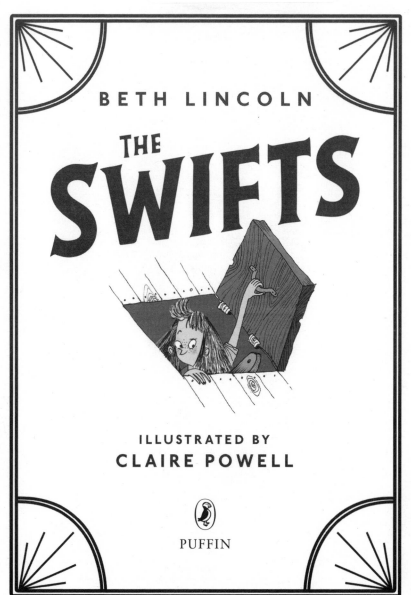

ILLUSTRATED BY
CLAIRE POWELL

PUFFIN

PUFFIN BOOKS

UK | USA | Canada | Ireland | Australia
India | New Zealand | South Africa

Puffin Books is part of the Penguin Random House group of companies
whose addresses can be found at global.penguinrandomhouse.com.

www.penguin.co.uk
www.puffin.co.uk
www.ladybird.co.uk

First published 2023
This paperback edition published 2024

001

Typeset by Jouve (UK), Milton Keynes
Printed and bound in Great Britain by Clays Ltd, Elcograf S.p.A.

The authorized representative in the EEA is Penguin Random House Ireland,
Morrison Chambers, 32 Nassau Street, Dublin D02 YH68

A CIP catalogue record for this book is available from the British Library

Paperback ISBN: 978-0-241-53645-2

All correspondence to:
Puffin Books
Penguin Random House Children's
One Embassy Gardens, 8 Viaduct Gardens, London SW11 7BW

MIX
Paper | Supporting
responsible forestry
FSC
www.fsc.org   FSC® C018179

Penguin Random House is committed to a
sustainable future for our business, our readers
and our planet. This book is made from Forest
Stewardship Council® certified paper.

For my family,
in blood and in bond

CONTENTS

PART ONE

PART TWO

PART THREE

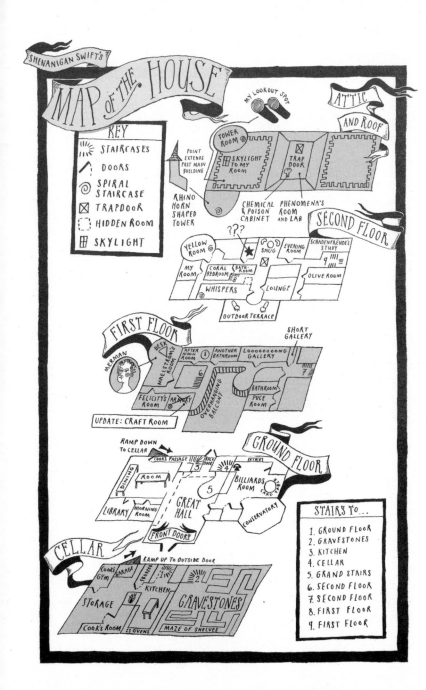

AN UNEXPECTED INHERITANCE

It was a bright, well-dressed morning in early May, and the Swifts were in the middle of a funeral.

The House looked very fine. The lawns had been swept clean of leaves, the hedge maze had been trimmed, and the statues had been scrubbed behind the ears. The Family had spent the morning practising their eulogies in front of a mirror, and now they walked in slow procession through the cemetery, faces professionally grim.

According to Arch-Aunt Schadenfreude, a funeral ought to look like a wedding upside down. The Swifts had done their best to honour her wishes. The path to Aunt Schadenfreude's grave frothed with flowers, and the trees dripped black ribbon. Cook had even baked a sombre cake with black icing, set on a table just to

3

the left of the headstone. To the right, a gramophone coughed out a melancholy tune.

Shenanigan Swift was carrying the front end of the coffin. She was considerably shorter than the other pall-bearers. At the back, her eldest sister Felicity gangled and her Uncle Maelstrom loomed, and although Shenanigan was doing her best to keep the coffin steady, it still tilted forward at a worrying angle. Phenomena, ahead of the procession and guiding her sisters through the cemetery like an air-traffic controller, shot her a wary look. Shenanigan tried to think herself taller, with limited success.

They wound between the graves like black floss through crooked teeth. Shenanigan read the names of her late family as they trudged past:

Calamitous Swift

1598–1652

Adjective

Causing, or fraught with, disaster

and

Godwottery Swift

1733–1790

Noun

i. Overly elaborate gardening or garden design

ii. Old-fashioned and affected language

She shifted the weight of the coffin, and it lurched alarmingly. Felicity hissed, so Shenanigan wobbled it again, just to annoy her. Her hand left a smear on the expensive, highly polished wood. Her aunt wouldn't have liked that – Aunt Schadenfreude believed you should spend more on a coffin than you would on a house, since you spent more time dead than alive – but then Aunt Schadenfreude wouldn't have liked a lot of things. Like the scuffs on Shenanigan's shoes, or the twigs in her hair, or the thoughts in her head.

To her right, Shenanigan read:

Faultress Swift
1860–1889
Noun
A female offender or criminal

Shenanigan probably would have got on with her.

They halted before the grave, and there was a flurry of confusion as each Swift lowered the coffin at a different speed. Maelstrom tried to set his end down slowly, with dignity, but Felicity was a bit too fast, and Shenanigan was still thinking about being a *faultress* and not paying attention.

'Shenanigan,' Felicity hissed again, 'can you *please*—'

The thing inside the coffin let out a yowl.

Felicity cried out and dropped her side. With a dull *thunk*, the head-end of the coffin hit the grass, teetered, and tipped over into the grave, the lid flying off as it went. Shenanigan leapt out of its path and straight into the black-frosted cake, her outstretched palms scooping up damp, vanilla-scented handfuls.

There was silence, but for the gramophone's wheeze. The Swifts peered cautiously into the grave.

The coffin lay wide open, revealing a gleam of black silk warming in the sun. Of course, there was no one in it – only John the Cat, who blinked sleepily, gave a luxuriant stretch, and trotted off in the direction of the woods. Shenanigan licked cake off her hands.

'Well,' called a voice behind them. 'That was an appalling rehearsal, I must say.'

The troupe turned guiltily towards Aunt Schadenfreude, perched on Vile's Monument. She had her walking stick in one hand and her opera glasses in the other, and she was peering through these at the mess they'd made of her final resting place.

'It'll be alright on the night, Auntie!' Uncle Maelstrom rolled his shoulders, his joints creaking like an old ship. He picked Shenanigan up with one hand, dodged her attempt to smear icing into his beard, and set her on her feet, grinning.

'Alright on the *morning* – you're burying me at eleven.' Aunt Schadenfreude grumbled towards them, tightening the thick iron collar round her throat. 'You are to have me in the ground by twelve, finish crying by half past, then head back to the House for a lunch you will all be too distraught to eat at a quarter to one. *That* is the schedule. You do not fill me with confidence, Maelstrom.'

Aunt Schadenfreude's life was highly organized. She expected her death to be the same. Since she would not be around to oversee her own funeral, she'd had the Family rehearse the ceremony every month for as long as Shenanigan could remember. They had never managed to get everything right.

'Shenanigan, Felicity, try to keep the coffin level next time. It looked like you were carrying me downhill.'

'It's *hard*, though, when Uncle Maelstrom's so much taller than us!' whined Felicity.

'Given the average rate of adolescent growth, we should be a bit taller by the time Aunt Schadenfreude dies,' Phenomena pointed out. She dabbed at the splattered icing on her lab coat. 'That should balance things.'

'Rank optimism!' snorted Aunt Schadenfreude. 'I could drop dead before you grow another inch. Felicity, the decorations will do, I suppose. A few more bows. As for Shenanigan . . .'

Shenanigan paused in her licking.

'I'm assuming *you* put John in there?'

Shenanigan shrugged. 'Cats like boxes.'

'Could you please wait until I'm *in* my grave before you desecrate it?'

This remark seemed very unfair to Shenanigan, who thought she'd improved a great deal. Last month, she'd got the coffin stuck in the front door and the whole Family had to limbo their way in and out of the House for several days.

Her aunt's sour expression mirrored her own. 'Well, you can't help your name, I suppose.' She sighed. 'We shall break for lunch. We still have to clean this up before tomorrow.'

With this dismissal, they trooped back to the House. Shenanigan ran a hand over the headstones they passed, reading the names. *Rubric. Catharsis. Endeavour. Ilk.*

You can't help your name.

She shook off the irritation that came with Aunt Schadenfreude's well-worn phrase. Nothing could annoy her today.

Today was the day before tomorrow, and *tomorrow* she was going to steal her Family's fortune.

'Watch where you're *going*,' Felicity snapped, as Shenanigan leapfrogged over a gravestone and into her path. 'How do you always manage to get underfoot?'

'Maybe 'cause your feet are so massive. Hard to avoid them, really.'

'My feet aren't massive! You're just small. It's like trying to keep an eye on an ant.'

Shenanigan started making clicking sounds, and lunged at her sister with her hands formed into pincers. Felicity recoiled.

'Ugh, you're so *weird*,' she groaned. She used her much longer legs to stalk away from Shenanigan.

'You shouldn't antagonize her, you know.'

Phenomena adjusted her glasses and gave Shenanigan a knowing look. Phenomena was a scientist, so all her looks were knowing. 'Don't forget what happened to your catapult.'

'Never,' said Shenanigan. She'd *tried* to explain that she hadn't been aiming at Felicity at all, but neither Schadenfreude nor Felicity had listened. Now the Siegemaster 5000 was ashes in Cook's furnace and Shenanigan had sworn her revenge. For starters, when she found the treasure, she would not be giving Felicity any of it.

As they drew close to the House, Shenanigan noticed two unusual things. The first was that there was a car in the driveway: sleek, low-slung, bottle-green, with a nose like a barracuda. It was pointing at the front door as if it was holding it hostage. The second was that Cook was coming towards them at a dead sprint. She had a smear of oil on one cheek – she must have been working on her motorbike – and her arms and legs pumped furiously. She skidded to a stop in a shower of gravel.

'She's here,' she panted.

Shenanigan gave a whoop of excitement and raced off in the direction of the House, leaving her Family in the dust.

As she ran she mentally went through the contents of the pack she kept ready on the roof. She had rope, a torch, lock picks, a trowel, paper and pencils, a letter opener, binoculars, a packet of biscuits, and a bottle of water in case she became trapped somewhere in the House. Her relatives would probably come better prepared. She wondered if Phenomena had bothered to build the metal detector she'd asked for.

At first, in the gloom of the hall, Shenanigan could only see a pair of white-gloved hands. When her eyes adjusted, she could make out the rest of the woman. She was almost as pale as her gloves, with skin like an apple that had been left in the fruit bowl for one too many days, dull and loose-looking. It made it difficult to guess her age. She was wearing a tweed suit, and had frizzy hair of a doubtful colour, inexpertly pinned back. As she turned towards Shenanigan, her little round glasses flashed.

'Matriarch!' she intoned. 'The time has come again! We – oh.'

She blinked at Shenanigan, who, remembering her manners, was walking towards her with her palm outstretched. The woman took one look at Shenanigan's hands, covered in cake and grave dirt, and put both of her own behind her back as if she was being offered a dead rat.

In the awkward pause that followed, the rest of Shenanigan's family caught up. Uncle Maelstrom sailed in under a pile of what must have been the woman's luggage: two battered suitcases of the kind people call 'valises', a hatbox, and several long leather tubes lashed together. Shenanigan's mind immediately ran riot over what could be in those tubes. *Telescopes? Stolen art?* She had recently read about a very long wooden instrument called a didgeridoo that was played in Australia. Maybe their guest was Australian?

When the woman spoke again, it was very clear she was not Australian. She had an accent that came from an English university and a voice that was used to libraries.

'Ah, there you are, Matriarch,' she said with some relief, nodding to Aunt Schadenfreude. 'And Maelstrom too I see! The time has come again! Once more, we gather—'

'*Inheritance,*' Aunt Schadenfreude interrupted. 'You were supposed to arrive tomorrow.'

Inheritance's nodding increased in speed and enthusiasm. 'Yes, yes, *but*, as I said in my letter, we have a matter of *great* importance to discuss—'

'I did not,' said Aunt Schadenfreude, with the tone of someone who found excuses personally offensive, 'receive a letter.'

'Oh.' Inheritance stilled. 'But . . . I sent it a week ago, with the rest of the invitations.'

The Family all groaned in understanding. Aunt Schadenfreude distrusted anyone in a uniform, be they police officers, soldiers, members of a marching band, sales assistants, schoolchildren, firefighters, or chefs. Postal workers were no exception. The only one permitted near the House was a local postie named Suleiman, and he'd had the flu for the past two weeks.

'Well, I suppose you're here now,' allowed Aunt Schadenfreude, 'and there's little we can do. Girls, this is your Aunt Inheritance. Inheritance, these are the girls: Felicity, Phenomena, and Shenanigan, in order of descending age and rising inconvenience.'

'Pleased to, ah, meet you,' Inheritance said.

This was a lie, Shenanigan knew. A lie is a mischievous thing with a life of its own, and no matter how hard you try to keep it hidden, it will surface on your face, or through your hands, or in the way you shift from one leg to another. Shenanigan had always been good at spotting them, and this one was hovering just underneath her aunt's left eye. Though she had been waiting for Inheritance's arrival for weeks, something about her made Shenanigan take an instant dislike – maybe it was her watery eyes, or her white gloves, or the way she was looking at Shenanigan as if she was something she'd found going mouldy in the back of a cupboard.

'And you're important?' Shenanigan asked doubtfully. She heard Maelstrom swallow a chuckle.

Aunt Inheritance drew herself up. 'I *am*,' she said, 'the *Archivist*. It's my job – no, my *calling* –' her white hands fluttered to her chest, and her eyes grew glassy with emotion – 'my *duty*, my – my *privilege*, to record the lives of the Swifts for posterity. I keep our Family history, I chronicle our legacy, I maintain our customs—'

Aunt Schadenfreude cleared her throat.

'Speaking of which, Inheritance, if you could get on with it. Briefly, mind,' she warned, seeming to sense another speech.

'Yes. I have an experiment waiting in my lab, and it's very time-sensitive,' said Phenomena.

'And I need to figure out what to wear tomorrow,' added Felicity.

'And I need my lunch,' said Aunt Schadenfreude.

Aunt Inheritance looked scandalized. 'Schadenfreude, this is Phenomena's and Shenanigan's first time! Tradition is everything!'

'Well, tradition doesn't have a mushroom omelette waiting for it in the kitchen.'

Aunt Inheritance's mouth puckered in disapproval. For a moment she looked as if she wanted to scold Aunt Schadenfreude but had wisely realized she might not survive the experience.

'*The time has come again,*' she intoned through gritted teeth. '*Once more, we gather.* I, Inheritance Swift, Archivist, having consulted my books, and interpreted the signs, and checked everyone's availability, hereby call the Swift Family Reunion. We return to the House of our House, to strengthen our bonds, to keep the peace between us, and to search for our lost fortune – as we have done for decades hitherto, and will do for decades hence, for as long as our names are spoken. Matriarch Schadenfreude, are we welcome?'

'Hm? Oh, I suppose so.'

'Then it is done!' Inheritance threw her arms wide. 'The Reunion is officially underway!'

Back in the old tights-and-doublets days of the Swift family, every child had been named either Mary or John. It got terribly confusing at dinner time when someone asked a John to pass the potatoes and ten hands shot out at once, and so Mary Swift XXXV had begun the tradition of naming her children using the Family Dictionary. The idea stuck, and the Swifts prospered. People often overlook a Mary or a John, but they seldom forget a person named Meretricious or Flinch.

Shenanigan couldn't remember the day she was born, but she could picture it very well: the hospital room, the nurses, her mother, tired and smiling as Shenanigan's father fussed over her pillows. She pictured herself too, wrapped up like a little peanut with a shock of disobedient hair already erupting out of her head.

She pictured the Dictionary – and this part was easier, because she was looking at it – an ancient, leather-bound monster of a book, bursting its bindings with pages of calfskin and parchment and paper, with entries in crisp modern fonts, wonky typewritten letters, and hand-scrawled script with long S's that looked like F's.

The Dictionary would have been brought in, set on the bed (Shenanigan pictured the nurses' noses wrinkling in distaste) and opened at random by Shenanigan's mother. Her eyes would have been closed. She would have run her finger down the page and stopped on the word and definition that would become her child's name.

Shenanigan could picture this so well because every Swift's first day began in exactly the same way. The only exception, as far as she knew, was Arch-Aunt Schadenfreude. She'd been born five weeks early on a Family trip to Germany, and her parents had had to make do with what was available.

Felicity dashed off upstairs before Aunt Inheritance had finished speaking, Aunt Schadenfreude was immediately embroiled in a menu discussion with Cook, and Maelstrom began to inspect the fountain-pen attachment of his penknife. Finding herself roundly ignored, Aunt

Inheritance approached the great glass case that housed the Dictionary. It was open at the title page.

'Illuminated' has two definitions, one being 'lit up' and the other 'decorated with intricate, coloured designs', and this page was both. The illuminated illuminated page had a dedication printed in complicated letters:

The
Dictionary
of the House of
Swift

Aunt Inheritance stepped forward until her nose was almost touching the case. She took out a small key from a chain round her neck. Carefully, reverently, she unlocked the door, and with trembling, white-gloved fingers reached out to touch a yellowed page.

From the floor above there came a sound like someone riffling through the pages of a large book, and a rising shriek, and then Felicity barrelled on to the landing. Behind her, pursuing her fleeing figure down the length of the grand staircase, were the moths.

Shenanigan smiled.

A few days after the Siegemaster 5000's destruction, Shenanigan had picked up the post from Suleiman. Addressed to her had been a small square package with holes poked in the top, and inside were dozens of caterpillars she had ordered from an advert at the back of a wildlife magazine. Shenanigan had crawled into Felicity's cavernous wardrobe, opened the box, and let the caterpillars feast on Felicity's clothes. They had chewed through wool and silk and cotton, growing fat and sleepy, spinning their cocoons inside the warm, dry, dark space.

Now it seemed the cocoons had hatched.

Shenanigan wished she had been there for the moment Felicity had opened her wardrobe to see the moths glaring back at her. Each velvet body was the size of Shenanigan's palm, with two enormous yellow eyes on the wings that were supposed to fool predators.

They moved in a furiously blinking whirlwind towards the chandelier, scattering dust. Their wings brushed Shenanigan's face. She thought it was rather nice – like being in the centre of a soft tornado – but, judging from the way her aunt was howling and batting at her hair, Inheritance disagreed. One of the moths, lured by the

light illuminating the Dictionary, had ⌐
case. When Aunt Inheritance saw it, sh
someone was holding a match to the N

Amid the noise and chaos, Phenomen
off the light switch. Confused, the mo   ──ιcu –
some further into the House, but most through the
open door and out into the noonday sun to terrify
the local birds.

Shenanigan burst out laughing.

Felicity spun round, her eyes bright and wet and
utterly furious.

'Look what you did!' she shrieked, holding up a scrap
of blue silk. It might once have been a dress, but the
moths had chewed so many holes that now it could
have been a swimsuit for an octopus. The sight only
made Shenanigan laugh harder.

'My clothes are ruined!' cried Felicity. 'I made half of
them myself!'

'Well, it serves you right!'

'Shenanigan!' Cook's leather jacket creaked as
she crossed her arms. Her expression was stern,
and Shenanigan's stomach shrank. She looked to
Maelstrom, her staunch ally. His disappointment was
even worse.

_r Felicity started it!'

_ou little beast! How would you like it if I destroyed something *you'd* made?' Felicity cried.

Shenanigan's stomach made a miraculous recovery. 'You did! That's for the Siegemaster 5000, you—'

'Your stupid *catapult*? You made it in an afternoon! Some of those clothes took me *weeks*!'

'It wasn't stupid! It was—'

Crack.

They fell silent at the sound of Aunt Schadenfreude's stick hitting the banister. Her eyes pinned Shenanigan in place. She felt like she was one of Felicity's moths, stuck in a display case.

'Inheritance, are you alright?'

Aunt Inheritance was still brushing imaginary moths out of her hair. There was dust on her previously white gloves. 'Yes . . . Yes, I think so.'

'Shenanigan,' growled Schadenfreude, 'apologize to your aunt.'

'I'm sorry,' said Shenanigan promptly. 'I don't have a problem with you yet.'

'Good. And to your sister,' said Aunt Schadenfreude.

'No.'

Aunt Schadenfreude glared at Shenanigan. Shenanigan glared at her aunt. She squared her shoulders, and got ready to kick and scream and shout.

But Aunt Schadenfreude only shrugged.

'Very well,' she said.

Felicity's mouth dropped open.

'*What?*' she cried. 'You're just going to let her off?'

'Oh, she'll be punished, of course,' said Aunt Schadenfreude, shooting a grim look at Shenanigan, who'd been doing a very small victory dance. 'But I doubt it will have much effect. It's who she is. She can't help her name.'

'That's not an excuse!'

'But it is a reason.' Aunt Inheritance clapped her hands together to rid them of some of the dust. 'The Dictionary has enormous power, after all. She wouldn't be called Shenanigan if the name didn't fit.'

Shenanigan frowned. She passed the Dictionary every day. It was just a normal book – a bit too big to read in the bath, but a book all the same.

'What d'you mean?' she asked warily.

'It named me Inheritance, knowing that I would be keeper of the Family records. It named your Uncle

Maelstrom, foreseeing his seafaring future. And it named you Shenanigan, knowing that you would cause trouble.'

Phenomena made a sceptical noise. 'So you're saying the Dictionary is *magic*?'

'No,' sobbed Felicity. 'They're saying that I'm just supposed to *put up with her!*' And she tore upstairs, weeping into her scrap of silk.

Shenanigan refused to feel guilty. Felicity would be fine in a few days. It was only a couple of dresses, after all. They couldn't have taken her *that* long to make.

'Poor Felicity. It's not her fault her name is mundane,' sighed Aunt Inheritance. She meant that Felicity's name, like Prudence, August, Rose, and Bill, was perfectly normal in non-Swift society. 'Such members of the Family always live perfectly boring, perfectly average lives. Why, I remember Arch-Aunt Hope! Lovely woman, but she tragically became an optometrist . . . which reminds me . . .' Her little round glasses flashed at Aunt Schadenfreude. 'About that matter I wished to discuss—'

Elsewhere in the House, there was a muffled *boom*.

'I told you the experiment was time-sensitive.' Phenomena sighed, and trudged off to see what had exploded.

3
MAPPING
THE
INTERIOR

If Swift House had ever been put on the market, the advertisement would probably have read as follows:

FOR SALE

Charming and quirky seventeenth-century manor house. Original building established 1602, with later additions. Strong personality, with plenty of character! Beautifully situated in an isolated location, far from earshot of the nearest village – perfect for anyone wanting to get away from it all! Some love needed.

To translate: the House was a massive, three-floor breadbox of a building on to which extensions had been stuck over the years like old bits of chewing gum. An east and west wing had sprouted a century after the original building was constructed. The Victorians had glued a conservatory to the rear. For reasons no one understood, Arch-Uncle Fustian had also stuck a turret on one end, so that, with its boxy outline and unexpected tower, the House now rather resembled the head of a rhinoceros.

Once upon a time, the Swifts had been rich and, despite its odd shape, the House had always had fresh paint and clean gutters. But the House, like its owners, had come down in the world and let in the rack and ruin. Mould and dust and shabbiness ruled. Mice, birds, and bats held their own obscure kingdoms in forgotten corners. The overall effect wasn't ugly exactly, but it was certainly only pretty if you tilted your head a bit and squinted.

Shenanigan loved the House, but she'd been trying to break out of it since she could stay on two legs for more than a minute at a time. It was expected of her, what with her name. Aunt Schadenfreude tried her best to stop her great-niece roaming the grounds at all hours of the night, but, luckily for Shenanigan, the Swifts hadn't just made changes to the outside of the building; successive generations had burrowed through the inside of the House like mice through a mattress, carving out secret passages, popping the eyes out of paintings to make spyholes, adding false walls to cupboards, and even throwing in the odd trapdoor. Shenanigan had found three secret ways out, and Aunt Schadenfreude had only managed to block off two.

Since few of these additions appeared on any plans of the House, its occupants lived in a state of mild peril. For instance, it was reckoned that a quarter of the books in the library were not books at all, but triggers for secret, sometimes lethal, traps. Arch-Cousin Lectern had found this out the hard way after a volume of Edgar Allan Poe stories dropped him into a pit.

The Swift children were taught to be careful what they read.

That afternoon, Shenanigan found herself drafted into the House-cleaning crusade, and so strapped on her shin pads. Cook's preparations for the Reunion involved marching about, bristling with feather dusters and smelling strongly of polish. Phenomena and Felicity were her other reluctant foot soldiers, and while Cook lifted sofas and tables one-handed (she was remarkably strong, with biceps like three ham hocks lashed together), the girls scurried underneath with dustpans, catching tumbleweeds of fluff and hair. Uncle

Maelstrom helped too, lifting Shenanigan up to rescue spiders in high corners.

Shenanigan wouldn't have minded the work if it wasn't for Aunt Inheritance. As a guest, she was excused from cleaning, but she very quickly began to infest the House. Every time Shenanigan turned round, she saw Inheritance's halo of no-colour hair bent over some knick-knack or other, as she lectured the others on its history. It was as if someone had added a new piece of furniture to the House and everyone kept tripping over it.

'Oh marvellous!' cried Inheritance, picking up an object from the mantle. 'This is engraved with the initials A. S., and a black lily . . . the personal signifier of Augury Swift! She emigrated to Spain in the sixteenth century and predicted the storms that destroyed the Spanish Armada – only she didn't speak Spanish, so old King Philip didn't listen. This is a key piece of Family history!'

'It's an air freshener,' Cook whispered to Uncle Maelstrom, who let out a noise that on a smaller person would have been a giggle. Inheritance looked round suspiciously. Her gaze settled on Shenanigan, who was perched on Maelstrom's shoulder and trying to look innocent.

'Hm. Wise to keep *her* occupied,' Inheritance remarked with a conspiratorial smile at Cook.

Cook frowned. 'What do you mean?'

'Well, it can't be easy running around after someone called Shenanigan.' She patted Cook kindly on the shoulder. 'With a name like that you'll have to keep an eye on her. Who knows what she'll grow into!'

Inheritance's smile wasn't cruel, but, nevertheless, Shenanigan felt a small sting inside. Felicity snorted from where she was polishing a sideboard. Cook weighed her feather duster in her hand, as if checking its suitability as a weapon. Uncle Maelstrom moved between her and Aunt Inheritance like an iceberg drifting between two battleships.

'Tell you what, why don't I tell the story of the Hoard as we go along?' he rumbled. 'I'm sure you'll keep me right, Inheritance.'

The girls perked up. Uncle Maelstrom was by far the best storyteller in the Family. They had each, at some time or other, pretended to be ill so he would sit by their bed and read to them. He always did voices.

Aunt Inheritance gave a dignified nod, and gestured for him to proceed.

'This is an old tale,' Maelstrom rumbled, 'almost as old as the Swift family itself, told so many times that it's as worn and well-used as the Dictionary.

'Long ago, when the Swifts were freshly named and the House freshly built, Mazzard Swift, the head of the Family, died. He left behind a small fortune, divided equally in three: a third each to his two sons, Gramercy and Vile, and the final third to his only daughter, Cantrip—'

'Who moved to Denmark after becoming obsessed with *Hamlet*,' interrupted Inheritance. 'Actually, her story is *fascinating*—'

Cook shushed her.

'As you say, Cantrip went out into the world, leaving the House to her brothers. Gramercy, the elder son, moved into the west wing –' Maelstrom swept a hand to the west, swinging a giggling Shenanigan around like she was perched on a yard-arm – 'and Vile, the younger, moved into the east. Now, these two brothers were like chalk and cheese. Gramercy was a decent man – as decent as a rich man can be, anyway – and he was a philanthropist, which means, girls, that he spent a lot of his money on orphanages and the like. But Vile . . .' Maelstrom shook his head with a hum of disapproval, as if he'd known Vile personally. 'He loved gold so much that if he'd found a buyer for his father's bones, he'd have dug up the grave himself, and he had big plans for his share of the fortune. He invested every penny of his share in businesses: mining, trading, industry, and it still wasn't enough. Vile was furious with the way his brother was wasting money, as he saw it. "Let me have your share," he said, "and I'll make us rich as kings." The brothers quarrelled day and night. Then one day Gramercy was found dead in the garden, an axe in his back.'

Uncle Maelstrom paused for effect.

'Vile was never arrested, and never tried. But he killed his brother, Gramercy, as sure as the sky is blue, as sure as water's wet, as sure as I'm standing here.'

Shenanigan always got the shivers at that bit. There were portraits of Vile in the House still. One large painting in the hall showed Mazzard with his three children standing in the shade of a huge oak tree that had once dominated the front lawn. Shenanigan had stared at the young Vile's face for hours, trying to see the murderer in it.

'Gramercy had left some money for his wife and daughter, but with no other male heir (which in those days seemed very important) everything else went to Vile – including Gramercy's half of the House. Vile's wealth grew and grew. He became a merchant, then a gentleman, then a lord. He married off his niece as quickly as he could, and sent her husband abroad. He built the monument to himself in the garden, supposedly right on the spot where he murdered Gramercy.

'But Vile's fear grew with his wealth. He became terrified of other members of the Family, and *especially* terrified that one of them would come along and rob him, the way he'd robbed his brother. He withdrew all his funds from the bank, and with it he bought gold, silver, jewels – all the riches he could get his hands on. He amassed a dragon's hoard of treasure and, like a dragon, lived atop it, because he never left the Swift estate again. He shut himself away, admitted no visitors, and communicated only by letter. When he finally died, it was a week before anyone dared to fetch his body.'

'By which time he would have been squishy,' added Shenanigan with morbid delight. 'His eyes would have collapsed inside his head, and he'd have started to swell up, and the rats—'

'Yes, alright,' said Aunt Inheritance queasily. 'I don't think we need to be *that* gleeful about the death of a relative.'

'When poor Cantrip learned of her brothers' deaths, her grief was terrible. She returned to England, and to the House she had inherited. Vile's actions had divided and scattered the Family, but Cantrip was clever – to draw them together again, she invited every living Swift to come to the House and hunt for the missing fortune. This was the first Reunion, and she the first Matriarch.'

'And the treasure?' prompted Shenanigan.

'The Family searched high and low at that Reunion, and at every Reunion thereafter,' recited Maelstrom, building to his final flourish, *'but no trace of Vile's Hoard has ever been found.'*

Maelstrom paused, until the silence rang. Then he clapped his hands, and Inheritance jumped. 'And so the story goes, and so the story's done.'

'Well told!' beamed Inheritance. Seemingly unable to help herself, she added, 'Though, of course, it's no substitute for the play Cantrip herself wrote, *The Tragical Tale of Gramercy and Vile*. Cousin Thespian is going to perform it on Saturday. And then the play isn't *nearly* as thrilling as the Family's old housekeeping books and tax records . . .'

As Inheritance began a lecture on the bookkeeping of centuries past, Shenanigan slid off Uncle Maelstrom's shoulder. He pretended not to notice. She slipped away through a passage behind a suit of armour to work on her secret project.

A year ago, Shenanigan had begun her map. It was a bold attempt to mark down every concealed nook, every hidden pathway, every hiding spot in the House. Most people would have said it was impossible, but Shenanigan wasn't most people. She had just the mix of stubbornness and curiosity that either rediscovered lost cities or landed a person in prison. Learning new escape routes had proved useful, yes, but *really* she was always looking for the lost Swift fortune, Vile's Hoard, hidden somewhere on the estate by Grand-Uncle Vile himself.

Shenanigan had plans for that treasure. They changed and shifted according to her mood, but always involved adventure. If one of her relatives turned up and found it before her, she was sure she would burst into flames of pure jealousy and die on the spot.

John the Cat sauntered past, carrying a dead moth the

size of a pigeon. Shenanigan idly scratched him behind the ears. She had already marked most of the hidden rooms and passages on the map, and now her focus was on suspicious paintings. In mystery stories, the secret wall safe or old treasure map was usually found behind the strangest, ugliest painting in the room and, since detective novels were some of the only books in the library *not* booby-trapped (they were considered educational), many Swifts had copied this idea when creating their own hiding places. The result was a house full of bad art.

On the back of the map, Shenanigan had listed her discoveries as she worked her way down through the House:

SUSPICIOUS PAINTINGS ON THE SECOND FLOOR

CORAL BEDROOM:

Pondscum (watercolour): wall safe, broken lock, empty

A Clown Laments His Lot in Life (oil on canvas): nothing

Sardine Cannery at Sunset (oil on wood): loose brick, contains old diary (boring)

Monkey on a Rocking Horse (pencil sketch): peephole into adjoining bathroom

BATHROOM:

The Sea on a Drizzly Day (pastels): nothing
Mermaid Eating a Hot Dog (watercolour): peephole
   into adjoining bedroom

SECOND-FLOOR CORRIDOR:

Still Life of a Bowl of Pistachios (pastels): one red
   button – DO NOT PRESS!
The Sour-faced Duchess (oil on canvas): wall safe,
   left open, contains mouldy remains of sandwich
A Study in Ink (ink on paper): message in what
   looks like red paint (?), illegible
Nun Picking Her Nose (oil on canvas): laundry chute

So nothing unusual yet.

Shenanigan leaned back against the wall, fished half a browning apple from the depths of her pocket, and considered her next move. On the floor below, she could hear Felicity trilling a song in French as she dusted. On the ground floor, Cook was calling out items to Phenomena as she prepared to do a last-minute grocery run. If Shenanigan hurried, she could make a start on the Chartreuse Room before anyone noticed she was missing.

She threw her apple core down the laundry chute behind *Nun Picking Her Nose*. Her hands were sticky, so she quickly wiped them on the wallpaper in the alcove behind her.

And paused.

Instead of wallpaper, Shenanigan felt the cool, slightly bumpy surface of oil paint on canvas. She took a closer look.

The alcove, she realized, wasn't an alcove at all, but an enormous floor-to-ceiling canvas painted to look exactly like an empty stretch of corridor. A slim crack ran round the edges where the painting had been set into the wall. She would never even have noticed if she hadn't rubbed her hands all over it.

Shenanigan's heart thudded. She dug the tips of her fingers into the tiny seam round the edge of the canvas, wishing for a brief moment that she had Felicity's nails. To her surprise, the painting swung outward easily, perfectly balanced on slim hinges. Behind the painting there was a door.

Shenanigan had been counting coins in her head before she even pulled back the painting, so it was a crushing blow to realize that the door had no handle or traditional keyhole, only a tiny, round hole at eye level, little more than the width of a toothpick. Like all decent explorers, Shenanigan carried a Swiss army knife, and, like all good escape artists, she also carried several paperclips to use on the tiniest locks. But though she picked and plied for several minutes, she could not get the door to open. Whoever had built the door had made it impenetrable to children, which is no mean feat.

Shenanigan may not have been able to get in, but this didn't mean she couldn't find anything out. First, she thumped hard on the door. Then she sprawled flat on the carpet and, pressing her nose to the crack between door and floor, sniffed mightily. After that, she pulled a mirror out of her pack and angled it *just so* beneath the door frame.

She now knew several things. Judging by the echo when she hit the door, the room was of a decent size. The air within was cool and dry and smelled like old books. The mirror had reflected only darkness, which told her there was probably no window.

Detective novels. The safest books in the library.

Shenanigan sat back and considered her next move. When you are faced with a problem, it can be very difficult to admit that doing nothing might be just as good as doing something. Shenanigan was a doing-something person, and walking away and leaving the door felt like defeat. Better to think of this not as walking away, she decided, but as regrouping for a second attack.

Shenanigan took out her pen. To her list of suspicious paintings, she added,

Floor-length Canvas, Camouflaged (oil on canvas): secret room????

Then she drew a large red question mark on the map of the second-floor corridor, on the spot where it told her there was nothing but a blank stretch of wall.

4

A Research Proposal

Dinner that night was a humble affair. Aunt Schadenfreude had chosen to eat in her room, and Maelstrom took to his bed early; he had run afoul of the stuffed deer in the taxidermy hall, and had been lightly gored by some falling antlers. His hands and arms – where his black skin was already richly dotted with scars from a lifetime of sailing mishaps – bore several new cuts. Shenanigan, who had no scars at all, was terribly jealous.

The remaining family members drooped around the kitchen table, exhausted from cleaning. Tragically, Inheritance wasn't in the least worn out. She sat steadily chewing on bits of Family history and steadily chattering over a single slice of bread. Shenanigan took the seat next to her with all the enthusiasm of a prisoner going to the guillotine. Cook gave her a sympathetic wink over her aunt's head, and mimed knocking her out with a ladle.

'Shenanigan! Hands!' cried Cook. 'Wash your hands first. And buck up! You girls have such long faces. You remind me of my first horse.'

Cook set a plate in front of Shenanigan, and slipped her an extra chunk of garlic bread.

'Rasputin was his name. Great big roan stallion, miserable as sin. Felicity, you look so like him I almost fed you a lump of sugar.'

Shenanigan had known Cook her whole life, and for a long time thought she was a distant cousin of some sort. It had been a great shock to learn that 'Cook' was not Cook's given name, and that she wasn't a Swift at all, but something called a Winifred. At first Shenanigan found this a great betrayal and refused to eat anything made by the hands of a traitor. But, after a week of living off hoarded biscuits and unripe fruits foraged from the orchard, she had rearranged some things in her brain and realized that Cook was not a traitor at all, but a great hero. Cook –Winifred – had not been born a Swift, yet she had come among them, taken a proper Swift name, and become a Swift by choice.

Cook rarely talked about her life before she'd come to live at the House, saying only that she had run away from home. Ruddy-cheeked and hard-jawed, she always spoke as if there was a marble in her mouth she was trying desperately not to swallow; she told Shenanigan she'd had something called 'electrocution lessons' as a child, and that was why she sounded so posh. Shenanigan thought it was pretty terrible to electrocute someone just to make them speak differently, and reasoned that was probably why Cook had run away.

Cook was family, even if she wasn't Family, and everyone in the House understood this – everyone, it seemed, except Aunt Inheritance, who was unable to grasp that Cook didn't work for them.

'Cook, for breakfast tomorrow I would like two boiled eggs, nice and runny,' said Inheritance.

'Would you?' said Cook mildly. 'Then we must show you how to work the stove. It can be a bit temperamental.'

A moment later, Inheritance noted, 'The Reunion must be a lot of work for you, Cook. Are you sure you can keep up?'

'It's very kind of you to worry, but we are more than capable.' Cook gestured to the bowls, trays, and pots crammed on the kitchen counter, the first line of defence against the Family's appetites. 'One's mettle is tested in times of trial – that's what I always say!'

And finally, as the girls were clearing away the plates, Inheritance rubbed at a smear on her glass and said: 'It does seem rather *odd* to have a House this size, and only one employee.'

The jar Cook was trying to open cracked in her hands.

'An employee?' She glanced around in mock surprise. 'I didn't know we'd hired anyone.'

Shenanigan got the feeling that conversations like this occurred at every Reunion. She also got the feeling she'd like to borrow Cook's ladle.

As the girls picked their way through dessert, Aunt Inheritance finally seemed to steel herself.

'Girls.' She folded her hands on the table. 'I can't help but feel that you are not treating the Reunion with the excitement it deserves.'

The girls looked at her blankly.

'Perhaps,' Inheritance tried again, 'your aunt has failed to impress upon you its *importance* to the Family.'

Shenanigan opened her mouth to say that of course she knew it was important – there was a massive pile of gold at stake – but Felicity jumped in.

'It's not that we don't want to see our relatives,' she said tactfully. At fourteen, she was the only one able to recall the last Reunion. She'd told her sisters that it was like being cornered by a hundred instruments, all playing out of tune. 'It's just that there are a lot of them. We'd rather they visited in shifts.'

'Or formed an orderly queue,' added Phenomena.

Aunt Inheritance's watery eyes had that manic shine to them again.

'Our Family may be a little . . . chaotic, but you heard the story. Our coming here, to this House, is *tradition*. Tradition, girls, is a living thing, a flame passed from the past to the future! It is our job to keep it alive. We must take pride in our history, in the honour of our forebears.'

'Why? Some of them weren't particularly honourable,' pointed out Shenanigan.

'Well, yes, there were a few bad apples. But you should know, Shenanigan, that Swifts aren't normal people. The rules don't apply to us in the same way.'

Cook snorted. 'Good Lord, it's like I never left the palace,' she muttered.

'As a Family, we are *blessed*,' continued Aunt Inheritance. 'Normal people go their whole lives trying to find themselves. Once we are named, we know ourselves, our role, from birth to death. Good or bad, we just . . . are. The Dictionary guides us.' She looked beadily at Shenanigan. 'Don't you find it a comfort to know exactly what you are?'

Shenanigan's stomach lurched, though if you'd asked her why she wouldn't have been able to say. Aunt Schadenfreude's words came back to her again: *you can't help your name.*

Cook politely suggested that perhaps Inheritance might like to borrow some light armour so she could visit the library before it was locked for the weekend. Their aunt left the table, oblivious to the upset she had caused.

'What a load of rot.' Cook looked at the three girls glumly considering the tablecloth and started rummaging in a nearby cupboard. 'Here. I popped to the post office, since Suleiman is still out of commission, and I brought something that might cheer you up.'

Part of Cook's air of mystery came from the fact that she was the only person who regularly left the House, gunning down the driveway on her boisterous red motorbike and returning with supplies in the sidecar. Today, she pulled out a large square package wrapped in brown paper. Shenanigan's mood lifted a little.

'If the Reunion starts tomorrow, does that mean Mum and Dad are coming home?' she asked hopefully.

Cook avoided her eyes. 'I'm sure they'll say in their letter.'

Opening post from their parents was a ceremonial affair, as it only arrived every few months and was always stuffed with gifts. Shenanigan liked to look at the customs stamps first, the record of the journey the package had taken. She would close her eyes and imagine what those places sounded and smelled like, things you could never learn from pictures in an atlas. Recently, most of the stamps had been in Portuguese and Spanish, of which Shenanigan could read a little, and had inked pictures of mountains blurred by rain or seawater. She carefully smoothed the paper, reading the labels. *Lima. Rio de Janeiro. Paris. London.* Perhaps, once she had Vile's Hoard, she could follow the postmarks back to her parents.

Cook pulled out and set aside a bottle of something dark for Maelstrom, a thick envelope for Schadenfreude, and a packet of seeds for herself. There was a gift for each of the girls too. For Phenomena, a new journal bound in leather, of the kind Charles Darwin had used. For Shenanigan, a large knife, almost like a sword, that widened towards the tip. It was immediately confiscated by Cook.

Felicity did not rush forward with her sisters. Instead, she took her letter and her sheaf of French fashion magazines bound up with a ribbon, and quietly headed upstairs. Over the past few years, she'd grown less enthusiastic about their parents' letters. They seemed to make her sad.

There was also a postcard addressed to each of them. Shenanigan's read:

> First at the site! Some wonderful glyphs, utterly spectacular logograms, very clear and undamaged. Your father's been bitten by something and won't stop complaining. Enclosed is a machete to use on the nettles.
>
> Love,
> Mother and Father
>
> PS: Don't run with the machete.
>
> PPS: Sorry we can't make it to the Reunion. Say hello to your cousins for us – and stay out of trouble, Trouble!

The postcard was of the staggered steps of a temple draped with greenery. Her parents were at the real temple, reconstructing dead languages with their university. Shenanigan pretended that the postcard was a window and that if she looked hard enough she could see her mother kneeling by one of the carvings, note-book in hand, or her father, rummaging through a first-aid kit. She hadn't seen either of them in over a year. The postcard would look wonderful on her wall with all the others.

The feeling Shenanigan had at every mention of her name had found a little dark corner of her mind, the part that got plenty of rainfall. It had been growing and growing for a long time, fed by Aunt Inheritance's words, until she felt like the temple on the postcard, disappearing into jungle.

But Aunt Inheritance's lecture had given her an idea. *From birth to death*, she'd said. Shenanigan opened her map under the table, just to double-check.

Then she kicked Phenomena on the ankle.

'*Lab*,' she mouthed at Phenomena's indignant look. '*One hour.*'

Aunt Schadenfreude had given Phenomena a room in the attic on the basis that bad smells, like heat, would rise, and keep the chemical stench of Phenomena's experiments away from the lower floors. Phenomena herself didn't mind. A mishap with chlorine gas when she was four had destroyed her sense of smell. No one ventured up there but Shenanigan, who was often summoned when Phenomena was working on her more dangerous experiments to do a similar job as a canary in a coalmine.

As Aunt Inheritance clattered about, settling into the Puce Room below, Shenanigan climbed the ladder to her sister's lab. She liked Phenomena's room. It had sloping ceilings, lightly scorched, with posters of the periodic table and serious-looking women in lab coats. A bed was tucked beneath the window, but Phenomena spent most of her time at a large, scarred bench surrounded by test tubes, vials, bottles, beakers, three Bunsen burners, and an old microscope that crouched in the corner like a great brass insect.

Shenanigan found Phenomena standing upright, safety goggles on, holding an empty test tube and snoring gently. She gave her a solid poke in the thigh with a thermometer, and Phenomena opened her eyes and turned on the Bunsen burner as if she'd never fallen asleep.

'Oh good! You're here.' She thrust a beaker at Shenanigan. 'How's this smell?'

Shenanigan sniffed. 'Sweet,' she said decidedly. 'A bit like Bakewell tart.'

'Drat,' sighed Phenomena. 'I've made cyanide. Again.' The poison went in a bottle with a glittery skull-and-crossbones sticker, and the bottle went in the cabinet with her other concoctions, helpfully labelled and tightly sealed.

'You're in a mood,' Phenomena observed, giving her sister a quick, piercing glance. 'You're fidgeting. If you're not careful, you're going to knock something over.'

Shenanigan shrugged. 'I probably will. You heard Aunt Inheritance – I can't help it. It's in my *name*.'

Phenomena snorted. 'Is that what you're upset about? Inheritance talks rubbish. All that guff about the Dictionary.' Phenomena brandished her thermometer like a wand. 'Correlation does not equal causation, Shenanigan.'

'What does *that* mean?'

'It means that just because two things *seem* connected, it doesn't mean they actually are.'

Shenanigan wasn't convinced. She fiddled idly with

a glass test tube. 'Hmm. What's the definition of Phenomena?'

'Oh, that's easy. I come across it all the time in research. It means "interesting events or behaviour that makes you want to do experiments".'

'So you have a science name, and you like science.' Shenanigan stuck her finger in the test tube and tapped it against the bench. 'Maelstrom's name means "a great big whirlpool", and he was a sea captain. You don't think Aunt Inheritance was right? That the Dictionary knows who we're going to be?'

Phenomena's eyes glinted behind her glasses. 'Of course not.' She pulled a pencil from her hair and opened her new notebook. 'But . . . I do think it merits further research. It brings up all sorts of questions about nature versus nurture. It's perhaps more of a metaphysical matter when you get right down to it, but aspects of it can probably be measured . . .'

Phenomena started rambling about things that Shenanigan didn't understand. Shenanigan tried to surreptitiously pull her finger out of the test tube. It was stuck. She shook her hand frantically under the bench.

'I thought there might be a way for us to check.'

'Well, if you wait long enough, you'll grow up, and then we'll know for sure,' said Phenomena.

There was a small crash as the test tube slid off Shenanigan's finger and smashed on the floor.

'Though maybe we should solve this sooner rather than later. Ooh, you could be a case study!'

Phenomena rummaged for her flask. In order to keep her brain in tip-top condition, Phenomena made herself a sort of smoothie to drink in her lab. It was the colour of mud and contained, among other things, spinach, kale, cod-liver oil, blueberries, certain kinds of algae, soy sauce, broccoli, and egg yolks. She called it her Solution Solution. Every time she took a swig, Shenanigan gagged. Phenomena insisted that it contained all the vitamins and protein she needed for a long day of mental exercise. Shenanigan insisted it smelled like a bin.

'Inheritance seems to think the Dictionary itself decides our names,' said Phenomena, 'so ideally the first step would be to look up your exact definition. But the Dictionary is behind glass, and probably fragile. Even if we do get to it, Aunt Inheritance might *actually* kill us.'

'She could try. But I've thought about this already,' said Shenanigan. 'Look.'

She spread her map over the table. There was another place in which the Swifts' definitions were written down, a place she was dying to get into.

She pointed to the bottom of her map, to the bit helpfully labelled CELLAR.

5

GRAVE MATTERS

The girls waited until midnight to put their plan in motion, knowing that anything secret ought to be done when the clock struck twelve and the House was safely asleep. There wasn't much risk of being heard, regardless. The only person who slept within earshot of the cellar was Cook, and since she believed the House to be haunted, a belief she held with the same unswerving faith she had in garlic, aspirin, and the post office, she would certainly blame any noises on spirits.

The challenge was getting into the cellar in the first place. It was kept locked, and there was only one key.

The girls had only been inside Aunt Schadenfreude's study a few times, and only when they were in trouble. As soon as Shenanigan put a toe over the threshold she shuddered, the echoes of previous tellings-off still ringing in her ears. The mahogany panelling and red wallpaper made it look like a courthouse, dominated by the large desk from which Aunt Schadenfreude had handed down her sentence on many occasions. The study was one of the few rooms Shenanigan hadn't mapped. Maelstrom had hinted that there was a secret exit to the grounds somewhere inside, and she itched to investigate the panelling . . . but she had to focus.

Aunt Schadenfreude was asleep in the straight-backed, red velvet armchair she used instead of a bed. Her iron collar shone dully in the light from the dying fire. So did the keys on her belt.

Phenomena lingered in the doorway. A lifetime of pouring chemicals had given her the steadier hands, but Shenanigan was far more accomplished in matters of theft: over the years, she had stolen every single one of Felicity's diaries, and had recently grown tall enough to pickpocket Uncle Maelstrom.

She clicked her fingers next to her aunt's ear to check she was deeply asleep, and when she didn't stir, Shenanigan lifted the keys in one hand. With the other, she tightly wrapped a strip of one of Felicity's ruined dresses around the keys to muffle their clinking.

Aunt Schadenfreude shifted a little in her sleep. Her iron collar thunked against the side of her chair. Shenanigan wasn't sure why her aunt even wore it. Cook said she didn't need to, medically speaking, and it couldn't have been comfortable. Perhaps she was worried that if she removed the collar her head would fall off.

Willing her fingers not to tremble, Shenanigan began to unbuckle the ancient leather belt tied at her aunt's waist.It was hob-hot in the study, as Aunt Schadenfreude kept the great fireplace stacked high, even in summer. Sweating, Shenanigan silently slid the keys off the belt and, biting her tongue in concentration, re-buckled it.

Not a twitch from Aunt Schadenfreude.

As she was about to make her escape, Shenanigan spied a small, well-worn book on her aunt's reading table. Ignoring Phenomena's tiny groan of frustration, Shenanigan picked it up and opened it at the bookmarked page.

It was a battered German to English dictionary. Underlined on the marked page was:

Schadenfreude (noun)
the enjoyment felt at the misery of others

That seemed about right to Shenanigan.

'Come on!' hissed Phenomena.

Shenanigan placed the book back on the table and slipped out of the room.

There was another tradition in the Swift family, that went along with the Naming. It was not as cheerful. A week or so after a child was born, a large, heavy package would arrive at Swift House, to be stored in the cellar until it was needed.

Their names were quite literally set in stone.

Staring down from the top step, Shenanigan decided the cellar must be where her Family stored all their extra darkness. She and Phenomena looked out over a room that spanned the entire length of the House, an endless space where shadows lived and breathed and were swallowed by bigger, hungrier shadows. Their torch was a bare thread of light twisting away into a labyrinth of steel racks, and on these were stacked gravestones like books on a shelf.

Shenanigan shone her torch at the nearest stone. It read: '*Ameliorate Swift*', and then there was a blank space where dates should be, and below that was her definition: '*Verb: To make something better*'.

A sweep of the torch down the shelf revealed hundreds more. Until now, Shenanigan hadn't really understood how large her Family was. The Swifts had scattered themselves across the world, and she had met so very few of them – while they were alive, at least. She usually made their acquaintance once they weren't.

'Well! We'll never find me in here,' she said cheerfully.

'Of course we will,' said Phenomena. 'Look, they're alphabetized. It's like a library!'

Shenanigan squinted. It was true: there were neat letters stamped into each of the shelves. It was exactly like a library, except you were only allowed to check out one book, and only once you had checked out yourself.

Even with the letters, it was difficult for the girls to find their way. They took a right at D and ended up at M. They turned left at M and found themselves at H. They passed through P, Q, R, and ended up back at A.

'O!' called Phenomena.

'Oh what?'

'No, just O. We've passed it already.'

'Oh. Can you see I?'

'It's "Can you see *me*".'

'You?'

'U's back that way.'

'I thought it was "You are"?'

'You're both ridiculous,' said a voice from the darkness.

The girls whipped round.

Felicity stood with her arms crossed, looking as bored as it was possible to be at midnight in a cellar full of gravestones.

'What are you doing here?' hissed Shenanigan.

Felicity scowled. 'What am *I* doing here?! I was up late, *sewing –*' she gave Shenanigan an especially vicious glare – 'when I heard someone galumphing about down here. I thought it might be burglars.'

'We weren't *galumphing*. And what would you have done if there *were* burglars?'

'I'd have asked them if they fancied being kidnappers instead, and pointed them towards your room.'

Shenanigan had learned a new word recently, which was *incandescent*. It meant both 'brightly lit', like a candle, but also 'furious'. With her torch angled up to her chin and her anger making her glow from inside, Felicity was most definitely incandescent.

Phenomena stepped between them.

'This is pointless. Felicity, are you staying or going?'

'Well, knowing you two, you'll knock over a shelf and get crushed under a pile of rubble,' snapped Felicity.

'So?'

'So I actually wouldn't enjoy that very much, even though you'd deserve it. You're my sisters. Now move out of the way.'

Before her sisters had come along, baby Felicity had had little to do except crawl around the hedge maze in the garden. She'd grown quite adept at labyrinths, and now found her way through the shelves with ease. Shenanigan and Phenomena followed close behind her, and the darkness brought up the rear.

After a while, Felicity said, 'Look, there's S! Give me a hand,' and, with an effort, the three of them turned Shenanigan's gravestone to face them. They crowded round to read.

It said:

Shenanigan Swift

Noun

i. Tomfoolery, skulduggery, mischief of all varieties
ii. A devious trick for an underhanded purpose

Shenanigan chewed her lip.

'Well?' said Felicity.

'That's me, alright,' said Shenanigan miserably. 'I don't know some of these words, but I can see *mischief* in there, and I know what that means, and I'm definitely it.'

'So why don't you look pleased?' asked Felicity.

Phenomena started explaining to Felicity all about nature versus nurture and predeterminism and a lot of other complicated things, but Shenanigan had stopped listening. She was staring at the slab of granite with her name on it.

For many people, looking at your own name on a gravestone would be a sad or frightening experience, but for Shenanigan, who had been rehearsing her aunt's funeral for years, it was just like looking at a jumper she hadn't quite grown into yet. Her finger traced the neat, carved S. According to this, she would be setting traps and causing trouble forever. Even if she liked her name (which she did) and even if it suited her (which it did) she would have preferred to have been consulted before she was stuck with it for life.

Shenanigan was feeling a lot of complicated things, and not enjoying it very much.

'I've got an idea,' she said.

Phenomena and Felicity stopped whispering. An idea from Shenanigan was a dangerous thing.

'We're going to need some rope, a skateboard, some matches, and some of Phenomena's chemicals,' said Shenanigan. 'Felicity, help me lift this down—'

'Absolutely not.'

Shenanigan sighed. 'Fe-*licity*, don't be a wet sandwich.'

'You're not going to . . . to blow it up or whatever it is you're thinking of doing. You'll get us all into trouble. And, anyway, I'm still cross with you!'

'Well, if you're not going to help, you can go,' said Shenanigan haughtily. She began to pull at the stone. It made a grinding noise as it began to tip slowly towards her. 'Phenomena, get ready to pick it up with me.'

'Er, alright,' said Phenomena uneasily.

'Shenanigan, you're not strong enough. And Phenomena *definitely* isn't strong enough.'

'Fine, I'll do it alone, then,' Shenanigan snapped. She braced her foot against a lower shelf and pulled again, grunting with the effort. The shelf wobbled slightly.

Felicity's eyes widened. She grabbed her sister's shoulder.

'Will you stop? You're going to hurt yourself!'

Shenanigan shook off her hand. 'Well, then you can say, "I told you so"! Won't that be—'

With a final tug, Shenanigan managed to pull the stone over the lip of the shelf.

As soon as its weight settled against her, she realized her mistake. It was far too heavy. It tipped in her hands, her name falling towards her face, and Felicity shrieked, and—

Shenanigan twisted out of the way just in time as the stone crashed to the floor and cracked neatly in two.

For a moment, they all stood stock-still. Shenanigan strained her ears, listening for movement within the House. Just as she began to relax, she heard a creak and the muffled thump of two legs and a walking stick making their way along a corridor, far above them.

'Oh, *great* job, Felicity.'

'You can't blame me for –' Felicity bit back a rude word – 'Oh, never mind. Do what you want, but I'm not getting caught down here.' She ran off into the dark.

Shenanigan and Phenomena had no choice but to go after her at a flat sprint, or stay lost among the shelves. They followed Felicity's swinging ponytail through the looming stacks of stone to the cellar steps, up them and out. Panting, Shenanigan closed and locked the door behind her. If she could manage to replace the keys in the morning before Aunt Schadenfreude noticed their absence, and if Felicity didn't tell, their aunt would never know.

Aunt Schadenfreude's study was on the second floor, at the far end of the east corridor. By the sounds of it, she was making her way down to the first floor. Shenanigan hauled Phenomena across the hall, up the grand staircase, along the west corridor to the right, and up the second set of stairs to the second floor, just as Aunt Schadenfreude's walking stick began to thump ominously down the grand staircase.

It was a close thing. They heaved ragged sighs of relief and separated. Phenomena headed to her lab on unsteady legs, Shenanigan to her own room.

The lights were all out, and it was difficult to see her way in the gloom, but that didn't matter. Shenanigan had lived in the House for so long that her legs knew the way on their own. She was getting along pretty well without using her eyes until, all of a sudden, they found something to look at.

Uncle Maelstrom had once shown Shenanigan a picture of an anglerfish. An anglerfish is a creature that lives deep underwater, in the parts of the sea the sun has forgotten about. It spends its whole life in darkness, and lures foolish prey by dangling a light from its forehead, right above its waiting jaws.

So when Shenanigan saw Aunt Inheritance floating along the corridor, a pale figure in an old-fashioned nightgown with a torch strapped to her head, her first thought was of the anglerfish. Her second thought was that whatever was in the mysterious tubes she had brought with her couldn't have been very heavy, because she had strapped every single one of them to her back.

Shenanigan watched as her aunt passed the *Sour-faced Duchess*, the *Still Life of a Bowl of Pistachios*, *A Study in Ink* and the *Nun Picking Her Nose*, and stopped in front of the painting that looked exactly like a blank stretch of wall. She swung back the canvas. Shenanigan waited for her to take out a key for the small, round keyhole, but instead Inheritance took off her spectacles. She twisted one of the arms, and it detached from the frame with a soft click. She placed the arm into the keyhole. Shenanigan heard the low grinding noise of heavy tumblers shifting in the lock.

Within seconds, Aunt Inheritance had slipped inside and closed the door behind her.

If Shenanigan hadn't been bound by a feeble human body that needed to sleep occasionally, she would have kept watch outside the secret room all night. As it was, she nodded off inside the large vase where she was hiding, and woke before dawn the next morning with a sore neck and a dead leg, still clutching Aunt Schadenfreude's keys. She heard low voices far below, Cook and her aunt at work in the kitchen, Uncle Maelstrom carrying tables into the hall.

She poured herself out of the vase, limped as fast as possible to Schadenfreude's empty study, and dumped the keys on the desk. Hopefully her aunt would assume that she'd left them there herself. Shenanigan then sauntered down to the kitchen, making a big show of yawning and rubbing her eyes as if she'd just got out of bed. She was given a hasty breakfast, an ugly velvet dress, and a stern reminder: the morning of the Reunion was upon them.

It was still dark when Shenanigan clambered to her perch on top of the roof, a greyish light seeping over the horizon as if the sky had sprung a leak. She settled into a cross-legged position with her notebook and a pack of biscuits, and fumbled for her torch.

There are many ways to pass messages across long distances without the use of a telephone. Yodelling is one, pigeons another. To save on throat lozenges and bird feed, Shenanigan had decided that the combination of a torch and a thorough knowledge of Morse code was the most effective means of communicating with the local postman.

She began to flash the torch on and off. Every short flash was a dot, every long flash a dash. All together, her message looked like this:

And meant this:

H E L L O   S

After a few seconds, several miles away in the attic room of the local post office, an answering torch flashed out:

\-\- \-\-\- .\-. \-. .. \-. \-\-. / ...

Or:
MORNING S

This was Suleiman. He was one of the only people up as early as Shenanigan, who hated being asleep at the best of times – she imagined it was like being dead and, since she intended never to die, it wasn't like she needed the practice. Each morning, she would clamber on to the roof, watch the sun come up, and signal to Suleiman to ask him whether or not he could make a delivery.

ARE YOU FEELING BETTER?

YES THANK U. DID COOK GET PACKAGES?

YES

PUT ME OUT OF A JOB

Shenanigan grinned.

W H A T ' S   F O R   B R E A K F A S T ?
she asked.

K I P P E R S   M M M, he replied.

Y U C K !

Shenanigan enjoyed talking to Suleiman, who sometimes painstakingly spelled out jokes, or told her about the antics of his small terrier, or asked for help with the crossword. But it took a long time to spell things out in Morse code, and soon it was almost too light for the torches.

D O N ' T   C O M E   N E X T   F E W   D A Y S,
she shone out. **F A M I L Y   R E U N I O N**

**O K   E X C I T I N G ! ! !   S A Y   H I   2   F A M
4   M E**

It was exciting, Shenanigan thought. It was really, dreadfully, horribly exciting.

The sky lightened further, and got a bit of colour in its cheeks. From her perch on the roof, lying flat with a flask of hot chocolate, Shenanigan felt like a lookout on the keep of a castle, watching enemy forces arrive. She fastened her eyes to her binoculars, and for most of the morning all she saw were cars: modern cars, old-fashioned cars, cars that were falling to bits, two-seaters, four-seaters, stretched-out many-seaters that reminded her of bristle-toothed fish. They looped around the flat silver mirror of the lake, and parked nose-to-tail down the gravel driveway, choking the path to the House. There were so *many* of them, and some had large tools strapped to the roof, as if they intended to get a spot of mining in before tea.

Shenanigan glanced again at the little pack she'd put together for her own treasure hunt and refused to be intimidated. She sat staring down at the skylight that led to her room for quite a while, listening to the low buzz of voices drifting up from below. Like Phenomena's chemicals, they made her dizzy and a bit sick.

She shimmied up a drainpipe and knocked on her sister's window.

'Are you coming down?' she shouted through the glass.

'PARDON?'

Phenomena was at her bench as usual, only this time she was wearing a pair of large, fluffy earmuffs.

'I said, are you coming down?'

'THE BOILING POINT OF SULPHUR IS FOUR HUNDRED AND FORTY FOUR POINT SIX DEGREES,' said Phenomena too loudly, which wasn't really an answer.

Shenanigan slid back down the drainpipe and looked in on Felicity, who was at her dressing table putting on make-up. Shenanigan did a very loud impression of a goose, which made her sister jump and smear a stripe of pink lipstick down the side of her face, then she hopped back into her own room before Felicity could throw a shoe at her. Beneath her bed, the orange tail of John the Cat twitched. She knew how he felt.

'You stay here, John the Cat,' she said solemnly. 'If anyone comes in, show no mercy.'

John blinked slowly to show he understood, and kneaded the carpet with his claws.

The sheer size of the House, with its east and west wings, conservatory, tower, and innumerable guest rooms, suddenly made sense to Shenanigan as she paused at the top of the grand staircase and looked out over the landing banister into the hall. The House had been built to be full. Now that the guests had arrived, the thick oak front doors had been propped open, and the House took great gulping breaths of people, sending them scudding between the billiards room, the lounge and the far side of the hall, where Cook had outdone herself with a magnificent buffet. Everyone was talking, laughing, drinking champagne, all packed tight as sardines. And yet it didn't seem cramped. The House felt comfortable, like an old cushion that finally had enough stuffing.

Shenanigan heard a small rustle to her left, and started as she saw a person sitting with their legs through the banisters, drawing a lizard on their arm. They noticed Shenanigan a split second after she'd noticed them, and froze.

They were about Shenanigan's age, she guessed. She'd never seen anyone close to her own age before, other than Phenomena, and Phenomena didn't count. They were wearing turned-up trousers and a bright blue-and-black patterned jumper that looked three sizes too big. Shenanigan wasn't sure if they were a girl or a boy, or if it would be rude to ask, and, if it *was* rude to ask, whether it would be the right kind of rude.

'Hello,' Shenanigan said uncertainly.

'Hello,' they replied.

The two of them stared at each other like wary cats.

'I'm Shenanigan. I like your jumper,' she said, finally.

'I'm . . .' They hesitated. 'Erf. I'm Erf. And thanks. I knitted it. The pattern is supposed to look like the markings on a blue poison dart frog.'

'Neat,' said Shenanigan, who'd never said 'neat' before in her life. 'I've read about them. They're one of the most poisonous animals in the world, aren't they?'

'Yes.'

'My parents are in Peru. I wanted them to send me some tadpoles so I could raise my own lethal frog army, but they said that if tadpoles were meant to fly they'd grow into birds, and anyway I didn't need the extra help.'

Erf grinned at that. Shenanigan grinned back.

Was this making a friend? It wasn't something Shenanigan had ever had to do before, so she had no idea how it worked. She stuck out a hand, with the vague idea they were supposed to shake. Erf hesitated. Before they could take it, someone else clattered up the stairs, scowling and munching on a bag of coffee beans.

'Oh. Hullo,' said the someone. 'Having a peek at the zoo?' She pretended to squint through the banister as if she was looking through the bars of a cage. She had very straight black hair and severe eyebrows. She must have been in the early stages of grown-up, as she only had the first faint symptoms around the eyes. 'The beasts are lively today.'

'That's pretty rude. They're my relatives,' said Shenanigan.

'Mine too. That's why I get to be rude about them.'

She popped three beans into her mouth. Shenanigan wrinkled her nose at the strong smell of coffee. The woman looked sidelong at her for a moment, then, as if this was a gesture of politeness, spat the beans out over the edge of the banister, *one, two, three*.

'Whoops. I think those hit someone!' She put the rest of the beans back in her handbag. 'I'm Flora, by the way. You two better get your name badges on. If Inheritance sees you without one, she'll blow a gasket.'

'Oh,' said Erf glumly. 'Is she insisting on those?'

Flora waved a small gold badge at the two children. 'Oh yeah. Repeatedly. You can pick 'em up over there.' She pointed. Near the front door was a long table, with a stack of papers, a large blue ledger, a row of gold badges, and Aunt Inheritance, who was flapping about and squawking at people to sign in. She looked in her element, which meant everyone else looked annoyed.

'This is your first Reunion, right?' Flora squinted at the children. They nodded. 'Then take my advice, as a veteran of these things. Keep your head down, trust no one, and don't play any games you don't know the rules to.'

That seemed a bit dramatic. 'But everyone here's a Swift.' Shenanigan frowned. 'They're Family.'

Flora squinted still further. '*Exactly*,' she said darkly. 'Quick, do I stink of coffee? I do, don't I? I can see it in your nose.' She rummaged in her handbag, took out a tiny bottle of perfume, and spritzed herself. Then she opened a little tin and popped three mints in her mouth at once. 'That's better. Mint? No? Alright.' She stood up straight, cracked her knuckles, and flicked coffee grounds off her dress. 'Once more unto the breach, I suppose.'

Shenanigan watched Flora descend the stairs, her shoulders squared as if she was going into battle.

'Do you know what a breach is?' Shenanigan asked Erf, but, when she turned, her new ally had vanished. Shenanigan tried to look for a face she recognized in the crush, or, failing that, part of a face – maybe a familiar nose or chin, or friendly ears, or a smile she recognized as her own. *Something* that tied all these strangers to herself. It took her a while to pick out the leonine head of Uncle Maelstrom, glass in hand, loitering by the buffet table.

He's shrunk, she thought. *He looks smaller than he did yesterday.* His suit was sharp, but it looked as if it hadn't seen the light of day since the last Reunion; he laughed readily, but his hands, which usually moved with a quick, sure expressiveness when he talked, continually retreated into his pockets to hide. The idea that her uncle could feel something close to what she was feeling – her uncle with a voice like a ship's horn through fog and a back as straight as a ship's mast – brought out the brave in Shenanigan.

She gave her head a quick shake, did a few star jumps to get her courage flowing, and followed Flora unto the breach.

COLLECTIVE TERMS

If you have ever been very small – which, unless you began life as a fully formed adult of average height, you must have been – and if you have ever experienced your smallness in a crowded place, then you will know the unpleasant feeling of being invisible to a lot of people with very sharp elbows. Shenanigan was experiencing that unpleasantness for the first time. It was like being underwater, all the talk passing above her head like waves breaking on the surface of the sea while below she was knocked back and forth. Clothes wafted around her in invisible currents. It was hard to breathe. Shenanigan struck out in the general direction of the buffet table to seek higher ground.

'*You! You scoundrel! You rogue!*'

She broke through a gap between relatives just in

time to see an extraordinary figure in a frock coat hurl a glove at another man's feet.

'Do not laugh at me, *monsieur!*' the man in the frock coat cried. 'This is an insult to my honour! Pistols! Pistols by moonlight!' He tossed his long curly hair like an angry poodle. His name badge flashed. It said: PAMPLEMOUSSE. As he struggled to unsheathe the sword at his hip, his opponent finished the canapé he was chewing and ambled away.

'Brigand! Cad! *Fleur du mal!* We shall settle this with arm wrestling,' Pamplemousse called after him. 'Vile cur! *Chien andalou!* Rock-paper-scissors – to the death!'

Shenanigan picked up his glove and handed it back to him. Up close, Shenanigan could see he had a waxed, curled moustache, and as well as the frock coat he wore a ruffled shirt and tights. He was also armed to the teeth. A long, thin sword was buckled on one hip, a pistol on the other, and he bristled all over with daggers.

'I like your clothes,' said Shenanigan. 'They were very fashionable a few hundred years ago. I read that people back then shaved their eyebrows and glued strips of mouse fur in their place, and that all their face powder contained lead and it poisoned them.'

The man blinked. '*Comment t'appelles-tu, petite?*'

'Is that French? I only speak a bit of Spanish,' said Shenanigan.

'I was asking your name. I am Pamplemousse de Pastiche Martinet,' he said, bowing so low his hair brushed against the floor. 'Combatant, raconteur, émigré.'

'Shenanigan. Er . . . humdinger, travesty, sloop.' She began to understand why everyone needed name badges. It probably saved time on introductions. 'What did that man do to make you angry? And why do you have so many weapons?'

'*Non!* Not weapons! They are what you call "rhetorical devices". I use them to make people listen to me. And that man –' Pamplemousse's face darkened – 'he took the last mini quiche. We shall have words!'

Fuming, he stalked off into the crowd, calling loudly for trial-by-backgammon. No one paid him any notice.

Shenanigan decided she'd better pick up her own name badge. There were a few people at the table: a pretty woman in a flowery dress was signing her name in the ledger with painstaking, tidy cursive. An engagement ring with a stone the size of a robin's egg made it hard for her to hold her pen. Beside her, Erf was staring intently at their own gold name badge. The name on the badge was not Erf.

Inheritance handed Shenanigan her badge and shoved a leaflet into her hand.

'There's your timetable and, Miss DeMille, here's yours. You and your dear fiancé shall be in the Coral Bedroom, which I do hope –' she glanced at the ring – 'will be up to your standards. Shenanigan, remember to sign in and don't lose your name badge.' She paused in her harried speech to frown at Erf. 'Aren't you going to put yours on, dear?'

'In a minute, Gran,' said Erf.

The fact that Aunt Inheritance had a grandchild threw Shenanigan a little. She had thought of Inheritance as more of a mushroom than a person – she just sort of happened if conditions were right – but now she felt that was silly. Of course Inheritance had parents and siblings and children. They all had to be related to each other somehow.

'What's that on your arm?'

Erf hurriedly rolled their sleeve down, but Aunt Inheritance was too quick, and pulled up the cuff of their jumper. She looked worried rather than angry.

'Have you been drawing on yourself again? Really, dear, you're going to give yourself ink poisoning. Actually, you look a bit peaky. Have you eaten? Or have you eaten something that disagreed with you? Maybe you should stay with me for a while, so I can keep an eye—'

'Oh look,' said Shenanigan cheerfully. 'Someone's drawn a rude picture on the Dictionary case.'

Aunt Inheritance dropped Erf's arm and, with a noise like a strangled crow, went haring off after the imaginary vandal. As soon as she was out of sight, Erf shoved their badge in their pocket.

'Thanks,' they said.

'Why don't you want to wear your name badge?'

Erf looked warily at Shenanigan, as if they were expecting an argument. 'Because Gran calls me by my Dictionary name, but I'd rather be Erf.'

'Is Erf like a nickname?'

'Not really. It's just my name. I picked it.'

'Oh.' Shenanigan hadn't known you were allowed to do that. 'I also wanted to ask if you were a boy or a girl earlier, but I wasn't sure if that was a rude question. Is it a rude question? I've never met anyone new before, so I'm not really sure how to do it.'

'It's okay. Meeting new people is hard for me too. And, um, I'm not a boy or a girl.'

Shenanigan hadn't known you were allowed to do that, either.

'Well then hi, Erf. We're cousins!' She grinned. 'I'm sorry Inheritance smudged your lizard. It was really good. I'm going to get tattoos when I'm older, like Cook. We could go get them together if you want, and then Inheritance wouldn't be able to rub yours off.'

Erf laughed. 'Gran's alright, really. Just over-protective. Hey, did you know that, when trapped, some lizards can detach their own tails to escape? They grow back later. I think that's amazing.'

'If you want to escape, head towards the very top of the House. My sister is in her lab with her earmuffs on. Don't scare her, though – she might be holding acid.'

'Neat,' said Erf with a wry grin, and finally held out their hand. Shenanigan shook it firmly. Then she kicked out towards the buffet.

For the first time in history, Shenanigan wasn't actually hungry. She was thirsty, but there were chewed-up coffee beans floating in the fruit punch. Everyone else was drinking champagne, and since there was no one around to tell her not to do so, Shenanigan took a sip. It tasted awful, and left an odd, sour ghost of itself in her mouth. Luckily, Flora was off to one side, adjusting her name badge.

'Can I have one of your mints?' Shenanigan said.

Flora looked at her quizzically. 'Excuse me?'

'The mints you have, for coffee breath. Can I have one, please?'

'I don't drink coffee,' Flora said, sounding mildly concerned. 'And you shouldn't, either! There's a lot of caffeine in coffee, and you're very small. Small people shouldn't really have caffeine.' Then she gasped, and plucked the still-full flute of champagne out of Shenanigan's hand. 'And drinking too! At your age! When your liver is only the size of a tennis ball!'

A woman with what looked like an entire stuffed pelican on her hat waved frantically at Flora, and Flora winced apologetically. 'You stay there. I'll just be a second,' she said to Shenanigan, and darted away.

Shenanigan really did try to wait for Flora, but, as at any party, the area with food was an area of high traffic, and she was soon buffeted away from the buffet and swallowed up by the churning sea of people once again, dodging legs and dropped food. At one point, she was carried past Felicity, who was smiling rigidly at an older woman who was offering condolences on her mundane name ('*Poor thing, it's not your fault, is it? Some people are just born unlucky, I suppose . . .*'), and in

85

an attempt to reach her, Shenanigan inadvertently crashed into someone else.

There are some people in the world who have made unpleasantness a hobby, and they practise it every day the way other people practise playing the trumpet or picking locks. Shenanigan had collided with one such person, and she knew it straight away. Her name badge said ATROCIOUS, and she had a figure like the newel post at the bottom of the stairs, curved and shining as if she'd been polished into existence. No one else was anywhere near as dressed up, and Shenanigan instinctively backed away from her clothes, clean and pressed and expensive enough to bite. She was arm in arm with a repulsively handsome man sporting a thin moustache and a sharp suit. His name tag said PIQUE. They had the same cruel smile.

'Pique, my dearest, what is this?' the woman said softly.

'Atrocious, my darling heart, I'm no expert . . . but it appears to be a small, grubby child.'

'Do we know her?'

'We don't travel in such circles, sister mine.'

There was a deliberate boredom to them as they sipped their champagne.

'Well? Who are you? Introductions!' said Pique.

'I'm Shenanigan,' said Shenanigan. 'Swift,' she added.

'Obviously,' said Pique.

'Can you sing?' asked Atrocious.

'No,' said Shenanigan.

'Can you dance?' asked Pique.

'No.'

'Can you play any instruments?' asked Atrocious.

'Not well.'

'And you clearly lack the wit for sparkling conversation. What exactly are you good at?' sneered Pique.

'Smuggling spiders in my sleeves,' said Shenanigan sweetly. 'I can show you, if you like.'

Pique took a step back, nose wrinkling, but Atrocious leaned forward.

'That might work on someone like Inheritance,' she said, her voice low and deadly, 'but you should see what *I'm* smuggling in *my* sleeves.'

Shenanigan wanted to stick her tongue out and run off, but their eyes were fish-hooks digging into her. She felt she couldn't leave without their permission, and they were enjoying her discomfort too much to let her go. She was going be stuck here forever, with the two of them watching her flounder and twitch like the catch of the day.

A hand clamped tightly on her shoulder.

'Atrocious! Always lovely to see you. *So* sorry to hear about your fifth husband,' said Flora. Her almost-genuine smile was still in place. 'And, Pique, your third? A heart attack at his age! You two do seem to have the worst luck in love.'

'I'm afraid your information is out of date, Cousin Flora. We have both since remarried.' Pique smirked over the rim of his champagne glass. 'Though I do notice you're here alone this year.'

Flora's smile didn't slip. She and Pique stared at each other for a long, tense moment. Her nails were digging into Shenanigan's shoulder.

Finally, Atrocious rolled her eyes. 'Pique, sweetheart, shall we go find someone a little more interesting?'

'You do have the best instincts, Atrocious, my dear.'

Shenanigan watched them go, making a mental note of where they were headed so she could be sure to walk in the opposite direction.

'What did I tell you?' said Flora. 'Beasts.'

'They're awful! They're horrible! They're—'

'Rich. *Disgustingly* so. With enough ex-husbands between them to crew a small yacht. You should see them in their element, swanning about with the rich and spoiled, pretending to like them. They leave a bad taste in my mouth.'

'Me too. Could I have a mint?' Shenanigan prompted.

'Hmm? Oh, of course,' said Flora distantly, dropping one into her hand. 'Ugh, I think I see Jilt coming this way. I'm off.'

But a split second after Flora vanished from beside Shenanigan's right elbow, she reappeared at her left, like a magic trick.

'There you are!' she said. 'Ta-dah!'

She held out a packet of chewing gum. 'Not a mint, but close enough. And chewing gum is supposed to help you give up caffeine, I think. Just be sure not to swallow it.'

Shenanigan looked back and forth between her elbows until she was dizzy with confusion.

'How did you – but you were just – I don't like coffee,' she finished lamely.

Flora laughed. 'I know.'

Shenanigan looked at the name tag pinned to the woman's dress. She could just make out an F, but the rest was hidden by her cardigan.

'You're teasing me,' she said slowly. 'You're not Flora, are you?'

Not-Flora took Shenanigan's hand in hers, smiling brightly, and bent down to look right into her eyes.

'Nope. But I am delighted to meet you, Shenanigan Swift. I'm Fauna.' She smiled brightly. 'We'll have a chance to talk again, but right now I think someone is trying to get your attention.'

Shenanigan turned and saw a huge hand waving. 'Uncle Maelstrom!'

'Hold on, Skipper!'

A *crack!* echoed around the hall and Shenanigan learned what it sounds like when a great many heads swivel round at once, which is similar to a cat skidding on a roll of taffeta. Arch-Aunt Schadenfreude stood beside the Dictionary, her walking stick in hand – the *crack!* had been the sound of it striking the banister. She did not have to speak. As one, the crowd of relatives arranged themselves around her in a rough semicircle.

Uncle Maelstrom scooped Shenanigan up one-handed, and set her on his shoulders. She tangled her fingers in his hair and looked around at her Family.

A collective term is a special name given to a group of animals, like a herd of cows. Many animals have their own strange terms. She knew the collective term for starlings was a murmuration, and the collective term for owls was a parliament. And then it was a murder of crows. A gulp of swallows. What was the collective term for Swifts, she wondered? A quarrel, maybe. Erf might know – they seemed to know a lot about animals.

Shenanigan thought she could see a flash of Atrocious's shining dress somewhere in the throng, and a stray flounce of Pamplemousse's frock coat. She spotted Flora over to the left of her aunt, and raised a hand to wave, but then saw Fauna – or was that Flora? – settle beside her. Looking at them made Shenanigan feel dizzy. They were identical twins, but *really* identical. The same height, the same weight. They had the same haircut. They wore the same clothes. One of the twins spotted a slight rip in the sleeve of the other's cardigan and reached down to tear a hole in her own to match. They linked arms.

The steady waves of talk that had filled the high arches of the hall rolled back. The House was quiet once again but for the faint humming sound that comes from many people standing together, waiting.

'Good,' said Aunt Schadenfreude. 'Most people seem to be here. And if they are late, then tough. I could die any minute. It's time to begin.'

8
ASKING FOR TROUBLE AND COURTING CHAOS

Aunt Schadenfreude towered before her Family like a national monument, straight-backed and funereal in her black dress and shawl. Her iron collar threw back electric light from the chandelier. No one so much as sniffed.

'Thank you all for coming. Few of you will remember my predecessor, my Arch-Aunt Gracious. She always called our Reunions "a great gathering-in". It was an expression that rather made me think of drawing the curtains, but she loved having you here. She believed that any Swift had the right to treat the House as their own – that it was what Cantrip would have wanted.'

She tapped a finger against her cane.

'With the greatest respect to her memory, that was both sentimental and foolish. I have lived here for more years than I care to remember, so listen when I tell you: *this House is dangerous.*'

Shenanigan felt a tingle of excitement travel from the roots of her hair to the soles of her feet. She heard soft *clinks* and *clanks* as people adjusted their tools.

'As you know, it is tradition, each Reunion, for the Family to search for the fortune Grand-Uncle Vile hid on the grounds. And while I wouldn't *dare* suggest that we break with tradition –' she cast a sidelong glance at Aunt Inheritance, overflowing with pride beside her – 'I want to be absolutely clear: any treasure-hunting is undertaken at your own risk. I suggest that if you intend to go poking around, you take first-aid supplies and ample provisions – we all remember poor Cousin Findal. Incidentally, if you do come across Findal, please let us know the location of his remains.'

Aunt Inheritance put her hand on Aunt Schaden-freude's sleeve as if she wanted to say something, but Aunt Schadenfreude waved her away irritably.

'Now, some housekeeping. The library shall remain locked for the duration of the Reunion, largely for the protection of the fools among you. Breakfast is served from seven until nine each day . . .'

Shenanigan knew all the House rules and wasn't

interested in hearing them again, so she tugged on Maelstrom's ear.

'Ow!'

'Uncle, what exactly does Aunt Schadenfreude *do*?'

'Do? Many things. Eats, breathes. Sleeps, so the rumour goes—'

'*Uncle.*'

'She's the head of the Family. If the head is female, they're called the Matriarch. If they're male, they'd be the Patriarch. If they were another gender, they'd be the first, and get to pick their own title, which I'm quite looking forward to.'

'That's just what she *is*. I mean what does she *actually do*.'

'You'll see.'

'. . . And finally, drilling is not permitted in the House after 9 p.m. I retire at that hour, and I will not have my sleep disturbed by you performing amateur masonry on our stone floors. Now . . .'

Aunt Schadenfreude eased herself into her red velvet chair. She thumped her walking stick on the floor, once, and half the assembled Swifts jumped.

'If you have any disputes to bring, come forward now. Form an orderly queue, please. No pushing.'

The crowd shuffled itself like a deck of cards and reformed as a straggly line. Aunt Inheritance stood at the front with her ledger, scribbling furiously.

'Step forward,' she called in her reedy voice.

Two Swifts did so. One had long, beautiful blonde hair down to her waist. She was smirking. The other was bald, and bubbled with rage like a pan of boiling soup.

'Covetous Swift and Vendetta Swift,' announced Aunt Inheritance. 'State your grievance.'

Vendetta pointed at her bald head. 'This is my grievance,' she spat. 'My sister cut off my hair as I slept and made it into a wig.'

Looking closer, Shenanigan could clearly see the irregular tufts where someone with very little hairdressing knowledge had hacked away at Vendetta's hair.

'Is this true?' Aunt Schadenfreude asked Covetous.

Covetous tossed her hair – or her wig, rather – and it rippled obediently. 'Vendetta was barely using it!' she sneered. 'She always had it tied up in this messy bun.'

'It's MY HAIR!' protested Vendetta. 'I can do what I like with it! You little stoat! You've always been jealous!'

'Of you? Please. I look better in it than you ever did.'

Vendetta howled with rage and snatched Covetous's wig from her head. Covetous's own hair uncoiled and cascaded down her back. The two women began to fight over the wig. It looked as if they were having a tug of war over an unfortunate Pomeranian.

'Enough!' shouted Aunt Schadenfreude, banging her stick. 'Covetous, you will allow Vendetta to shave your head. You can match, and hopefully your dignity will grow back with your hair. Next!'

Aunt Inheritance ushered the two squabbling sisters away, confiscating the wig in the process. Neither sister looked happy about the solution, but they didn't object, either.

Next up was a frazzled-looking woman carrying a newborn baby in a sling round her middle, and a stocky bearded man Shenanigan took to be her husband.

'Renée Swift, née Carter, her husband Fortissimo Swift, and their daughter Finicky Swift,' announced Aunt Inheritance.

'Hello,' said Renée nervously. 'Um. My husband and I recently had our first child, as you can see, and you know how hard it is to get babies to sleep. We're exhausted. But every time we manage to get her down, my husband's voice wakes her. We need your advice.'

Aunt Schadenfreude turned to Fortissimo. 'Well?'

'I CAN'T HELP IT,' boomed Fortissimo. Several people close by winced. 'MY VOICE JUST SORT OF CARRIES, NATURALLY.'

Little Finicky Swift began to cry. Renée hushed her gently, looking despairingly at Aunt Schadenfreude.

'Fortissimo,' said Aunt Schadenfreude. 'Do you sing?'

'DO I SING?' bellowed Fortissimo. 'I SING BEAUTIFULLY. LISTEN . . .'

Fortissimo opened his mouth wide, and the Swifts covered their ears in anticipation. But to their surprise, the voice that emerged was soft and tender.

> *'Hush, little baby, don't say a word,*
> *Papa's gonna buy you a mockingbird . . .'*

Little Finicky quietened immediately.

'Well, that settles that. Fortissimo, you will have to communicate in song until the child is old enough to sleep through the night. Next!'

Aunt Schadenfreude dispensed justice for the next hour. People aired their bickerings, their disagreements, their squabbles and feuds; they laid them all out before Aunt Schadenfreude and she found solutions.

'She stole my identity!'

'We can't decide who's more indecisive!'

'He shot my tailor!'

The solutions were not always popular, but not one person argued with her judgement. Not all of Aunt Schadenfreude's pronouncements made sense. She had one pair settle their disagreement via rock-paper-scissors. She made another pair stand on one leg and apologize to each other continuously for five minutes. One tangled group of cousins were fighting so badly she said she couldn't possibly solve their dispute until they had each brought her a single four-leaf clover, and why didn't they get started with that right away?

Then a young couple stepped forward. The man was tall, symmetrically handsome, with square glasses and a broad smile. The lady with the ring who Shenanigan had seen by the ledger was on his arm, looking like a spring day come to life with a gold flower pinned in her natural curls. They looked like the kind of people about whom old ladies said, 'Oh, they make *such* a handsome couple!' and they clung to each other as if they were entering a three-legged race.

'State your grievance,' said Aunt Schadenfreude.

The man grinned. 'Hi, Auntie!' He gave her a half-wave, and pushed his glasses up his nose. 'It's more of an announcement than a grievance! We just wanted to tell you, ah—'

'State your name, please,' said Aunt Schadenfreude, sounding bored.

'Well, I'm Candour Swift – you know me, Auntie, obviously – and this is my fiancée, Daisy DeMille of New York.' Daisy wiggled her fingers, where the diamond ring gleamed. 'And we wanted to ask your blessing. For our marriage.'

Candour and Daisy grinned shyly.

'It's a pleasure to meet you, ma'am,' added Daisy.

Aunt Schadenfreude looked keenly at the two of them.

'Absolutely not,' she said.

Candour and Daisy's smiles faded by several watts.

'What?' said Candour.

'I cannot bless a marriage in which one person is so blatantly leeching off another,' said Aunt Schadenfreude, glaring at them.

This was rude, even for Aunt Schadenfreude. Daisy gasped. A few people murmured.

'Goodness!' cried Candour, still just holding on to

his smile. 'You're being a right pastry today.' Aunt Schadenfreude didn't respond. 'Get it? Because you're a *cross aunt*!'

'Ma'am—' began Daisy, but Candour patted his fiancée's arm soothingly.

'Don't worry, Daisy, you'll grow on her. After all, Auntie doesn't even know you.'

'I *know* more than you think,' said Aunt Schadenfreude darkly. She fixed her stare on Daisy, whose mouth had fallen open in shock. 'And I suggest you leave this House at once.'

More murmurs filled the hall and Daisy's eyes filled with tears. But, surprisingly, Candour just laughed.

'Well, you're a card, Auntie!' he chuckled. 'Come along, Daze, we'll ask again tomorrow.' He began to tug Daisy away, but Aunt Schadenfreude half rose from her chair.

'Candour. You *aren't* marrying Miss DeMille,' she said curtly. 'In fact, I expressly forbid it!'

'Alright, alright.' Candour rolled his eyes, as if Aunt Schadenfreude was playing a little joke. Aunt Schadenfreude never joked. 'We'll chat later, Auntie! It's good to see you!'

He slipped away, hand in hand with Daisy, who was

still looking rather shocked, while the rest of the Swifts muttered to each other.

Aunt Schadenfreude dismissed the remaining complainants with a wave of her hand.

'That's enough for now,' she said. She looked worn out. 'Settle down and listen. Inheritance has provided you all with a timetable of organized games and events to keep you out of trouble. You are welcome to attend or not – I don't care. However, in addition to the usual . . . frivolity,' (Aunt Schadenfreude pronounced *frivolity* as if it was a dirty word), 'I have an announcement to make.'

She hauled herself upright, leaning hard on her walking stick. Inheritance moved to touch her shoulder, but Aunt Schadenfreude waved her off again.

'I am an old woman. I have lived a long and adequate life, but I am far, far closer to my end than my beginning. I am tired. Tired of sorting out all your problems, certainly.' Her fingers moved to tighten her iron collar. 'In three days' time, I will choose my replacement. That is all.'

The crowd fizzed like champagne, restless and sharp. Everyone began talking at once, so Shenanigan was required to shout her most pressing question into her uncle's ear.

'Could I be Matriarch?'

'Ow! Ask again in a decade or two. Though I'm sure you'd hate it, Skipper.'

Shenanigan wasn't sure of that. She liked the idea of bossing people around. Uncle Maelstrom pulled a compass out of his pocket, checked it, pulled a fob watch out of his other pocket, checked it, and then pulled out a sextant, which he laid on the buffet table and squinted at. 'Hmm. Winds are changing,' he murmured. 'If you're interested in Family law, you should ask Aunt Inheritance.'

'Yes, I should,' said Shenanigan. She'd add it to her list of other questions for Inheritance, along with *What is the secret room behind the painting in the second-floor corridor?* and *What were you doing in it?* and *What exactly is in those tubes?* But she would have to wait her turn to ask them. Aunt Inheritance was, at that moment, squashed into a corner having a pinched discussion with Aunt Schadenfreude. She looked upset, and kept waving her timetable in Aunt Schadenfreude's face.

'What do you suppose they're arguing about?'

Candour and Daisy had sidled up to Maelstrom. Daisy looked rattled, but she offered up a brave smile.

'Aunt Schadenfreude springing her retirement on us all, probably,' said Maelstrom, chuckling. 'She keeps things close, does Schadenfreude.' He clapped Candour on the back so hard that Candour's glasses slipped down his nose. 'It's good to see you, lad! I haven't heard from you since you were in medical school.'

'Oh, I've been a real nomad these past few years,' said Candour. 'But there's never a dull moment back here, is there? Auntie's news has caused rather a fracas.'

'A hullaballoo,' added Daisy.

'A brouhaha!' he cried, smiling at her. The look they shared was like treacle, sweet and sticky.

Maelstrom cleared his throat. 'Miss, you have been standing here nearly an entire minute and your companion has not introduced us properly. I must take on the task myself. I'm Maelstrom, and the girl I am wearing as a hat is called Shenanigan.'

'Well, aren't you just the sweetest thing!' Daisy said to Shenanigan, unwittingly making an instant enemy. 'And such a pretty dress!' She gave no indication of noticing all the grime on it. Her own dress was pristine, her make-up perfect, her deep brown skin glowing and flawless. She waved up at Shenanigan with the neatest hand Shenanigan had ever seen. The gold flower in her hair was, in fact, a daisy. Her earrings were also daisies. The only thing that wasn't shaped like a daisy was her massive engagement ring. Shenanigan was surprised she could lift her perfect hand to wave.

'I guess I've already been introduced,' Daisy said, wincing. 'Though it's not the "hello" I would have chosen.'

Candour planted a kiss on her temple. 'Now, Daisy, don't wilt. I warned you she might be a little sharp. You usually have to ask more than once with these things.'

'I don't know. She seemed very certain she doesn't want me to be part of her – of *your* Family.'

'It's not like Schadenfreude to be quite so rough,'

Maelstrom said, shaking his head. 'I think there must have been a misunderstanding – you're even named Daisy! Wonderful.'

'I know. I'm very, very lucky,' said Candour proudly.

'Felicitous,' said Daisy.

'Fortunate,' said Candour.

In the Swift family, where names carried such importance, finding a partner with a name that could also be a word in the Dictionary was considered a good omen. It was funny, Shenanigan thought. Being a Swift called Felicity was unlucky, because there were plenty of other Felicitys running around in the world. But the moment one of those non-Swift Felicitys wanted to marry into the Family, they'd be welcomed with open arms.

Candour and Daisy's sweetness was giving Shenanigan a toothache. With Schadenfreude's speech over, people were already pulling out shovels and pickaxes. If she didn't get a move on, someone might strike it lucky, and she had better things to do than sit on her uncle's shoulders and listen to the discussion he and Daisy were having about yachts.

'Why don't you show the happy couple to their room,' suggested Maelstrom, after Shenanigan had kicked him in the collarbone one too many times.

'You go ahead,' said Daisy to Candour. 'I'm just going to – to go make some coffee.'

Candour offered to go with her, and Daisy said it was alright, and Candour said he would miss her in the ten or so minutes it would take her to get a cup of coffee, and then Daisy said that she would miss him too. Then Candour took so long kissing his fiancée goodbye that Shenanigan began to suspect that Daisy was actually hollow, and had to be blown up every few hours, like a balloon.

Finally, *finally*, Shenanigan was free. She was up the stairs so fast Candour had to take long strides to keep pace.

'I say, what's the rush?' he huffed. 'Worried they'll find the Hoard while you're gone?' It sounded like a joke. Shenanigan scowled.

'I'm not worried, because I don't need to be. *I'm* going to find the Hoard.'

'That's the spirit!' Candour beamed.

Shenanigan sped up. First Daisy had spoken to her as if she was a baby, and now Candour was patronizing her. This was a word she had learned recently; it meant 'being kind or helpful, but in a smug, superior sort of way'. Felicity did it a lot.

'I *am*,' she said hotly. 'No one knows this House better than me. I know where all the secret rooms are, all the trick floorboards and hidden levers, so you'd better watch out!'

Candour stopped walking, and raised his hands in surrender. 'I've offended you, and I'm sorry. You seem very smart, and determined besides.'

Shenanigan looked him over. She couldn't see any lies hiding on his face, and she softened; it was nice to have someone believe in her.

'Apology accepted. What about you? Are we going to be rivals?'

Candour smiled a lopsided smile. 'Oh no, I'm no prospector. I'm happy just being a doctor.'

They paused on the landing, and watched someone try to convince Inheritance to let them bring their industrial drill through the front door.

'I would like *someone* to find it, though,' he said. 'It seems a shame that a piece of our history has been hidden for so long. And goodness knows, Aunt Inheritance will be giddy if we do dig it up.'

'Aunt Inheritance would be giddy over a pair of old boots if a Swift once wore them,' Shenanigan said bluntly.

'Ah, Inheritance is fine, really. She's a bit *straight-laced*, but she's got a *good sole*.' Shenanigan groaned at the joke. 'She cares about tradition, anyway. That's important nowadays. It's pretty much all we have left. I say, look at her!' He stopped at the painting of the *Sour-faced Duchess*, leaning towards it as if they'd just met. 'Are you feeling alright? You look a little *drawn*.'

There was, obviously, no response.

'I feel like I should draw a moustache on her. What do you think?'

Shenanigan had had the same thought, many a time. She stubbornly swallowed her giggle, but Candour spotted it bubbling inside.

'I *will* make you laugh, Shenanigan Swift! No matter how long it takes. I'm a doctor – we have a lot of *patients*.'

Shenanigan shoved him through the door to the Coral Bedroom. Candour declared everything from the bed to the skirting boards to be 'charming!' and 'just wizard!', and shook her hand solemnly before she left.

'Remember, an apple a day keeps the doctor away! But only if your aim is good.'

Shenanigan decided she liked Candour. Like Daisy, he was neat and well pressed, and this was a mark against him. But he also had an odd, lopsided smile, and this made everything else bearable.

Shenanigan had wanted to have another go at breaking into the secret room while everyone was busy, but she hadn't considered how difficult it would be to sneak around the House now it was full. As she approached the second-floor corridor, two women rounded the corner and shrieked with the excitement of aunties everywhere upon seeing a child at a family gathering. Shenanigan ducked down the adjacent corridor towards the Upper Lounge, only to find an old man with a squint inspecting one of the paintings. He waved a trowel at her. It felt as if everywhere she moved, eyes followed.

In the end, she pulled a lever disguised as a candle-stick, and was swung into one of the small, tight hidey-holes that were scattered about the House. The sounds from outside were muffled. Shenanigan took a deep breath of the musty air and sat. For the first time all day, she had a moment to consider what Inheritance could be doing in the secret room. She took out her map and a pencil, and drew a rough sketch of Aunt Inheritance's round glasses next to the question mark. The best idea would be to stake out the room again that night, she decided, and wait to see if Inheritance went in again.

She yawned. In that case, she would just take a moment to rest. She had only snatched a few hours' sleep last night, after all, and that had been in a vase. She would just take a moment. She would just . . .

As had been the case many, many times before, hunger woke Shenanigan up. Her appetite had not enjoyed its brief holiday and had returned with serious complaints. She could tell it was late – she might even have missed dinner – but she could still hear everyone downstairs, a steady hum that she now knew would not go away for the entire week and was the reason Phenomena had been wearing earmuffs.

She wiped drool from her face and swung out of the hidey-hole, pulling her map from her pocket. The House was full of dumb waiters and laundry chutes, put in when the Swifts had had servants. Rich people have a terrible fear of housework. What they want more than anything is to believe that their food and washing and waste appears or disappears by magic, so measures are put in place to preserve that illusion. Shenanigan had found many of these old measures long-abandoned but still useful, like the laundry chute down the corridor that ended up by the bottom of the stairs near the kitchens. She could whizz down it and grab some dinner from Cook without having to sneak past all the guests or, worse, Aunt Schadenfreude.

It was then that, with her head down and looking at her map, Shenanigan was almost flattened by the shape that came hurtling round the corner in a streak of blue dressing gown. She leapt into a doorway just in time as Daisy whistled past, hauled open the door to the Coral Bedroom, and disappeared inside.

That was strange, noted Shenanigan. She hesitated for a second, wondering if she should follow Daisy. But she was too hungry for spying. She pulled back *Nun Picking Her Nose* and chucked herself down the laundry chute without a second thought.

The second thought came when she was already plunging into the unknown at a tremendous speed. It was pitch-black, and everything echoed – her breath, the squeak of her shoes against the metal chute, the thump of her head and arms hitting the sides. Shenanigan was just wondering what would happen when she needed to stop when she did, the chute taking a sharp turn that wedged her tight.

Shenanigan hadn't been scared before getting stuck and it didn't occur to her to be scared after. But as she assessed her situation she heard shouts of alarm.

'What was that?'

'*Saperlipopette!*'

'I heard a thumping noise and—'

Rats! They had heard her rattling her way down. Shenanigan kicked herself in the shin with the heel of her other foot. This was exactly the kind of fuss she'd been trying to avoid.

'It's okay!' she called. 'I'll be out in a second!'

She kicked off her shoes and let them clunk away below her. Then she pressed her hands hard against the sides of the chute and began to work herself free. It took time, and all the while the shouting grew louder and more agitated.

'Should we try to help?'

'We should call an ambulance! And the police! And the fire brigade!'

'Don't be absurd! We should just leave her where she is, at least for now!'

Eventually, with an embarrassing squeak, Shenanigan came free, and plummeted. She hit the bottom of the chute toes first, stubbing them badly, and slithered unceremoniously out.

'I'm alright, everyone,' she said, wiping dust and grime across her face. 'You can stop panicking.'

But no one was looking at her. Shenanigan had come out from behind a painting near the entrance to the kitchen, and from here she had a very good view of what everyone *was* looking at.

They were looking at the body of Arch-Aunt Schadenfreude, lying in a crumpled heap at the bottom of the stairs.

'Excuse me, please! Excuse me! Out of the way! I'm a doctor!'

Candour's long stride swallowed three stairs at a time, and he dropped to his knees beside Aunt Schadenfreude's body. After a few attempts, he gave up trying to squeeze his fingers under the metal collar at her neck, felt for the pulse at her wrist, and finally put his ear against her chest.

It was so quiet and still that Shenanigan could hear the blood rushing in her ears. She spotted Phenomena and Felicity, grey with shock, and the steady shape of Uncle Maelstrom nudging his way forward. Whatever had happened to Aunt Schadenfreude must have happened during dessert, because more than one guest had brought their crystal chalice of ice cream out of the dining room and were mechanically spooning melted fudge sundae into their mouths.

Shenanigan felt as though she had brain-freeze. She kept coming back to tiny details: Schadenfreude's grey bun was still fixed tight, but her left shoe was half off, exposing the worn heel of her tights. Her walking stick was gone. Her shawl was askew. Candour's eyes were squeezed shut behind his glasses as he listened for her heart, and relief broke over Shenanigan as she spotted a curl of his hair stirring with her aunt's faint breath.

'She's alive,' Candour announced, sounding faintly astonished. A sigh – of relief or disappointment – rippled through the crowd. Shenanigan realized she was twisting the hem of her dress and made herself stop. She began to shove forward, but before she could reach her aunt, another shape shouldered its way into the tableau, and Cook folded beside Schadenfreude's prone body with a soft cry. Maelstrom laid a comforting hand on her bicep.

'Her collar probably saved her life,' Candour murmured quietly. 'A fall like that? She should have broken her neck.'

Cook nodded. Her lips were tight as she expertly felt Aunt Schadenfreude's arms and legs for breaks, the same way she had when Shenanigan had fallen out of a tree last year.

'Nothing broken. She's a tough old bird, the toughest . . .' She cleared her throat. 'She wouldn't like to make a scene.'

Candour peered over her head at the audience of spoon-lickers. He got the hint.

'Everyone!' His voice was calm and authoritative. He spread his arms. Maelstrom moved beside him to block the Family's view of Aunt Schadenfreude. 'I need to get Auntie somewhere quiet so I can have a proper look at her. Go back and finish your meal – I'll let you all know how she's doing as soon as I can. Alright?'

People began to disperse, muttering among themselves. Candour blinked, and ran a hand through his hair, ruining its perfect side parting.

'Alright,' he said again.

He and Cook exchanged a nod, and with barely a grunt Cook scooped Aunt Schadenfreude up in her arms. Maelstrom hoisted Phenomena and Felicity on to his shoulders and followed. As they turned down the corridor to Schadenfreude's study, Shenanigan saw Phenomena swivel round, eyes flashing, to scrutinize the twisted carpet at the top of the stairs.

The study was warm and quiet, the fire already crackling expectantly, and a fresh cup of tea waited on the table by Aunt Schadenfreude's chair. Maelstrom swept everything off the desk, and he and Candour piled up cushions and blankets so Cook could lay Aunt Schadenfreude down on top of it. Even unconscious, she was frowning.

Candour struggled with their aunt's iron collar. 'How do I get this thing off?'

'You don't,' said Cook. 'She had it fitted years ago.'

'And I bet she's never looked back since.' Candour chuckled weakly. 'Sorry, bad joke.'

'She put it on when she became Matriarch,' Cook said shortly. She didn't elaborate.

'When will she wake up?'

Shenanigan was startled by the sound of her own voice. It seemed to come from very far away.

'We don't know,' Candour said. 'But I'm sure she will. Many people recover from accidents like this.'

That didn't make Shenanigan feel better. Everything was wrong. It was as if the floor and the ceiling had changed places. Her aunt was the most upright person Shenanigan knew. She even *slept* upright. Seeing her lying down was almost the same as seeing her dead.

Out of the corner of her eye, she spotted Phenomena and Felicity whispering. Shenanigan left the adults debating what to say to the rest of the Family.

'Her cane was at the top of the stairs, not the bottom,' Phenomena hissed to Felicity. 'And the carpet is wrong too – remember when Shenanigan was a toddler and tripped on a loose edge? She fell the entire length of the staircase.'

'Yes, I remember,' said Felicity crossly. 'She bounced.'

'And to keep it from happening again, Cook nailed the edges of the carpet in place.'

'So?'

'*So*, when I looked, those nails had been pulled free. Someone would have to have done that deliberately. And her cane was *metres* away from the top of the stairs – she didn't just drop it.'

'What are you saying?' asked Shenanigan.

Phenomena looked at her gravely. 'I'll need to grab my Junior Forensics Kit to be certain, but it looks like *before* she fell someone grabbed Aunt Schadenfreude's stick from her and tossed it aside. And it looks like *after* she fell someone pulled up the carpet to make it look like she tripped.'

'And in between?'

'And in between they pushed her. It's attempted murder, Shenanigan.'

One of Phenomena's favourite games to play with Shenanigan was called 'post mortem'. In it, Shenanigan would stage her own grisly death and let Phenomena work out how she'd been killed from the clues she left behind. Sometimes Shenanigan would fake-murder one of Felicity's stuffed toys, and together they would be Holmes and Blackbeard (Shenanigan was nobody's Watson).

Felicity hated this game, as did Cook, since it usually involved finding Shenanigan lying in out-of-the-way corners of the house, drenched in ketchup and with her eyes bulging dramatically. Much like the rehearsals for Aunt Schadenfreude's funeral, this wasn't really a game; it was more like practice. There had never been any doubt in Phenomena's mind that, someday, she would be called upon to act as detective – and when that time came she would need an assistant.

So when Phenomena pronounced that there was an aspiring murderer in their midst, Shenanigan wasn't surprised. Despite the horror of the situation, despite their aunt's body lying in state on the desk, despite Cook's pinched face and Maelstrom's heavy concern, Shenanigan felt a thrill of anticipation. She supposed that was her name, acting up again, but at the back of her mind was a quiet voice saying, *Finally. Finally, something is happening to you.*

The fear and the fog that had been threatening to surround her cleared, just a little, and she saw with clarity all the objects that had been swept from Aunt Schadenfreude's desk to the floor: her pens, her keys, her ink bottle, the battered German-to-English dictionary. She saw the strand of grey hair that had escaped from Aunt Schadenfreude's no-nonsense bun and straggled across her cheek, and more than anything it was that strand of hair, disobeying her aunt while she was too unconscious to do anything about it, that chased away the last of Shenanigan's paralysis. Someone had dared to attack Aunt Schadenfreude in the House she ruled – and by pushing her down the stairs, no less! This was the part that offended Shenanigan most. Aunt Schadenfreude was a feared and respected enemy, and anyone who wanted to kill her should at least have the decency to come at her from the front.

Shenanigan made a solemn vow to her aunt's

indomitable eyebrows: *I will find out who did this, and I will have revenge.*

'No,' said Felicity flatly.

'What?'

'Don't give me that look. I know you're swearing vengeance, and you're not allowed.'

'Fine. I'm swearing . . . justice.'

'I'm not sure you know the difference.'

'I do! They're spelled differently, right, Phenomena?'

'Vengeance is purely selfish. Justice is in service of a greater good. Catching the would-be killer would be justice, as long as we didn't kill them back,' said Phenomena reasonably.

'Well, I do want to kill them back, though,' said Shenanigan.

Felicity shook her head so hard her hair whipped about her face. 'Listen to me, *for once,*' she pleaded. 'You can't run around trying to solve this by yourselves. You're too young. *We're* too young. You need to tell an adult, and they will call the police, and *they* will deal with this.'

'We will *not* be involving the police,' said a voice.

They turned. Aunt Inheritance stood in the doorway, ledger clutched to her chest. Peering over her shoulder was Daisy, blinking sleepily in her blue dressing gown, and a man in a long, beige raincoat with the collar turned up. He was wearing a fedora, which is a type of wide-brimmed hat worn by detectives, and this was how Shenanigan guessed what he was.

Aunt Inheritance coughed. 'Apologies. I don't mean to be . . . Oh, what's the word?'

'Commanding?' asked Daisy.

'Imperious,' said Candour.

'Forceful,' added Daisy. 'Darling, what's going on? I was sleeping, and then I heard this awful racket – Oh,' she said as she saw Aunt Schadenfreude. Her hand flew to her mouth. She ran to Candour and buried her head in his shoulder.

Shenanigan frowned. Daisy hadn't been sleeping – she'd seen her not ten minutes ago. So, unless she was prone to sleep-sprinting, Daisy had just told a lie. They had their first suspect.

'We're not calling the police,' repeated Aunt Inheritance. 'It just isn't the way things are done. We Swifts take care of ourselves.'

Felicity stared at her, dumbfounded. 'You can't be serious.'

'In Family matters, it is the job of the Matriarch to

settle disputes, find solutions, and dispense justice,' said Aunt Inheritance firmly.

'But Aunt Schadenfreude is the Matriarch!'

'Yes.'

'And she's the victim!'

'Yes.'

'And she's unconscious!'

'Yes.'

'Surely you can see the problem here!'

'Well,' said Aunt Inheritance, 'in *The Lore and Law of the Family Swift*, it *clearly* states that, in the absence of the Matriarch, the Archivist is to make any and all decisions regarding the Family. And the Archivist is me. So I shall be organizing everything from here on.'

Felicity's hands balled into fists. 'Aunt Schadenfreude would want—'

'*Aunt Schadenfreude* would want to maintain our Family's traditions in a time of crisis!' said Aunt Inheritance sharply.

Felicity looked beseechingly at Cook.

'She's right. If your aunt hates anyone more than doctors and door-to-door salesmen, it's the police. She'd never allow it,' said Cook, but she looked pained. 'Buck up, Fliss.'

Felicity sagged, beaten by the immovable illogic of adults. 'Do you know,' she said, 'sometimes . . . sometimes I hate this Family.'

'Of course you do, dear,' said Aunt Inheritance. She reached out and patted Felicity's shoulder in what was probably supposed to be a comforting gesture but which instead looked as if she was petting a small dog. 'Poor Felicity. I know it's in your nature to look for a mundane solution to this, but you mustn't worry. Everything shall be done according to—'

But Felicity did not enjoy being patronized any more than Shenanigan, and flounced out of the room.

In the silence that followed, the man in the hat spoke.

'It was about ten o'clock on a night in May, with the sun well sunk below the horizon. Downstairs, guests were enjoying coffee and a nightcap. Upstairs, their hostess was dead.'

'She's not *dead*,' corrected Phenomena, but the man held up a hand for quiet and pulled a notepad from the depths of his coat. He started making notes.

'I'd arrived late to the party, but right on time for the action. Blood is thicker than water, as they say, and I had a feeling the old broad would only be the first to spring a leak. Had Aunt Schadenfreude's sins come home to roost? In this

family of Swifts, was there a cuckoo in the nest? I'd found another case, and this one . . . was a family matter.'

Aunt Inheritance cleared her throat. 'This is Gumshoe Swift,' she said. 'He's a private detective. He's kindly offered to take the case and, given his name, I believe he will be well-suited to the task.'

Gumshoe was already crawling about on the floor, picking up objects and pocketing them.

'I'll want to interview you all later,' he said. 'The maid first. I try to talk to the help right off the bat.'

'My *name* is Cook, I'm *not* a maid, and if I may – what the *hell* are you doing?'

Gumshoe was leaning over Schadenfreude, attempting to look up her nose. Cook hauled him up by the scruff of his neck until the tips of his shoes brushed the floor.

'Now, miss, I understand you're protective of your employer, but—'

'She's not my employer – she's my *friend*,' snapped Cook. 'My best friend. You've no idea – she took me in, she gave me a home when I had nowhere, she . . .'

To Shenanigan's horror, Cook began to tear up – Cook, who hadn't cried even when she chopped off her little finger with a meat cleaver and sewed it back on herself.

Uncle Maelstrom was at her side in an instant, arm round her shoulder. 'Cook is family,' he stated, with the finality of a slamming door. 'You won't speak to her like that again.'

'Sure. Well, I guess I'll check the body later,' said Gumshoe as Cook lowered him to the ground. 'The first thing we have to figure out is how she was killed – I mean, injured.' He pulled another object out of his coat, and Phenomena gasped.

'That's evidence!'

Gumshoe twirled Aunt Schadenfreude's walking stick round his fingers.

'No it's not – it's a stick.'

'I left it at the scene so I could get some fingerprint powder!'

'But why would you need fingerprint powder?' Gumshoe snorted.

'For fingerprints! In case the attacker left any behind!'

'Oh, I doubt he'd do that. Seems like an easy way to get caught! That's one thing I can tell about this would-be killer already: he doesn't want to be caught.'

He tossed the stick up in the air and caught it. Aunt Inheritance clapped.

'You've *ruined* the crime scene,' groaned Phenomena.

'It's cute that you want to help, though,' said Gumshoe. 'Maybe you two can be my junior detectives?'

Phenomena glowered. Gumshoe didn't know it, but he'd made a mistake. He reached out, chuckling, to ruffle Shenanigan's hair – and made a second. Shenanigan bared her teeth and threw herself towards him, but Cook placed a heavy hand on her shoulder.

'Alright, girls. Bedtime for you two, I think.' Smiling tightly, she steered them out of the room. 'Now, don't get any ideas!' she said loudly, so those still in the study could hear. But then she bent towards them urgently. '*Do* get some ideas. Get as many ideas as you can. The pair of you have a better chance of catching the culprit than that twit in there.' She glanced around furtively. 'I don't trust anyone in this House except us, your sister, and Maelstrom. We—'

Cook shut up abruptly as Gumshoe strode past, and began measuring the stairs with a ruler.

'We need to keep this between ourselves,' finished Phenomena. 'Make the not-quite-killer relax.'

Gumshoe licked the banister, and made a small noise of suspicion.

'Jolly good,' agreed Cook. 'I'm going to stay with your aunt, for protection. They may try again.'

Soft, murmuring voices rose and fell. It was getting late and, despite all the excitement, people were beginning to drift off to bed.

Cook lowered her voice even further. 'Be subtle, girls. The last thing we want is a panic on our hands. Let everyone continue to think this was an accident.'

'Right.'

'Attention!' announced Gumshoe from the top of the stairs. 'Attention, folks! I've got grave news. Aunt Schadenfreude's fall was *not* an accident!'

Cook's swearing was drowned out in the uproar.

11
Suspicious
Characters

In the lab, Phenomena wiped some equations off the chalkboard with the elbow of her lab coat and started hunting around for chalk.

'The first thing we need to do,' she stated, 'is establish the time of the incident.'

Shenanigan settled on a bench. This was Phenomena's area of expertise: dates, details, and durations.

'Those of us who were in the dining room heard a crash at 8.53 p.m., so we have to assume that's the moment she fell. I, along with most of the Family, arrived at the scene a minute later.' She took a long, long gulp of her Solution Solution. 'Luckily, that means we can rule out anyone who was at dinner – we were all eating dessert. We just have to go through all the guests and write down anyone missing.'

Shenanigan goggled. 'All of them?'

All of them, apparently. Shenanigan listened to her sister recount the seating plan and tried not to drop off. This wasn't the kind of detective work she'd had in mind.

'. . . Next to him it was one of the twins, but I couldn't say which one, and then that woman with the furry handbag—'

'That's Aunt Malaria, and it wasn't a handbag – it was a dog. A Bichon Frise, actually. It's French.'

Felicity sat on the lip of the attic's open trapdoor. Below her, Erf waved awkwardly. They were wearing pyjamas patterned with beetles.

'Oh hello, Erf,' said Phenomena. 'Shenanigan, Erf was helping me with some experiments earlier. We had a fascinating discussion about hagfish while *you* were off doing . . .' She frowned. 'Actually, what *were* you up to all afternoon?'

Shenanigan didn't want to say 'napping' or 'getting stuck in a laundry chute', so she just shrugged mysteriously. She tried not to be upset that Phenomena had asked for Erf's help with her experiments; after all, Shenanigan *liked* Erf, and she had met them first, so if Erf was going to be anyone's best friend – best cousin? – they'd obviously be Shenanigan's.

The best cousin in question was inspecting the chalkboard. Shenanigan made a snap decision, based on her gut and her nose, which both told her that Erf was trustworthy.

'That's our murder board. Someone tried to kill our aunt,' she said.

To their credit, Erf didn't look too surprised.

'I thought there was something up, to be honest. On my way here I saw a man in a fedora sniffing the carpet. Are these your suspects?'

'You haven't even put down Maelstrom or Cook, and neither of *them* were at dinner,' noted Felicity, also eyeing the board. 'That's what a professional would do.'

She picked up a spare piece of chalk, but Shenanigan snatched it from her hand.

'Don't be ridiculous. If you're not going to help, then go *away*, Felicity.'

Felicity didn't go away, and she didn't help. She folded her arms and sat on a bench, glaring as if she could convince them to give up the investigation through psychic attack.

Erf raised a tentative arm.

'Erm, Felicity *is* right, though. You should really put everyone down and then eliminate them as suspects.'

They shifted from foot to foot. 'I'll start. Gran wasn't at dinner, because she was cross with your aunt. Something about Schadenfreude not listening to her, and not having the best interests of the Family at heart. I don't think she'd *hurt her*, or anything,' they added hurriedly, 'but we should still put her down. She's a bit too obsessed with all the Family stuff, but not enough to kill over it.'

Shenanigan thought about the manic light in Aunt Inheritance's eyes, and wasn't so sure. Now would probably be the time to say something like *By the way, there's a secret room on the second floor, and I saw her going in there with a lot of strange tubes, and I think she may be up to something sinister.*

But she couldn't. Whatever was in that room felt like *her* secret and, selfish as it might be, she wanted whatever was in there all to herself. Besides, it was more likely to be treasure-related than murder-related, she reasoned. The not-quite-murder had knocked her off-course, but Shenanigan still had a pack waiting for her on the roof, a map in her pocket, and an unshakeable belief that she would be the one to find Vile's Hoard. She would just have to do it at the same time as solving a murder – that's all. Easy-peasy, lemon simple.

She also had someone else to add to their list.

'Daisy was lying. She wasn't asleep. I saw her run past me on the first-floor corridor just before I, er, made my way downstairs. Maybe she's angry with Aunt Schadenfreude 'cause she wouldn't let her marry Candour?'

'Hmm. That's a little suspicious, but it might just be a coincidence,' said Phenomena. 'I'll note it down.'

After an hour of arguing and cross-referencing, they finally had their list, with some helpful notes from Shenanigan:

Aunt Inheritance (sorry, Erf)
Daisy (SUSPICIOUS)
Uncle Maelstrom
Flora/Fauna
~~Man with Impressive Moustache~~ Uncle Ferrier
Candour
Atrocious - UGH
Pique - ALSO UGH
Cook
That Lady in the Pelican Hat

Despite Felicity's protests, Shenanigan immediately crossed out Uncle Maelstrom and Cook, because it obviously wasn't them.

'This is all good, but don't we also need clues and things?' asked Erf, chewing on the cuff of their pyjamas. 'Otherwise, we'll just be going around accusing everyone.'

'We could always torture them for information,' offered Shenanigan. She'd come across a lot of interesting books on medieval history when learning how to build her catapult. 'Erf, if you've brought your knitting needles, I could probably make an iron maiden.'

'We don't need an iron maiden,' said Phenomena. She brought out a vial from the pocket of her lab coat. 'Before Gumshoe got his sticky feet and fingers all over the crime scene, I did manage to find a little something.'

She shook the vial. The little something inside rattled.

'Dirt!' cried Shenanigan happily.

'I don't think it's dirt, but I need to run some tests to be sure. Maybe it fell from the pusher's shoe, or a fold of their clothing.' She shoved her glasses up her nose excitedly. 'The most important thing is that it's a clue.'

She began to haul over her microscope, beakers, and a pair of safety goggles.

'Do you know, I was dreading this Reunion,' she said, taking another swig of her Solution Solution. 'I thought I'd be horribly bored, and have to make lots of dull conversation about my growth rate and dental status. Thank goodness someone tried to murder our aunt.'

12
A FINE CHARADE

Shenanigan woke early the next day, gritty-eyed and grumpy, at the end of Felicity's bed. She hadn't slept well with so many people in the House. All the breathing and shuffling made her feel as if she was sleeping in a zoo. Still, there was a brief moment between waking up and sitting up when Shenanigan forgot the events of the day before. For a few minutes, everything was sweet and mellow in the morning sun that filtered through the curtains, warming a lazy stripe on Shenanigan's arm.

Then she remembered.

She scrubbed her nose with the back of her hand. They had been holed up in the lab well into the wee hours, and afterwards it had been too much trouble to clean the rubbish off her own bed and get in it. When Shenanigan had been very small, she often used to creep into Felicity's room and curl up at the end of her bed like a cat. When she awoke, her sister would have put a blanket over her and plaited her hair. She reached up to her head, but her hair was the same tangle it had been yesterday, and Felicity was still asleep, clutching tightly to her pillow.

Shenanigan picked her way towards the door through piles of magazines and fabric scraps, past the accusing eyes of the models on Felicity's wall, past the sewing bench where her moth-eaten clothes awaited repair. In the doorway, she tilted her head to listen to the House.

So this was what the morning after a not-quite-murder was like. It was a lot quieter than Shenanigan had expected, though it was still early. There were a few stirrings and sighings on the upper floors, and the wet rattle of more than one snoring guest. The old pipes shuddered and clanked as the boiler struggled to heat enough water for every bath and shower in the building.

Shenanigan tiptoed to her room, shoved her party dress under the bed for John the Cat to shred, and put on the first cleanish pair of trousers and shirt she could find. She made sure her pockets were full of useful things like lock picks and string and her map. She had important business to do before breakfast. She headed to the east wing to consult one of the only people in the House she trusted with knowledge of the secret room.

'Permission to come aboard, Captain?'

'Permission granted!'

Uncle Maelstrom had been writing his memoirs for as long as Shenanigan could remember. She'd been allowed a peek just the once, and even then only at the first page. It began: *As the pickle barrel bobbed in the warm waters of the Caribbean Sea, I thought that perhaps my father had been right, and eight was too young to leave the island. But by that point my fate, like the lid of the pickle barrel, was sealed.*

It was entirely possible he hadn't written further.

Maelstrom worked among teetering stacks of books, maps, and papers, and since these piles shifted position daily, it was often hard for visitors to find him in all the mess. Shenanigan wound through the maze, trying to follow her uncle's voice.

'Marco!' she called.

'Polo!' came a muffled reply to her left.

She dipped past an old wooden figurehead of a handsome merman, sadly separated from his ship. Every time she went into Maelstrom's room, she found something new to fascinate her: old wheels and rigging, pipes and paintings, statues and souvenirs of a life at sea. Maelstrom's chief fascination was globes, of which he had dozens. Shenanigan had fond memories of sitting on top of these when she was much smaller, being spun round and round the world until she was dizzy.

'Amelia!' she called.

'Earhart!' To her right this time.

Shenanigan secretly hoped Maelstrom had been a pirate. If the navy or the Armada or whoever was in charge of policing the sea ever came to arrest him, they would flee together in the middle of the night, steal a boat at the nearest port, and spend their days sailing the high seas – even if that meant living off ship's biscuits, which Shenanigan had read usually had weevils in them. Maelstrom had her complete loyalty because he never told her to be good. Instead, he told her wild blue tales of misadventure, and she loved him dearly.

'Olaudah!' she called.

'Equiano!' Just ahead.

Shenanigan rounded a last tower of papers and finally reached the man at the centre of the maze. He was at his desk, a vast oak vessel shaped like the prow of a ship.

'What ho, Skipper!' greeted Maelstrom. It was a lively-sounding voice from a tired-looking person. It was hard to tell, but the hammock in the corner looked as if it hadn't been slept in.

'Any news?' Shenanigan couldn't bring herself to say her aunt's name. Her uncle shook his hair out of its tie and sighed wearily.

'No change. Cook said I was hovering, and sent me to bed,' he said sheepishly. He looked Shenanigan over, as if he was worried she was hurting somewhere he couldn't see. 'And you? All shipshape?'

'I'm fine.' Shenanigan pushed down her worry and pulled out her map. 'Uncle, take a look at this.'

Uncle Maelstrom was the one who'd taught Shenanigan cartography ('An excellent pastime for a young lady. Or a young man, come to think of it!') and, as such, was the only person allowed to see her map. He picked up a pair of spectacles and peered at her latest work.

'Hmm, the ground floor looks finished! And you've made real progress with the first and second. I'd have said this was an impossible task, but you're an

impossible person, so I should have known you'd manage.'

Shenanigan glowed. 'It's true – I'm brilliant. But look what I found!'

She pointed to the large red question mark she had drawn and told him about the painting that looked like a wall, and what little investigation she'd been able to do. Uncle Maelstrom sat in his chair looking very grave until Shenanigan told him how she'd seen Aunt Inheritance sneak in there two nights before. Then one of his mighty eyebrows shot up.

'Does anyone else know about this?' he asked.

'No, that's why I came to you. I couldn't stake the room out last night, and now I've got a murder to solve, so we're going to have to break down the door and see what she's hiding. What if it's something to do with the treasure?' She hopped excitedly. 'You showed me how to make the map in the first place, so if what's inside helps us find Vile's Hoard I'll split it with you, seventy–thirty. But *only* you.'

Uncle Maelstrom looked at the map for another few moments, but it seemed to Shenanigan as if he was staring through it, at an invisible horizon – or, at least, one she was not permitted to see.

'Shenanigan, I need you to make me a promise. A sailor's promise, which is definitely a real and serious thing.' Maelstrom leaned forward. He fixed Shenanigan with a gimlet stare from below his gathering brows, but his voice was strained. 'Tell no one about this room. Don't try to get in, not until our guests have gone home. And whatever you do, don't show this map to *anyone* but me.'

This was not the reaction she'd been expecting.

'Why?'

There was something twitching against her uncle's left temple – not a lie, not yet. But a dishonesty. She had never seen one on his face before, not in her whole life.

'Uncle Maelstrom . . . do you know something about the room?'

'Ask me no questions and I'll tell you no lies,' he said seriously.

This wasn't like her uncle at all.

'But if Aunt Inheritance is hiding something . . .'

'Aunt Inheritance is the Archivist. She acts in the best interests of the Family, and we should leave her to it.'

'But—'

'Shenanigan.' Her uncle's face was pained. 'I am asking you as my niece, friend, and crewmate. It hurts my heart, but we have to be –' he shuddered – 'sensible.'

'No!'

'I'm afraid so. Do we have an accord?'

Shenanigan hesitated.

'Aye-aye,' she said at last. She held out her hand, but Maelstrom chuckled softly.

'Nice try. Spit first! A dry handshake isn't much of a sailor's promise.'

Shenanigan had told Phenomena and Erf she'd meet them at breakfast. When she entered the dining room, Phenomena was sitting upright and snoring, with a spoonful of porridge halfway to her mouth, while Erf stared at her in fascination. Today, their jumper was striped yellow and black – a wasp, Shenanigan guessed, or a hornet. Shenanigan prodded Phenomena in the back, and she opened her eyes and continued eating as if she hadn't fallen asleep.

'Ah, you're here, good – ugh, why is this porridge cold?'

Phenomena had dark smudges under her eyes, but her gaze was sharp. She had been busy – her new notebook was by her bowl, open at a small diagram of the crime scene. There was also a crude drawing of a man in a big hat looking the wrong way through a telescope. Next to that was a fresh flask of Solution Solution, and the vial with the speck she'd picked up the night before.

'Have you been at it all night? Looking at dirt?' asked Shenanigan.

'Yes. I mean, no.' Phenomena picked up the vial. 'I was hoping it would be dirt, as then we could analyse the mineral composition of the soil and pinpoint where it came from. But I ran my tests, and it turns out this is a small bit of the dried fruit of the plant *Coffea arabica*.'

'Which is?'

'A coffee bean!' Phenomena grinned. 'Gosh, murder is fun! I mean,' she added hurriedly, 'of course it's terrible that Aunt Schadenfreude is hurt and that everyone's so upset, but I so rarely get to do anything interesting.'

Phenomena's excitement made Shenanigan feel better about her own. Glancing around the room, she noted that the news of an attempted murder hadn't dampened the mood much. The grimmest faces belonged to Candour, tiredly working his way through his cereal at the end of the table; to Daisy, picking solemnly at a pastry; and to Inheritance, who kept reflexively shooting glances at Erf, as if worried they might have choked on their toast in the thirty seconds since she last checked. Opposite them, Pamplemousse was telling a rude joke, and Fortissimo was trying to keep little Finicky's hands out of his porridge. It was all quite normal.

Erf slid over Phenomena's notebook, and wrote down *Uncle Ferrier*, *Lady in the Pelican Hat*, *Candour* and *Daisy* on their copy of Aunt Inheritance's timetable.

'Everyone's getting ready for advanced charades right now,' said Erf, 'so it might be a good time to check out alibis. Gran won't let me out of her sight, but she's too distracted organizing the game to keep a close eye. I should be able to talk to a few people.'

'Perfect,' said Phenomena, but it didn't sound perfect to Shenanigan. She looked at Erf's timetable (she'd already lost hers) and saw that at 2 p.m. there was a performance of the play Vile's sister Cantrip had written: *The Tragical Tale of Gramercy and Vile*. Shenanigan might have promised not to investigate Inheritance's room, but Maelstrom had said nothing about looking for Vile's Hoard. If she was going to stay ahead of her Family, she needed every scrap of information about the treasure she could find – and there could be some hidden in Cantrip's play.

She was torn. On the one hand, avenging her aunt's almost-death was top priority; but, on the other, riches. It wasn't like she'd *abandon* the investigation, she reasoned. She just needed to take a short break after lunch.

But first, she had an idea of who could tell them all about *Coffea arabica*.

They found Flora and Fauna in the conservatory, limbering up for advanced charades among the colourful effusion of hothouse flowers. The light filtering through the glass turned their skin green. One of them was sipping a mug of coffee and stretching a leg towards the orchids, and the other rose from a rattan chair to greet them as they entered.

'Shenanigan! It's *so* lovely to see you again.'

Her hand was warm, and it closed over Shenanigan's as gently as a bird's wing. 'If you're wondering who's who, I'm Fauna. I promise we won't play tricks on you this time.'

It is common to say, 'it's good to put a name to a face', and considerably rarer to say, 'it's good to put two names to the same face twice'. Nevertheless, it's true. Fauna had a way of looking right into a person's eyes when talking to them. It could have been unnerving, but it wasn't. She was just paying attention.

'Morning, all.' Flora waved, spilling coffee on her shirt in the process.

Fauna sighed. 'I really liked this shirt.' She wandered over and, wrinkling her nose, poured a bit of Flora's coffee down her own front.

'We like to match,' Flora explained as the two of them dabbed at the stains.

Now they were side by side, Shenanigan looked hard for anything she could use to tell them apart. They didn't just *like* to match. Everything about them was identical, down to the last detail: the loose thread on their skirts, the mole above their left eyebrow. They wore the same clothes, and had their hair styled the same way, long and straight. They both had brutally short nails. If there was any difference at all, it was that Flora had the beginnings of frown lines on her forehead while Fauna had faint smile creases at the corners of her mouth. Their name badges were half hidden. Shenanigan supposed the badges would spoil their fun.

'We've come to question you,' Shenanigan said.

The coffee bean was in a vial in Phenomena's pocket. Phenomena had decreed that twins were typically suspicious in cases such as this, and a good place to start.

'Question us? Golly.' Flora smirked over the rim of her cup. 'Has old Gumshoe got you working as his muscle?' Phenomena let out a short, undignified noise that made Flora's smirk widen. 'He's already been to see us, y'know. Something about twins being "typically suspicious".'

Phenomena coughed. 'Well, that's . . . silly.'

'Isn't it, though? Still, I suppose you can question us while we practise charades,' said Flora. 'We're aiming to beat Atrocious and Pique this year.'

In case you are not familiar with charades, the rules are simple. One person acts out a word or phrase through movement and gesture, and their partner interprets what they are trying to say. Often, they compete alongside other pairs, and whoever guesses their partner's message in the shortest time wins.

Phenomena took out her notebook, which had, via its use the night before and the application of several stickers, transformed into a casebook. 'Only one of you was at dinner last night,' she began. 'Flora, was it you?'

Flora rolled her eyes, and shook her head.

'That's a *No*,' interpreted Fauna unnecessarily.

'Then where were you?'

Flora made a very creative hand gesture.

'She says, ah, *None of your business*.'

Shenanigan rolled up her sleeves in warning. Flora began to move more erratically.

'*But I wasn't killing Aunt Schadenfreude*,' translated Fauna. '*It's just private*.'

Phenomena raised a questioning eyebrow at Shenanigan. What Flora was doing wasn't charades, of which half the fun was watching someone struggle to act out a word like *notwithstanding*. Nor was it sign language, which has established rules and vocabulary and is used in various forms all over the world. It was more like interpretive dance, designed for only one person to interpret.

But then the timetable did say *advanced* charades. It was typical of the Swifts to take a game and make it several times more complicated.

It was much harder to spot lies when someone was moving rather than speaking. Shenanigan shrugged helplessly at Phenomena, who flipped to a new page.

'Can you think of any people who would want to hurt our aunt?'

Flora snorted.

'Tons. Aunt Schadenfreude had many enemies, and she deserved most of them – Flora, that's not very nice! She made a lot of people angry.'

'Because she was Matriarch?'

Flora wobbled on one leg, nodded, and only just managed to stay upright.

'Yes. Plenty of people weren't happy with her decisions, or with the way she settled grievances. She once had someone resolve their argument through crocodile – sorry –' Fauna corrected as Flora made a slightly different snapping motion with her arms – 'through alligator wrestling. That was the kind of person she was. Is. She likes to watch people suffer.'

Shenanigan thought back to the German-to-English dictionary. Her aunt could be strict, but Shenanigan had never thought of her as cruel.

Fauna apparently agreed. 'That's just not true. Flora has a grudge against her because we stayed here one summer and she made us eat peas.'

Flora gave up flapping her arms about.

'We *hate* peas,' she said crossly.

'No, *you* hate peas – *I* quite like them.'

Flora folded her arms. 'Listen, the point is you will never meet anyone more iron-willed, iron-hearted, or iron-clad as our iron-necked aunt. And if someone wanted to bend her out of shape a little? Well, I can understand that.'

'Can you?' asked Shenanigan.

Before Flora could respond, the blare of a car horn cut her off. *Complication* was not the name of a Swift, but it was nevertheless an unwelcome guest.

The quickest way to the noise was through the conservatory's cat flap, which was just the size for a large cat or a small person. Shenanigan wiggled through. On the drive, Pique was leaning through the window of his low-slung, snub-nosed sports car, mashing the horn repeatedly. Red-faced, his moustache a thin, furious slash above his bared teeth, he was literally hopping mad.

'What *barbarian*? What *vandal*?'

Atrocious glided from the crowd in a black silk dressing gown, curlers still twisted in her hair.

'Pique, dear, you're making a scene,' she drawled. 'What is it?'

Pique flung open the door to the car.

'See for yourself!'

Atrocious peered inside.

'Someone,' she said mildly, 'has stolen the steering wheel of my brother's car.'

A few people laughed, Shenanigan among them. Atrocious suppressed a smile.

'I'm glad you think it's funny, sister,' Pique hissed. He stalked past her to the car parked with its nose to the bumper of his own. This one was compact and the shiny, dark red of fresh lipstick. 'Yours is gone too.'

Atrocious's smile vanished from her face in an instant. She ran forward and peered through the windshield. When she saw Pique was right, she cried out in fury and dashed to the car behind hers.

'They're all gone!' she cried. 'Every single one!'

The Swifts soon discovered that in the long line of cars that snaked down the driveway, not one of them had been left with a steering wheel. Those that had not been unclipped from the dashboard had simply been sawn off, leaving sad stumps behind.

'When did this happen?' cried Uncle Ferrier, stroking his Rolls-Royce as if it was an injured thoroughbred.

'They must have come in the night as we slept on, oblivious,' said Pique.

'But why?'

'Isn't it obvious?' Though Atrocious didn't shout,

her voice carried down the drive. 'They don't want us to leave.'

'What? Who doesn't?'

Atrocious shrugged one elegant shoulder. 'Whoever tried to kill Arch-Aunt Schadenfreude. The murderer among us.'

There was a surge en masse towards the phone as everyone rushed to call their friends, lawyers, partners, parole officers, travel agents, doctors, and employees. But in the comfortable little nook by the billiards room, morale was dealt a second blow: the cord connecting the receiver to the old rotary phone had been neatly severed, and the receiver itself was missing. The Swifts could dial all the numbers they liked, but they could talk to no one.

A scouting party pulled on their boots and made the trek to the edge of the estate, only to return with news that the gates had been locked tight and looped with heavy chains. They could not even rely on passing locals for help, as over the years Aunt Schadenfreude had made it clear – with the aid of a blunderbuss and some harsh words – that no one was allowed to set foot on the Swift estate unless expressly invited by herself.

Without the phone or the cars, they were now totally isolated from the outside world.

Suspicion settled upon the House like a fog. The Swifts were no strangers to murderous disputes, so the attack on Arch-Aunt Schadenfreude wouldn't have been all that worrying if it had not been for this latest offence. Killing a rival was one thing – who *didn't* know someone who knew someone who'd engaged in a little casual assassination? – but preventing the entire Family from escape was another thing entirely, a sinister second move in a game with rules uncertain, its object unknown. In different pockets of the House, Swifts were eyeing each other warily, the same question buzzing in the air of every occupied room: *What next?*

Someone had an answer, and that someone was Aunt Inheritance. With her white gloves and her blue ledger, she waved everyone to and fro like a teacher on a school trip.

'We can't let murder get in the way of Family time!' she called, a desperate edge to her voice. 'Advanced charades has been moved to tomorrow afternoon! The next activity, a performance by Thespian of *The Tragical Tale of Gramercy and Vile*, starts in the morning room in fifteen minutes!'

Pleas for an explanation went unanswered, and Inheritance practically fled from her relatives' questions. In her absence, Fauna flitted among the harried Swifts, patting shoulders, pouring tea, offering a word of reassurance here and there. Flora watched her sister with a smile.

'Poor Fauna,' she said. 'She can't help herself. Always trying to take care of everybody.'

'You're very different,' observed Phenomena. 'Not in looks, of course, but Fauna seems quite nurturing. Sweet. You're more . . .'

'Acidic,' said Shenanigan.

It was a good word; it could mean someone who said sharp things, or a substance that burned what it touched, or something that tasted sharp, like the coffee beans Flora chewed.

'Acidic! I like that.' Flora seemed to come to a decision. 'Look, you two. I can't stand Aunt Schade, but I don't wish her dead. Even if I wanted to hurt her, can you imagine how upset Fauna would be? I'd never do that.'

This time, Shenanigan got a good look at Flora's face, and could give her sister a proper answer. 'She's telling the truth.'

Phenomena accordingly made a note in her book.

'My sister is very good at spotting tells and micro-expressions. If you were lying, she'd know,' she said.

As people started to shuffle towards the morning room, Erf tramped up the stairs, the list of suspects clutched in their hand.

'Well, we can cross a few people off. Uncle Ferrier has an alibi. He was hunting for the treasure last night and fell through a trapdoor by the Avocado Bathroom. He was stuck through there for a good two hours. The Lady in the Pelican Hat is called Dither, and it's not a pelican, by the way, it's an African grey parrot. I asked her why she wasn't in the dining room and she burst into tears. Apparently, she has deipnophobia.'

'Which is?' asked Shenanigan, one eye on the people filtering into the morning room for the performance.

'A morbid fear of dinner parties. She was in her room most of the night. "Just the knowledge that a dinner party was going on below me was enough to send me into fits," she said. Candour's a doctor, so he went up to give her something for her nerves at eight – sorry, Phenomena – 8 p.m. He stayed for nearly an hour, playing backgammon with Dither and her brother – which I suppose means we can cross Candour off too.'

'And Daisy?'

Erf shook their head. 'I didn't get a chance to speak to her alone. She says she had a migraine. Candour confirms it, so as far as he's concerned she was in her room all night. At least, until she ran past you in the corridor.'

Flora, who had been getting her coffee beans out of her pocket, suddenly jerked, scattering them everywhere.

'*Ten minutes till curtain!*' a voice called from several rooms away. Shenanigan wriggled, desperate to get going.

'Are you going to tell us your alibi now?' she asked Flora.

Flora hesitated.

'I was in my room, reading,' she said.

Shenanigan stared hard at Flora again. This time, something was off – she could see a lie, a small one, hovering near the mole by her left eyebrow. And Flora could see that she could see, and Shenanigan could see that she could see that she could see, and so they both sat seeing each other for a few moments, until Shenanigan felt something like trust.

'Alright,' said Shenanigan, which meant: *I know you're not telling the whole truth, but I have decided to give you the benefit of the doubt.*

'Alright,' said Flora, which meant: *I know you don't believe me, but I appreciate your trust.*

'Alright,' said Phenomena, which meant: *I'm not sure what both of your faces were doing just then, but I don't care because I want to move things along.*

She produced the vial from her pocket. 'What can you tell me about this? It's a bit of a coffee bean we found at the scene of the crime.'

'Five minutes till curtain!'

Phenomena handed Flora the vial. Flora opened it and took out the piece of coffee bean. She sniffed it, then popped it into her mouth.

Phenomena yelped. 'Why does *no one* respect the evidence?'

Flora moved the coffee bean around her mouth for a few seconds, brow furrowed in concentration. Then she wrinkled her nose and spat the crumb back into the vial.

'That's *kopi luwak*. Civet coffee,' she added, seeing Shenanigan open her mouth to ask. 'I've only had it a few times before. It's . . . not my favourite, but it is pretty unusual.'

'How?'

Flora poured a few of her own beans in her mouth,

chewed, and swallowed. 'Have you ever heard of the Asian palm civet?'

Shenanigan hadn't, but Erf, who was proving to be a great asset to the team, had.

'The Asian palm civet, or *Paradoxurus hermaphroditus*, is a medium-sized viverrid common to South-east Asia.' Shenanigan got the feeling Erf was reciting this from memory. 'It is an omnivore, and it looks a bit like a cross between a cat, a ferret, and a lemur.' They smiled. 'It is extremely cute.'

Flora nodded. 'Well, *kopi luwak* is usually produced in regions native to the civet – Java, Bali, places like that. It's made by a pretty unique method. You see, they feed the coffee cherries to the civet . . .'

'Oh no,' said Shenanigan, who had begun to see where this was going.

'. . . and something happens to the coffee beans as they pass through the civet's digestive system. Fermentation, it's called. When the civet . . . *passes* the beans, they are collected, cleaned off, and sold. That's why it's called civet coffee! Supposedly, the trip through the civet's innards improves the flavour, but I can't say I'm a fan. I like my coffee acidic –' she grinned – 'much like me.'

Shenanigan was still struggling with this information. 'People . . . drink coffee . . . pooped out by a civet?'

'Don't knock it till you've tried it, I always say. Though you'd struggle to afford it in the first place – *kopi luwak* is considered a delicacy. It's some of the most expensive coffee in the world. Whoever dropped this bean is probably rolling in cash.'

'*One minute till curtain!*' called Aunt Inheritance.

'Well then, we know who to talk to next, right, Shenanigan?' said Phenomena. 'Shenanigan?' She caught her sister edging towards the morning room and grabbed her sleeve. 'Hey! Where are you going? We need to continue the investigation!'

'But . . .'

'You're not seriously going to wander off in the middle of this, are you?' she demanded.

Shenanigan looked from the morning room door to her sister, and then to Erf, for a bit of variety. The longer she went without answering, the darker Phenomena's expression became. It was on the tip of her tongue to say *Yes, actually*, but then she remembered her aunt, lying flat on the table.

Shenanigan cast a last longing look at the morning room, sighed, and let herself be pulled away.

14

LESSONS IN VILLAINY

Atrocious and Pique had ignored their allocated rooms and staked their claim on the tower as soon as they had arrived. Phenomena and Shenanigan weren't the first investigators to make the hike up to the rhinoceros's horn. As they neared the doorway to the tower, it spat out a beige-coated figure.

'*I came out of the siblings' room revivified,*' muttered Gumshoe, scribbling vigorously. '*A brand-new lead and we hadn't even hit lunch. I was hot on the heels, tight on the tail, fast on the footsteps of whoever had gone after the old lady. The dame had pointed me at a motive; I had to hit the books, shake a few dead trees and see what came loose.*'

The sisters flattened themselves against the wall to let him past, but, like a trip to the dentist, he could not be entirely avoided.

'Hey, it's the petite PIs!'

Phenomena pretended to be terribly interested in a spot on her lab coat. Gumshoe was undeterred.

'You giving the sibs the buzz?'

'We're questioning suspects, if that's what you mean,' interpreted Shenanigan.

'Suspects?' Gumshoe laughed. 'Atrocious and Pique? Nah. That Atrocious has the face of an angel – she could never be a killer. Dames are never killers!'

From what she'd read in detective novels, Shenanigan thought that dames, in general, were fairly likely to be killers, especially if you called them dames.

'She did give me something to chew over, though. A clue, sort of.' He winked. 'But that's detective business. Now scram. I've got some research to do.'

He loped away, jingling something in his pocket and whistling.

'Shenanigan,' said Phenomena gravely, 'I detest that man.'

Shenanigan knocked on the siblings' door, a daunting iron affair at the tower's base. A soft, bored voice called, 'Come in.'

The Sort-of-Yellow Suite had always been thoroughly unremarkable. It was made up of a plainly decorated, unused lounge, with two bedrooms stacked one on top of the other into the tower's point. The wallpaper had been patterned with tentative flowers, and the curtains had been an uncertain green.

Atrocious had clearly not found the lounge up to her standards. Three large crocodile-skin suitcases stood in a corner of the room, and from them she had pulled a portable boudoir. The wallpaper was now black and gold, the curtains – still shut – a heavy, dark-red velvet. Shawls draped over the lamps suffused the room with a bloody glow. Expensive-looking, densely patterned rugs were overlaid on the floor, and Shenanigan lost her balance if she looked at them too long.

On the sofa lounged Cousin Atrocious, in a dress so shiny and dark it looked like oil. Shenanigan saw with a shock that she was turning the pages of Felicity's sketchbook with one long, perfectly manicured nail. Even more shockingly, Felicity herself was perched on a chair next to her, looking excited and uncomfortable.

'Felicity!' blurted Shenanigan.

Atrocious flicked her eyes over the two younger siblings. 'Oh. It's the little goblin from last night. And another sister! We have all the makings of a fairy tale.' She took a sip from her glass. 'Once upon a time, there were three sisters. One had the gift of brains, one had the gift of beauty, and one had . . . well –' she smirked at Shenanigan – 'I'm sure you have *something* going for you.'

Shenanigan really, really hoped Atrocious was their killer. She would love nothing more than to shove her in an iron maiden.

'A little bird told me you're . . . What was the word Gumshoe used, dear brother?'

Shenanigan started. She hadn't even noticed Pique, who was helping himself from a makeshift bar in the corner of the room stacked with interesting bottles, a teapot, and a coffee machine.

' "Meddling", I believe,' he replied.

'*Gumshoe*'s the meddler,' protested Phenomena. 'He couldn't solve a crossword, never mind a murder.'

'Phenomena!'

'It's alright, Felicity, dear,' purred Atrocious. 'Clearly standards slipped after Schadenfreude raised you.' She turned back to the sketchbook, tapping a drawing of an orange sundress with one long fingernail. 'Pique, look at this one! Isn't it just charming?'

'So simple, and yet so striking,' he agreed, peering over her shoulder.

Felicity beamed and stared shyly at her feet, but

Shenanigan caught the mocking laughter hiding behind their cousins' back teeth. Felicity didn't realize she was being teased. The cruelty of this knocked Shenanigan sideways. If she didn't like something Felicity made, she told her so to her face. She didn't snigger about it behind her back.

'If you keep at this, you might even see your designs in a department store one day!' said Atrocious.

'Do you really think so?' Felicity's eyes were wide and hopeful.

Shenanigan couldn't watch this go on any longer. She walked over to the bar and picked up a bottle. Then she deliberately let it slip through her fingers and crash to the floor.

'Oops,' she said. She picked up another, this one with a drunk octopus on the front. 'Clumsy me.' It clattered to the rug, spilling dark liquid. 'That looks like it will stain. Sorry!'

'You little hooligan!' cried Pique, moving towards her.

'I can't apologize enough, but I'm very thirsty,' said Shenanigan, picking up a third bottle. 'I'm just – uh-oh!'

Pique cursed and ran for a cloth. While he was distracted, Shenanigan picked up a bag of coffee beans and studied it. The bag was silk, and felt heavily expensive. Nowhere on the label did it say anything about civets.

She looked up to see Atrocious watching her coolly. While her brother fretted over the liquid soaking into the rug, and Felicity fell over herself apologizing for her sisters, Atrocious and Shenanigan had what felt like a staring contest.

'Why don't you sit down?' Atrocious said, finally. 'You have a question for me.'

Shenanigan sat. She held up the bag of coffee beans. 'This isn't *kopi luwak*.'

Atrocious snorted. 'Civet coffee? Goodness, no. I only drink the *very* best.'

'But isn't it the most expensive coffee in the world?' asked Phenomena.

'It is. But I don't pay for my coffee, dear. I grow my own on a private island, in the shade of an active volcano. The ash in the soil makes for a wonderfully smoky taste.' She sipped her drink. 'I wouldn't swallow any other brand.'

Shenanigan slumped. Atrocious wasn't lying.

'You weren't at dinner last night, either,' Phenomena tried.

'No.'

'Where were you?'

'Hogging the phone,' interrupted Pique, holding a sopping towel in each hand. 'She was talking to her husband for hours, which was very unkind of her, as she knew I wanted to talk to *my* husband about some of his investments.'

'So you were the last to use the phone before it was sabotaged?'

Felicity put a hand to her mouth. 'Phenomena, are you accusing our cousins of—'

'Most likely I was, yes. You can check the phone records, if you like,' said Atrocious. 'That's what they do in the movies, isn't it? Check phone records?'

'I'm not sure we can do that.'

She shrugged. 'Not my problem. Although, your cook walked past me, carrying a tray upstairs, at one point – she can confirm my story. Gave me such a dirty look too, and all I did was tell her to turn down the sheets. You might consider new staff.'

Atrocious and Pique were without doubt the most unpleasant people Shenanigan had ever met. It would have given her great pleasure to clap them in handcuffs, or put them in the stocks for the rest of the Family to throw rotten fruit and vegetables at, as people had done in medieval times. Their innocence would be really inconvenient.

'You could have paid someone to kill her,' countered Phenomena.

'My word. What are they teaching you nowadays?' Atrocious handed her empty glass to Pique, who carried it over to the sadly emptied bar. 'Take it from someone who has been on the wrong side of a lot of detectives. When a person is murdered, the very first thing they look for is a motive. Ask yourself: what motive could a person possibly have for killing Aunt Schadenfreude?'

'Flora said people don't like her,' put in Shenanigan.

'Oh, *Flora*,' said Atrocious scornfully. 'People don't kill other people just because they don't like them. They do it because they have something to gain from their death. Like power. Like money.'

'Aunt Schadenfreude doesn't have any money.'

'No?' Pique handed Atrocious a fresh drink. 'She has the House. And if she has the House, she has Vile's Hoard, doesn't she? At least until it's found. Legally speaking, the House and all its contents belong to the Matriarch or Patriarch. That's true of the treasure as well, regardless of who finds it.'

'*What?*' Shenanigan had never considered this.

'Yes. Although –' Atrocious's eyes slid over to Shenanigan – 'there's always a chance the Hoard will be found by an enterprising young Swift who'll clean out the trove without telling anyone.'

It felt as if Atrocious was looking right into her. Shenanigan had the uncomfortable feeling that Atrocious understood her better than anyone else she knew.

'No one in this Family would do that,' said Felicity stoutly.

Some of the scorn finally showed through on Atrocious's face.

'Vile did. Vile robbed and murdered his family, and many more besides. Oh, he didn't take an axe to all of them, but how do you think he made his wealth?' Atrocious shrugged. 'The Hoard is made of gold and silver, yes. But it's also made of textiles and tobacco, mines and machinery, spices and blood. The history of our Family, as Inheritance could tell you, is one of heroism, intrigue, adventure. But it's also one of deceit, and theft, and plain old nastiness.'

Shenanigan thought about Gramercy, Cantrip, and Vile, painted in a solemn line beneath the oak tree. She thought of Vile's Monument, erected on the site where he killed his brother, and still there all these years later.

'Money and power. You want a motive? There's a motive. I'll tell you what I told Gumshoe: find who's after the Hoard and you find who hurt your aunt. But it's not me. I'd much rather earn a dishonest living.' She flicked her fingers. 'You can leave now,' she said. 'You're all very tiring – and reminding me why I don't have children.'

Felicity retrieved her sketchbook from where Atrocious had been using it as a coaster. As soon as the door closed, her shy smile tipped over into a scowl.

'I cannot believe the way you two behaved in there!' She glared. 'You were just so needlessly rude!'

'Not needlessly,' said Shenanigan.

'Well, I expected this from you, Shenanigan, but Phenomena? You know better!' Felicity hugged her sketchbook to her chest. 'The first time I meet anyone who might appreciate fashion, who can give me advice, who likes my designs – and you two spoil it!'

Phenomena and Shenanigan glanced at each other. Neither could bring themselves to tell Felicity the truth: that Atrocious and Pique saw her as nothing more than a little mouse, squeaking for their amusement.

'They were on our list of suspects.'

Felicity closed her eyes. Somewhere, very near now, was the end of her tether.

'Of course. Your investigation. Have you even visited Aunt Schadenfreude today? To see how she is?'

Shenanigan opened her mouth, then shut it again. In their rush to treat Aunt Schadenfreude's death as a murder, Shenanigan had almost forgotten she was still alive. She banished the twinge of guilt to the back of her mind.

'There's no point! She's just as unconscious as she was yesterday. The best thing we can do for her is catch whoever attacked her!'

'*Unbelievable*,' bit out Felicity. 'You are the most selfish, the most pig-headed . . . I can't.' She turned on her heel and stalked off.

'She keeps doing that,' remarked Phenomena.

Atrocious's words followed Shenanigan back to the main body of the House. It was true that Shenanigan had never considered who the treasure truly belonged to, or how Vile had got it. The House echoed with the sound of knocking as people tapped on walls to check for hollow spaces. Even now, she felt the urge to ditch

Phenomena and run off to a dim and cobwebbed nook to see what she could dig up.

She wondered if this was what her parents felt when they entered one of their beloved historical sites. They were translators, not treasure hunters, but translation can be a sort of treasure if words mean more to you than gold. Maybe this feeling was in her blood. Or maybe – Shenanigan's pace slowed – maybe it was in her name. Since she had always thought the treasure fell under the finders keepers rule, all her fantasies had involved telling people she'd found it so they could seethe with envy. But now she knew that she was legally supposed to hand it over to Aunt Schadenfreude, she wasn't so sure what she'd do. Perhaps perform *a devious trick for an underhanded purpose*, as her definition said. Keep quiet, and keep the treasure for herself. It was what everyone was expecting, after all.

'Is our experiment still going?' she asked Phenomena.

'The one with the mould or the one about your name?'

'The one about my name.'

'Yes. Actually, I've been making notes.'

Phenomena flipped to the back of her notebook where she had drawn up a table. It was titled *Nominative*

Determinism in the Case of Shenanigan Swift, which, as usual, made no sense to Shenanigan. There were two columns: one said *In Character*, the other *Out of Character*. There were a lot more marks in the *In Character* column.

'I'm still gathering data,' explained Phenomena, 'to see if you live up to your name. For example, pouring drinks on the floor to annoy Atrocious and Pique was a very *In Character* thing for you to do, because you were acting like your definition.' Phenomena made a little mark in the *In Character* column. 'You trying to ditch the case so you could look for clues about the treasure in Cantrip's play – yes, I *know* that's what you were doing – was also very *In Character*. Do you see? When all this is over, we'll look at the totals and I can draw some conclusions.'

Shenanigan wasn't sure how she felt about that. She had agreed to this experiment, and she was still interested in the results, but didn't much like the idea of everything she did being boiled down to *In Character* or *Out of Character*. And if, once the study was over, the *In Character* column had the most marks in it, Shenanigan would have to face the fact that none of her decisions were really decisions at all, just her moving along the track the Dictionary had laid out for her the day she was born.

'In terms of the case, I think we should next try to corner Aunt Inheritance,' Phenomena went on. 'She was angry with Aunt Schadenfreude for an unknown reason. I'm not sure she likes the way our aunt runs things as Matriarch . . . maybe she's after the job?'

If Shenanigan was going to tell Phenomena about the secret room, now was the time. It could be relevant to the investigation, and if she wanted to prove that she wasn't selfish and devious, she should share what she knew. But she couldn't. Sailor's promise or not, her uncle's words had just made her more determined to get inside. She heard his voice in her head: *'You have to promise me you won't tell anyone.'*

Shenanigan stopped. That voice was familiar, but it was far too high-pitched to be her uncle, and far too loud to be in her head.

'I'm serious,' said the voice. 'Promise!'

As this was the sort of thing people expected her to do, Shenanigan had no problem with pulling Phenomena back behind a corner so they could listen to it.

'I promise. Who would I even tell?'

The second voice was also familiar, though there were two people it could belong to. She'd spoken to both only an hour or so ago. The speakers were in the Coral Bedroom, where Daisy and Candour were staying. Shenanigan signalled to Phenomena to wait, and then darted into the Coral Bedroom's next-door bathroom. Climbing on top of the sink, she peered through the peephole behind *Mermaid Eating a Hot Dog*.

'The important thing is to stay calm,' said Flora-or-Fauna. 'We just have to adapt the plan.'

Daisy sat on the bed, rubbing her temples. Shenanigan wriggled into a better position and nearly knocked a pair of toothbrushes off the sink. Each one had bristles shaped like half a heart, so when you put them together they made a whole one.

Ugh, she thought. *Soppy* and *unsanitary*.

'I know.' Daisy sounded wretched. 'And I know I've got to keep it together, but I just keep thinking *God, what have I done?* This'll ruin me, Flora.'

'It won't, because no one is going to find out.' Flora perched next to Daisy, and patted her gingerly on the shoulder. 'Um . . . there, there?'

To Shenanigan's (and clearly Flora's) surprise, Daisy leaned against Flora and laughed wetly.

'*There, there?*'

'Well, I don't know!' Flora didn't seem to know what to do with her arms. 'Comforting people isn't really . . .'

'In your wheelhouse? It's a baseball term,' she explained at Flora's blank look.

'Right.'

'Thank you, though.' Daisy dashed the tears from her eyes, and took a deep breath. 'Seriously. If you hadn't helped me out last night . . .'

Shenanigan's ears perked up. Fauna had been at dinner, but Flora had said she'd been in her room all evening, reading. Maybe this was her secret alibi – she'd been helping Daisy with something.

'Oh, er. Don't mention it.' Flora's hand moved to touch Daisy's, but she pulled back at the last second, aggressively chewing on her nails instead. 'But now you really need to stop feeling guilty. What's done is done, and we're dealing with it. Okay?'

'Okay. Yes.'

'The important thing right now is to make sure Candour stays oblivious. Reckon you can do that?'

'I can,' Daisy said in a steadier voice. 'Do you think anyone else is suspicious?'

'Not sure. Aunt Schadenfreude always kept – keeps? – her cards close to her chest. We've no way of knowing if she told anyone.'

Daisy sighed. 'Then we keep playing the game, I guess.'

'Just for a little longer. Once this Reunion is over, you'll be home free. That's the phrase, right? Baseball?'

'Sure.' Daisy hiccupped.

'I'll get you some water,' said Flora.

To Shenanigan's horror, she began walking towards her – or, rather, towards the bathroom door to her left. As quietly as she could, Shenanigan scrambled down from her perch on top of the sink. She opened the door to the corridor just as Flora opened hers, but in the second it took Flora to enter the room, Shenanigan had slipped out and silently shut the door behind her.

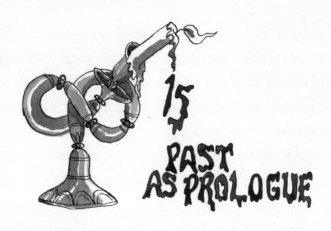

15
PAST AS PROLOGUE

Trust is not something you have or do not have. Trust is something you give precisely in small measures, teacups and egg cups at a time.

For example, Shenanigan trusted Cook to feed her and care for her every day, but she didn't trust her not to tell Aunt Schadenfreude about her smearing Felicity's lipstick on the statues. She trusted Phenomena to know the answer to any maths problem, but she didn't trust her not to start a fire in her lab. And she trusted her parents to love her no matter what, but she didn't trust them to make it to her next birthday party.

That morning, Shenanigan had poured a teacup's worth of trust into Flora, and it was as if Flora had poured it all over the floor. The betrayal she felt was new and awful. She had known Flora was hiding something – she had seen it in her face. Now she knew it was something to do with Daisy, and a guilty secret, and Shenanigan would have to be very bad at maths to put two and two together and not come up with: *Daisy shoved Aunt Schadenfreude down the stairs, and Flora is helping her cover it up.*

Shenanigan hadn't had time to form a solid opinion on Daisy, other than her natural distrust of someone who wears matching jewellery. But Aunt Schadenfreude had seemed pretty determined that Candour should end their engagement, to the point of outright forbidding their marriage. Though Daisy had played innocent, she clearly knew the reason Aunt Schadenfreude was so opposed to the match, and it was a bad one. Now she and Flora were worrying whether she'd told anyone else.

Atrocious had said that all murderers had a *motive*. It sounded as if Daisy had one. With Aunt Schadenfreude out of the way, Daisy would be free to marry Candour, and Flora would be free to . . . not eat her peas? Shenanigan hadn't thought that part out yet.

'Well,' said Phenomena, and then didn't say anything else until they were in Aunt Schadenfreude's study, where Cook sat in a chair as close to the desk as she could manage, reading ghost stories aloud to Erf.

Phenomena began firing off questions with a determination that would have made Gumshoe change careers.

'Daisy wasn't at dinner. Why?'

'She was feeling ill,' said Cook. 'Candour said she had a migraine, and he had to see to Dither, so I took her up a tray.'

'Right. And what time was that?'

'About half past seven.'

'What does *about* mean? I need exact timings. In decimals, if you please.'

'I don't know, Phenomena. 7.30 p.m. Roughly.'

'Did you pass Atrocious, on the phone?'

'Yes, the stuck-up—'

'And Daisy, how did she seem?'

'I – not well. She thanked me, and asked if she could borrow something to read, but all I had were my ghost stories, and of course the library's locked. Though why she'd think it was a good idea to read with a migraine—'

Phenomena turned abruptly to Shenanigan. 'And what time did you see Daisy running down the corridor?'

'A few minutes before 9 p.m.'

'What does "a few minutes" mean? And was she running away from her room, or back towards it?'

'Back towards it.'

'From?'

'How am I supposed to know?'

Phenomena snapped her book shut with a huff. 'You are both useless,' she said. Then, seeing their faces, added, 'At this specific thing. You are useless at this specific thing.'

Shenanigan understood this process must be frustrating for Phenomena, who treasured exactness. Shenanigan didn't need exact. At a few minutes before 9 p.m., Daisy had run past Shenanigan in the corridor, reappearing in the doorway to the study fifteen minutes later. She could have shoved Aunt Schadenfreude, run back to her room to hide, then pretended she had just woken up when Schadenfreude's unconscious body was brought upstairs. Now she was having hushed conversations with Flora and worrying about looking suspicious. As far as Shenanigan was concerned, this was an open-and-shut case, and she was ready to throw the book at Daisy – the book, in this case, being the Dictionary, which weighed as much as Shenanigan herself and could likely do some serious damage.

She could barely look at her aunt lying on the desk. Each time she did, she had a horrible swooping feeling, as if she'd missed a step somewhere inside. Schadenfreude's chest rose and fell so slowly it was hard to tell whether she was breathing, and the only noise she made was the faintest wheeze out of one nostril. Shenanigan couldn't help but feel that the longer the person who had done this was allowed to walk free, the more Aunt Schadenfreude would fade away, until only her shapeless black clothes would be left.

'What if we take too long?' she asked quietly, and she hated how small her voice sounded. 'What happens if whoever did this comes back to finish the job?'

Cook took an iron candlestick from the table. With the barest grunt of effort, she twisted it into a pretzel.

'That,' she said.

'. . . Well, it isn't a Family Reunion without some drama.'

'This isn't drama. Forgetting to invite Bellicose to a wedding, that's drama . . .'

' . . . Everywhere I turn I see what's-his-face, Flatfoot, skulking about with a magnifying glass . . .'

'I for one am glad he's on the case. He was very helpful when I lost my Pekingese, Buttercup.'

'He found it?'

'No, but he found me another one, with a much sweeter temper than the one that went missing.'

The three investigators caught snatches of conversation as they headed to the kitchen. Cook had sent them to 'check on Maelstrom', which sounded ominous. As soon as they were unobserved, Erf elbowed Shenanigan.

'Psst, I got something for you.' They pulled from the depths of their jumper a small, green book, very old and bound in leather. 'You didn't miss much, by the way,' they said casually. 'Thespian forgot his lines five times and had to read from the script for most of it. Then the scenery fell on his head.'

Shenanigan looked at the book.

The Tragical Tale of Gramercy and Vile
by Cantrip Swift

Shenanigan grabbed Erf by the shoulders. Erf looked alarmed, until they saw Shenanigan's manic grin.

'Erf,' she said. 'You are brilliant.'

Erf shrugged. 'Well, you seemed so upset about missing the performance. And I had to be there anyway, or Gran would have had a conniption.'

'What's that?'

'Not sure, but it sounds painful. I stuck around, and while Thespian was taking his bows I just sort of . . . took the book.' They looked abashed. 'I've never stolen anything before. Gran would probably say you're a bad influence.'

The thought made Shenanigan quite proud.

She opened the book. The first page read:

PROLOGUE

Gather ye close, and lest we lose our heads
In fumbling for ill fortune ill begot,
We first speak in dishonour of the dead,
Our fortune's fools, our old Familial rot;
Of violence and vile deeds, and of Vile's deed,
When he in envy, for a shilling's lack,
Hacked off the branches of our Family tree
And buried the hatchet in his brother's back.
Good kin, on blood I beg you: keep our ways,
Be rich in kindness, and be rich in kind;
Mark well the well-marked meaning of our days

And each Reunion riches shall ye find.
But as you seek your pocketful of crowns,
Recall the poor man floats, the rich one drowns.

Too late, and with a sinking feeling, Shenanigan realized two things. First, that Cantrip had been alive in the 1600s, and people talked differently then; and, second, that she'd been obsessed with Shakespeare.

'Is the whole thing like this?' she asked, dismayed.

''Fraid so. Sorry.'

Shenanigan groaned. The play could be full of clues, yet she wouldn't have a hope of understanding them.

She read the prologue over and over on the way to the kitchen, trusting her feet to navigate for her. When they stumbled down the steps, Felicity and one of the twins were sitting at the scarred table. Behind them bustled Uncle Maelstrom, his stormy hair swept beneath a bandanna and Cook's apron tied about his waist. Flora-or-Fauna slid over a plate of biscuits. Her nails were cut short, not chewed – Fauna, then. She had Felicity's sketchbook open in front of her.

'I'm serious, Felicity,' she was saying. 'You have a real, rare talent.'

While Atrocious had been teasing Felicity when she

said this, Fauna clearly meant it. Shenanigan ate her biscuits and watched Fauna exclaim over Felicity's work. She asked about her design influences and inspiration. She listened attentively as Felicity shyly admitted her desire to study in Paris.

'I wonder if that's where Daisy gets her clothes,' sighed Felicity. 'The dress she was wearing yesterday was so *chic*! I don't think I could pull it off, though.'

'Oh, I refuse to hear that kind of talk,' said Fauna. 'You can wear whatever you want, and you'll look beautiful doing it.'

Shenanigan hoped that, whatever Flora was up to, Fauna wasn't part of it. She also hoped that, one day, Felicity would learn there was a difference between well-dressed and well-intentioned.

It was maybe time to address the elephant in the room, which was wearing an apron and shaped like Uncle Maelstrom.

'You might be surprised to learn,' said Maelstrom with the air of someone imparting precious knowledge, 'that I was executive chef on the *Drunken Noodle* when I was younger.'

'Really? What was your signature dish?' asked Erf curiously.

'Seagull Surprise!' he said. 'Food was scarce, but there were always plenty of seagulls about.'

'Not in our kitchen, though, Uncle.'

'Well, there's chicken. And what is chicken, if not the seagull of the land? Now, the first thing we need is gunpowder, and lots of it—'

Felicity jumped in. 'Cook and I prepared a lot of dishes already. They'll be in the freezer, Uncle M. You won't need to do much more than heat them up.'

The girls and Erf headed into the frozen reaches of the walk-in freezer, which was cavernous and bigger than any of their bedrooms. They brought out a cornucopia of vegetables, ruby sides of salmon, avalanches of potato, and huge bowls of dashi stock like frozen lakes. There was a lasagne as big as a table, a vat of black-bean stew, dumplings the size of tennis balls, blocks of mushroom risotto, bricks of tofu, skewers of Moroccan lamb. They thought that was probably enough, but they poured a sack of rice into the old washing machine Cook had converted into a rice cooker, just to be safe.

The greedy jaws of three ovens gaped wide, and into them Maelstrom thrust each dish, like an engineer shovelling coal into a steam engine. When everything was ticking over nicely, and everyone but Phenomena had gone upstairs to change, Uncle Maelstrom prodded Shenanigan gently in the shoulder.

'A word?'

They left Phenomena reading a cookbook at the table. Maelstrom beckoned Shenanigan into the freezer and shut the door. He tried to lean casually against the wall and almost slipped on the ice.

'Shenanigan,' he said seriously, 'do you remember our sailor's promise?' She nodded. 'I need to know – have you told anyone about your map?'

'No!' cried Shenanigan, indignant. Promises were hard to wrangle from her, but the ones she made she kept. 'Why?'

'No reason,' said Maelstrom, clearly relieved. 'An idle wonder.'

Everyone assumed Shenanigan lied a lot. This was unfair, because, in fact, Shenanigan never lied. Since she could spot lies so easily in other people, she reasoned it was better to avoid discovery by always telling a version of the truth, or by saying nothing at all. Maelstrom clearly had never learned this trick, because his lie was curled up comfortably in the corner of his mouth, making it twitch.

'Uncle, what's going on?'

Uncle Maelstrom struggled. 'Nothing. Well, something. Some people here are untrustworthy – that's all.'

'Which people?'

'Just some of them,' said Maelstrom. 'Could I see the map for a moment?'

Shenanigan could feel the folded paper in the pocket of her trousers. Ordinarily, she would have handed it over without a second thought. But there was that lie again, making her uncle's familiar face feel strange and wrong. She wasn't sure what to do.

She was saved from decision-making by the smell of burning.

'Oh no,' they both said at once.

Maelstrom ran for the freezer door, but there wasn't a handle on the inside, as food usually doesn't try to escape. He pounded hard on the metal. 'Phenomena!' he yelled. 'Phenomena!'

But Phenomena, engrossed in her book, did not hear. Maelstrom and Shenanigan hammered for several minutes, and all the while the burning smell leaking through the vent grew stronger. Ice crystals began to form in Maelstrom's beard. Eventually, Phenomena opened the door, cookbook held loosely in her hand.

'Why are you in the freezer?'

Uncle Maelstrom and Shenanigan pushed past her into the kitchen. The smell was overpowering. They opened the doors of the three ovens and smoke belched forth in an acrid cloud. Phenomena stood bemused in the centre of the room as Maelstrom pulled out tray after tray, but they were too late. Every piece of food was blackened to a crisp.

'I'm sorry, Uncle,' Phenomena said miserably. 'I didn't realize.'

'It's not your fault, Phenomena,' said Maelstrom. 'You couldn't smell anything wrong.'

The three of them stared at the ruined food cooling slowly on the kitchen table.

'What do we do now?' asked Shenanigan.

'I don't know,' said Maelstrom. 'To tell you the truth, I'm not sure how to cook anything that isn't seagull.'

'Well,' said Phenomena hesitantly, 'this book says that cooking is just applied chemistry. Maybe I can muddle through.'

'We don't have many ingredients left,' warned Maelstrom.

'Then we'll make soup. Soup should be easy, surely?' Phenomena began rifling through the spice rack, which took up one wall. 'Besides, the benefit of cooking over chemistry is that if I make a mistake nothing should blow up.'

'Just try not to make cyanide,' said Shenanigan.

16

AFTER-DINNER HINTS

Maelstrom disappeared to his room and came back hauling a huge tin bath. This they scrubbed down, filled with water, and heaved on to the massive hob to boil. They threw in everything they could find that hadn't been cooked by Cook or burned by Maelstrom, and soon had a dark, spicy broth the colour and consistency of gravy. It bubbled lazily, so thick that it sucked at the ladle as Shenanigan stirred. Into this concoction Phenomena dropped the uncooked dumplings, which swelled to the size of footballs until the soup resembled a swamp, the dumplings floating like stepping stones.

Uncle Maelstrom lashed two mops together with a tablecloth as a makeshift stretcher. They heaved the bathtub of hot soup on top, and began the long trek to the dining room, carrying the stretcher as gingerly as they'd carried Aunt Schadenfreude's empty coffin so many times before.

Shenanigan had slept through last night's meal, so was startled at the spectacle of the dining table, fully laid. Usually it was just their little family-with-a-small-*f* clustered at one end around a tattered yellow tablecloth. Now the table was blanketed in a cloth as white as fondant icing, with gleaming silverware and crystal and the occasional candelabra – though Aunt Schadenfreude's high-backed seat at the head of the table was empty.

With all that finery, it would be natural to assume the Swifts had excellent table manners. In fact, it was a mad scramble to the tin bath. Elbows and cutlery were employed often and savagely. They swarmed the tub with bowls and goblets in hand, dipping them into the soup, not caring about drops or dribbles. They hoisted out dripping dumplings and plonked them on to plates, slicing them like birthday cake. Within fifteen minutes, the bathtub was empty, and the tablecloth utterly ruined.

As she mopped her plate, Shenanigan kept an ear on the conversations going on around her, tuning in and out as if she was flipping through radio stations.

'. . . a migraine, I'm afraid, but it does help to have a doctor as a fiancé!'

'. . . I do think their cook is rather rude . . . difficult to get staff . . .'

'. . . somewhere in Peru, I heard . . .'

'. . . job like that needs a can opener and a button man . . .'

'. . . Miss DeMille, of the New York DeMilles?'

Shenanigan made herself tune in fully. Halfway down the table, Atrocious had occupied the chair next to Daisy. She was separated from Candour by several seats, and her fiancé looked understandably worried, fiddling with the clasp of his doctor's bag.

'I see your Aunt Hyacinth all the time at society functions. How wonderful that our families will soon be connected!' beamed Atrocious. 'They say you've done *very* well for yourself with Candour.'

Daisy glanced along the table to her fiancé, who was clearly eavesdropping. 'I certainly think so.' She smiled, and fluttered her fingers at him. Her engagement ring winked flirtatiously in the light, and Atrocious eyed it with a faint look of distaste.

'I must apologize for your having to deal with our musty old traditions. I imagine you think we're *quite* ridiculous.' Atrocious gave a practised laugh. 'But our

Family goes back a long way. You accumulate ideas over time. Like plaque.'

'Oh, all families have their own special brand of strangeness,' said Daisy diplomatically. 'And it's helped me understand Candour better, seeing where he comes from. I get why he moved to New York.'

Shenanigan found it eerie watching Daisy and Atrocious. Their mouths were smiling, their words were bland, but it was as if a fight was taking place. It was weaponized politeness.

'How kind. But still,' Atrocious pressed, 'I hope you don't feel *unwelcome*, especially after what Schadenfreude said. I'd be appalled if people were being beastly towards you. Talking about you behind your back, that sort of thing. Treating you like a suspect.'

Daisy's smile remained firmly in place. She patted Atrocious's hand, and somehow it was like a slap.

'That's very sweet of you,' she said, 'but I can handle myself around a bunch of stuck-up, self-absorbed high-society types. *If* I encounter any.'

Atrocious's dark gaze was assessing. A corner of her mouth twitched upwards.

'Candour misjudged you,' she said finally, soft enough

that only Daisy could hear, or only an amateur lip-reader like Shenanigan could interpret.

'Ah, children.'

A shadow fell across Erf's plate. Shenanigan blinked as Aunt Inheritance did her best to loom.

'I have heard you children are investigating Aunt Schadenfreude's . . . *incident* . . . despite my explicit instructions.' Their aunt looked worse than before, worn thin and shabby from a day of wrangling her relatives. 'While I knew that would hardly stop *you* –' she eyed Shenanigan – 'I would have thought the rest of you might be more sensible. Phenomena, you are older and better-named. You must know that you're not qualified. Gumshoe *means* detective – he's the most logical choice to sort all of this out.'

Phenomena took a long sip of her Solution Solution, and did not deign to answer. Shenanigan didn't see the point in being tactful.

'Why weren't you at dinner the night of the murder, Aunt Inheritance?' she asked as innocently as possible. 'Where were you?'

Aunt Inheritance's mouth dropped open.

'How—I—That's none of your concern!' she snapped. 'I am the Archivist! I'm trying to run this Reunion, *and* conduct my own research, and *now* someone has stolen *The Tragical Tale of Gramercy and Vile* right out from under Thespian's nose! It was a first edition! I don't have time for your shen—for your mischief!'

Shenanigan felt Erf shrink into their jumper, and gave them a friendly pinch. It was important not to admit to anything unless there was proof.

'And you, dear –' Inheritance's voice softened when she turned to Erf – 'I hope you're not involved in this. It's too dangerous. You are my only grandchild, and if anything were to happen to you . . .'

Erf looked down at the tablecloth.

'I can't watch out for you on top of everything else.' Inheritance sighed. 'So once again, as Archivist, I am *ordering* you all to stop poking around, before there are consequences. And *do* put on your name badge,' she added to Erf. 'People won't know who you are otherwise.'

Erf made a show of digging in their pockets, but stopped as soon as Inheritance left the table.

'She's just being overprotective,' they muttered.

The coffee cups were brought out, used, then cleared away. People drifted off, or loosened their belts and lay back, picking their teeth. Shenanigan opened *The*

Tragical Tale of Gramercy and Vile under the table, and tried to figure out whether 'fortune's fools' referred to the treasure or just bad luck.

Then there came a scream.

It was as if someone had thrown a stone into a pool. For a second, there was silence, a dip as the scream dropped through everyone's conversation – and then all the voices rushed back into place, crashing over each other as the Swifts scraped back their chairs and ran towards the noise.

Shenanigan was quick, but not quick enough. A dozen people were out of the door before she thought to leap up on to the table and sprint. The screaming didn't stop, and they were all pulled towards it, down the hall, past the morning room to the double doors of the library, which now stood wide open and clogged with people. Shenanigan dropped to her knees and crawled towards the entrance, poking a few ankles with her spoon to get them to move.

Renée Swift, née Carter, was slumped and sobbing just inside the doorway. Fauna had reached her first, and was patting her hair and making soothing noises. Shenanigan couldn't see much further – only a sliver of the room, with something wet and red on the floor.

Fortissimo pushed through, little Finicky cradled in his arms.

'LET ME THROUGH,' he boomed, then, to Finicky, '*rock-a-bye baaaaby, on the treetoooop* . . . THAT'S MY WIFE!'

Fortissimo knelt at Renée's side, shielding the baby's face from the library interior. '*When the wind blows, the cradle will* . . . DARLING, IT'S ALRIGHT. I'M HERE . . . *roooock. When the bough breaks, the cradle will* . . . DON'T LOOK.'

But now Shenanigan could shuffle a little to the left and, for a brief second, before Maelstrom's hand descended like a claw machine to pull her away, she could look. She could look right into the room at the shiny tips of Gumshoe's shoes, the sprawl of his trench coat against the carpet; at his hand, loosely holding a book; and the white marble bust of Grand-Uncle Vile, stained with red, that now occupied the spot where Gumshoe's head used to be.

Shenanigan was pretty sure most people's family reunions didn't have a body count, but, then again, most people's libraries didn't require a helmet. Renée and Fortissimo were led away by Fauna, who continued to whoosh softly like a washing machine, and then the Swifts ushered Candour towards the library door. He stared down at the headless corpse with his doctor's bag clutched in hand. Everyone waited expectantly as he looked from corpse to crowd to corpse again. Finally, he felt Gumshoe's neck for a pulse.

'I'm afraid he's dead.'

The crowd gasped obediently. Candour cleared his throat, snapping on a fresh pair of white surgical gloves. 'Massive head trauma, if I had to guess. I think – it looks like a shelf collapsed, and one of the statues fell on him.' He stared at the body. 'What a horrible accident.'

'That shelf is hinged, look,' said Maelstrom, pointing at the site of collapse. 'Poor lad set off one of the traps.'

'Crikey. So you're saying this was –' Candour winced, even as the joke came out of his mouth – 'shelf-inflicted?'

Maelstrom's face did not twitch. 'Yes.'

Candour had the grace to look embarrassed. 'Could you help me get this statue off him? I can't lift it by myself. The rest of you, please go back to the dining room. You too, Daisy. I'll be alright. We'll . . . we'll be with you shortly.'

Shenanigan felt a tug on her elbow.

'I'm going upstairs for my Junior Forensics Kit,' Phenomena whispered. 'Whatever happens, don't let them remove the body!'

But this was easier said than done, because Uncle Maelstrom was taking his vow of sensibility very seriously. When Shenanigan and Erf tried to walk in under the poor pretence of wanting an encyclopedia, Maelstrom simply picked one of them up in each hand, turned them round, and planted them back on the other side of the door, apologizing as he closed it behind them. Shenanigan was reduced to squinting through the keyhole as Inheritance drew a chalk outline around both Gumshoe and his fallen hat. They all agreed that he would have appreciated that.

Then one of the throws from the back of the chaise longue was repurposed as a winding sheet, and between them – Maelstrom carrying the feet, Candour carrying the no-longer-a-head – the adults lugged Gumshoe out of the library. Shenanigan made a last-ditch attempt to slow their exit ('What was that? I'm blocking the door? Oh, I'm so sorry. Silly me, standing right in the doorway like this when you're trying to get past with something heavy . . . Alright, Uncle. I'm *moving*. Fine—') and when that didn't work, watched the melancholy crew disappear down the hall.

Still, Shenanigan knew an opportunity when it was left unlocked in front of her. She and Erf darted into the library and ducked behind the chaise longue. Soon, Phenomena returned to the scene with her Junior Forensics Kit – a large tin box that had been a gift from their parents. It had a cartoon of a dog in a deerstalker hat on the front, sniffing a bloodied pawprint.

Phenomena frowned at the empty chalk outline.

'Really,' she said loudly, 'the degree of unprofessionalism here—'

Shenanigan grabbed the hem of her lab coat and yanked her behind the chaise.

'Now is hardly the time for subterfuge and pranks, Shenanigan,' Phenomena huffed.

'Shh! It's exactly the time!'

They waited. But instead of the returning clomp of Maelstrom's boots they heard soft footsteps outside and a soft click of the door handle, and then a soft someone crept into the room. She looked about her, quick and furtive as a mouse, and skittered towards one of the shelves.

It was Daisy.

Shenanigan's blood fizzed as she watched Daisy cross the room in her stockinged feet, heels held loosely in one hand, and run her fingers over the spines of the books with mounting confusion. The Swifts did not arrange their library by genre, like some book collectors, or by author and title, like other book collectors, or by colour, like misguided interior decorators. Instead, they were organized by their important features. Small plaques on the shelves proclaimed which were *Books with Tigers in Them* or

Books About Doomed Voyages or *Books You Can Tell Other People You've Read to Seem More Intelligent*. This made finding a specific title quite difficult, and Daisy hadn't found whatever it was she looking for by the time a second set of footsteps approached.

She looked wildly around the room for a hiding place. Her eyes alighted on the chaise longue, and she stepped towards it – Shenanigan was sure they were about to be discovered – but at the last second Daisy changed her mind and darted behind one of the floor-length curtains flanking the window.

'Did we really have to put him in the freezer?' Inheritance sighed as the adults returned. 'We're going to have to walk past him every time we need some ice. And what if he haunts the sprouts?'

'I don't think that'll happen,' said Maelstrom. 'There are far more sinister vegetables.'

'Parsnips,' said Candour grimly. 'Always thought there was something off about parsnips. Though, given the circumstances, he might feel more at home with the squash.'

He polished his glasses, cleared his throat, put his hands on his hips, and then promptly sat down in the armchair.

'I'm sorry. I've come over weak all of a sudden. It must be because of all the head puns.'

'*Gather ye close, and lest we lose our heads . . .*' thought Shenanigan. She fought the hysterical urge to giggle.

'I'm not supposed to get . . . squeamish,' said Candour, looking grey. 'But his head . . .'

'Smashed like a melon,' said Maelstrom bluntly, inspecting the carpet where a large brownish stain marked Gumshoe's position. He picked up the bust of Grand-Uncle Vile, careful not to touch the mess at the base. He turned it in his hands. 'Yes, this is what did it. Heavy.'

'I couldn't even lift it,' Candour said wonderingly.

Maelstrom took an old sack from his pocket. 'Never liked having this around anyway,' he said, and dropped the statue inside. Erf pinched Phenomena to keep her from groaning aloud as yet more evidence was whisked away.

'And so the library claims another Swift,' intoned Aunt Inheritance. 'First Cousin Lectern – may he rest in peace – and now Gumshoe.'

'A terrible tragedy,' added Candour morosely. 'A great mind, taken from us too soon.'

'Yes, well,' said Inheritance. 'Let's have a look at what outsmarted him.'

Shenanigan's mapmaking mission hadn't reached the library yet, but she was aware of many traps there, nonetheless. For example, when taking *Siege Weaponry of the Norman Conquest* off the shelf, you had to immediately leap backwards to avoid the great big battleaxe that swung down from above. *The Bumper Book of Japes and Jokes* did something lethal with a rubber chicken. *The Phantom of the Opera* dropped the chandelier, and Felicity always forgot about that one, which was why their chandelier was so sorry-looking.

Maelstrom pointed out the shelf from which the statue had fallen. It looked to have been propping up several *Books with Significant Libraries in Them*, but one side of the shelf had tipped up, and most of the books had been knocked to the floor.

'You can see the hinge, just there,' said Maelstrom. 'It's a pretty simple trap, and an obvious one, if you're used to looking out for them. Works like a see-saw. Normally, the shelf is perfectly balanced – but remove the wrong book, and the balance shifts, the shelf tilts, and the statue falls. The girls would have seen through that in a second.'

There was a polite pause where they all thought, but did not say aloud, that Gumshoe had been an uncommonly stupid man.

'Well, we know which book triggered it, at least,' said Candour. 'He had it in his hand. *The Body in the Library* by Agatha Christie.'

Beside her, Shenanigan felt Phenomena poke her in the side excitedly. Her sister's eyes were wide with the effort of not communicating something out loud.

Shenanigan put a finger to her lips, which meant: *You have to be quiet. Tell me when it's safe.*

Phenomena squeezed her eyes shut, which meant: *AUUUUGGGGGGHHHH!*

Erf raised their eyebrows, which probably meant: *You two are incredibly weird.*

'Well, there we go,' said Aunt Inheritance hurriedly. 'What a shame! Such a terrible accident. We should go and reassure the others.'

'Belay that,' said Uncle Maelstrom, frowning at her. 'We should at least consider the possibility of foul play. Gumshoe was investigating an attempted murder!'

'Belay that "belay that",' said Aunt Inheritance. 'I'm telling you it was an accident. Gumshoe was a detective. He wouldn't allow himself to be murdered on a case.'

'Cook would agree with me,' countered Uncle Maelstrom. 'We watched Schadenfreude lock the library the night before the Reunion. How did Gumshoe even get in here? Schadenfreude keeps the only set of keys on her belt, and Cook says they've been missing since her fall.'

'Maybe Gumshoe found them. As a *detective* would.'

'Perhaps we should ask Cook to come down and offer her opinion?' ventured Candour.

'She won't leave Schadenfreude's side,' said Maelstrom. 'But there are other things missing. One of my compasses, and the keys to Cook's bike. So unless we have a kleptomaniac ghost—'

Aunt Inheritance bristled. 'The ghost does not *steal*. I'm sure Cook just mislaid them.'

That flipped Shenanigan's stomach like a pancake. Someone *had* taken Aunt Schadenfreude's keys, and that person was Shenanigan. She had used them to get into the cellar, and then, on the morning of the Reunion, she had run into her aunt's study and thrown them back on the desk. What if Schadenfreude never picked them back up? They could have sat there all day while all the commotion was going on downstairs. *Anyone* could've swiped them. A hot, sick feeling crept up Shenanigan's spine.

That seemed to be the extent of the adults' investigation. Maelstrom and Candour left, grave-faced and talking in low voices, but Aunt Inheritance lingered, frowning at the room as if it had vexed her in some way.

As soon as their aunt made her exit, Phenomena went to leap up. Shenanigan snatched her back. They waited. After a few moments, Daisy emerged from behind the curtain. For a moment, she too looked at the bloody carpet, a frown creasing her perfect face. Then she flitted to the *Books to Tell You Where You're Going* section, grabbed an atlas, and fled the room.

Finally, Phenomena could lose her temper.

'Those fools!' she snapped, leaping to her feet. 'Those absolute amateurs! That was like watching a fish try to make fire. Inheritance is in denial, Maelstrom is NOT cut out for detective work, and Candour is a medical man, so I'd have expected him to have at least SOME knowledge of the scientific process, but he *mmfffmff.*' She stuck the end of her ponytail in her mouth and chewed furiously.

Shenanigan agreed. Something didn't add up. She might not be able to put her finger on it with the same scientific accuracy as her sister, but that didn't mean she couldn't point in its general direction.

'Tell us what they did wrong, then,' she said.

Phenomena spat her ponytail back out. 'Number one: they assumed it was an accident right away. Every scientist knows that you look at the data first, then you come to a conclusion. They were looking for the data that would *prove* their conclusion.'

'*Riiiiight.*'

'But, if you think about it, this whole scene is nonsensical. Consider the way Gumshoe was found: flat on the floor with his head crushed, holding—'

'*The Body in the Library* by Agatha Christie.' Shenanigan realized what had been nagging at her.

'Is the title important?' asked Erf.

'Shenanigan and I both know detective novels are the safest books in the library,' said Phenomena grimly. 'That book couldn't possibly have set off the trap that killed Gumshoe. Maelstrom and Aunt Inheritance should both know that, so why were they pretending not to?'

Erf scuffed at the bloodied carpet. Their gran was looking more suspicious by the minute.

'So . . . what does this mean?' they asked.

'There is a principle in medical science: Occam's razor. It basically means the simplest solution is usually right,' said Phenomena. 'So, what seems a simpler explanation to you – that none of the detective books are booby trapped *except this one*, or that there wasn't a booby trap at all? Isn't the simplest explanation that someone just picked up the statue and bashed Gumshoe's head in themselves?'

'And then . . . collapsed the shelf to make it look like an accident?' asked Erf, brow furrowing.

'Precisely! It didn't matter what book they put in his hand, because it was all staged anyway.'

'They could have just grabbed the first one they saw. And – oh!' Erf blinked. 'That means they *aren't* that familiar with the House, because if they were they would have picked anything other than a detective novel. That makes Gran a lot *less* likely, right?' Erf looked momentarily winded by their own genius – but then their smile faltered. 'That doesn't explain why she'd pretend this was an accident, though.'

'You're right. That I can't explain.'

'Daisy wouldn't have known about the detective books,' Shenanigan butted in, desperate to get her top suspect back in the running. 'She's not a Swift.'

'Yes, she is looking better and better as a suspect,' agreed Phenomena. 'Though I still can't work out her motive. And if she killed Gumshoe, why sneak back to the scene of the crime?'

'To see if anyone figured out she did it,' said Shenanigan. 'It's what I'd do.'

Erf looked alarmed. 'It is?'

Shenanigan nodded vigorously. 'Obviously. It's like, what's the point of setting up a prank if you don't get to see it?'

She saw Phenomena turn a page in her book and put another little mark in Shenanigan's *In Character* column.

'It would help if we knew *when* he was murdered,' mused Erf. 'Or how the murderer, or Gumshoe, got into the library in the first place.'

'He was killed hours ago,' said Shenanigan, staring at the brownish smear on the carpet. As Phenomena had told her repeatedly, blood did not behave like ketchup. It went brown once it dried. 'And I think they had the keys. I think . . . they might have taken them off Aunt Schadenfreude's desk, where I left them.'

'Oh, *Shenanigan*,' sighed Phenomena, which only made Shenanigan feel worse. 'Well . . . if it was Gumshoe who took them, he certainly doesn't have them now.' Her scowl returned. 'I can't believe they took the body. *And* the statue.' She pulled out a device of her own invention, a sort of clip that could be attached to the front of her glasses, thick with magnification lenses. 'Oh well. Our turn.'

They searched. They crawled across the carpet, they looked under chairs, they inspected the collapsed shelf and the books that lay splayed open on the floor. They dusted every millimetre of the shelf and book for fingerprints. There wasn't much to go on at all, but after ten minutes Shenanigan spotted something.

It was a small, round hole, about the width of her thumb. It was halfway up the wall, just within Shenanigan's reach. She nearly stuck her finger inside before considering that Phenomena might actually scream at her for tampering with the crime scene, so she waved her sister over instead.

'Hmmm,' said Phenomena. She took a long cotton swab from inside her Junior Forensics Kit, and wiggled it about in the hole. It came out covered in plaster, and a brownish stain.

'Blood?' asked Erf.

'I think so. I'll need to analyse it in the lab.' Phenomena frowned, and put the cotton swab inside a glass vial marked EVIDENCE! The vial had a frog in a lab coat on it. 'But I have no idea what this hole is. It doesn't look like it was drilled . . .'

'A bullet hole?' Shenanigan grinned. That would be exciting.

'No – no, it wouldn't be this neat. There'd be a little crater round it from the force of the impact.' She put the swab and its vial back in her kit, snapping the lid closed. 'I don't know what it is, but we're missing something here. I know we are.'

'You have a hunch?' asked Shenanigan.

Phenomena sniffed. 'Don't be ridiculous,' she whispered haughtily as they tiptoed from the library. 'Hunches are unscientific.'

While Phenomena, Shenanigan, and Erf had been in the library proving that Gumshoe's death wasn't an accident, Inheritance had been in the evening room, telling everyone that it was. Judging by the argument now taking place, no one was convinced. Paranoia had been growing all day, fed and watered in the gossipy little groups that had formed all over the House. By the time the three investigators slipped into the room, things were tipping over from suspicion to outright panic.

'You expect us to believe this rot?'

'*Alors!*'

'Is anyone doing anything about this?'

'I demand to speak to the manager!'

'Everyone, please, calm down,' said Fauna. 'I've made tea. We can discuss everyone's concerns, and—'

'Bother to that!' roared Uncle Ferrier. 'Someone here is a murderer!'

Little Finicky began to cry.

'Please,' said Renée quietly. 'Could we lower our voices? We're upsetting the baby.'

'Oh, bother the baby, as well,' sneered Ferrier. 'Weren't you the one who found Gumshoe? Makes you pretty suspicious, in my book.'

'I got lost on the way to the dining room! All I did was open the wrong door!'

'A likely story!'

'YOU CAN'T SPEAK TO MY WIFE THAT WAY!' boomed Fortissimo.

'Why not? She isn't Family. Not by blood.'

'Hey,' said Daisy sharply. Candour was gripping her hand so tightly his knuckles were white. 'With respect, I think you should keep your opinions to yourself.'

'Oh, aye?'

'Yes. People might listen to them, and then we're all worse off.'

'I'd watch it, sunshine – you're not married yet. Won't ever be, if old Schadenfreude gets her way. Come to think of it, if anyone has a motive—'

'Daisy didn't mean it – she's just upset,' said Candour hurriedly. 'You're just upset, aren't you, Daisy?'

Daisy's expression flickered. 'Distressed,' she agreed.

'Overwrought,' said Candour.

For a second, Shenanigan saw real anger on Daisy's face. Renée didn't look as if she could hurt a fly, Cook had been with them for almost twenty years and was practically an honorary Swift, but Ferrier had a point about Daisy. When Shenanigan had first met her, she'd dismissed her as nice. The more she saw of her, however, the more certain she was that Daisy possessed an inner steel she was keeping hidden. She was like a bouquet of flowers with a crowbar in the middle. Atrocious had seen it, Flora had seen it, and Shenanigan did too.

'Ferrier's right about one thing,' said Cousin Dither, straightening her parrot hat. 'Someone here must be a murderer, or else why would they try to trap us here?'

'They mean to pick us off!'

'It could be any of us!'

'At any time!'

Crack!

For a second, Shenanigan thought it was Aunt Schadenfreude, striking her stick on the nearest piece of furniture for quiet. But it wasn't a stick. It was a gunshot. Pamplemousse stood on a table at the far end of the room, legs apart, arm raised. A tiny pistol lay against his palm. A light trickle of plaster dust fell from the hole he'd put in the ceiling and powdered his wig.

'*Écoutez, s'il vous plaît!*' he snapped. The guns and swords and nunchucks on his hips jingled as he lowered his hand. '*Mes amis,*' he trilled. 'I can let this stand no longer! I address you now as your blood, as your Family, and with a heart full of love . . . and fury.' He tossed his hair dramatically. 'One of you is a traitor of the highest order. One of you has betrayed the ideals of *fraternité*. One of you . . . is a killer.'

People looked at each other nervously.

'Someone in this very room,' said Pamplemousse, 'has hidden among us, has broken bread with us, while all the time they are plotting our end! While all the time they are an *assassin*! I cannot let this insult stand!'

His moustache quivered in indignation. He pulled off one of his gloves with his teeth, and flung it to the table. It landed in his tea with a splash.

'For the honour of *Tante* Schadenfreude, I challenge whoever is responsible . . . to a duel!'

There were murmurs throughout the room, some of excitement, some of dismay. Pamplemousse braced his hands on his hips.

'*Oui!* Tomorrow at dawn, I shall meet *le* snivelling *froussard* on the front lawn for a deadly contest of wits. Yes, it shall be Scrabble – to the death!'

When Shenanigan told Cook she was going to bed, it wasn't technically a lie. She did go to her bed – even if it was just to bring John the Cat some food and water. Erf came along, eager, as expected, to meet anything on four legs. It took a lot of coaxing, but eventually one orange paw emerged from under the bed, then a pair of luminous green eyes, narrowed suspiciously, and finally the whole mass of John the Cat himself, who ate the food and drank the water as though they were barely up to his standards. He butted his head against Erf's hand and even allowed his belly to be rubbed, but as soon as the children rose to leave, he retreated under the bed again.

'I put him on guard duty,' explained Shenanigan. 'He's under strict instructions to protect my room from invaders.'

'He's such a hefty boy! He'll make a good guard cat. He definitely doesn't like it that there are so many people in his House.' Erf reached beneath the bed to give John the Cat's head a last scratch. 'Cats can be very territorial. He should be fine once everyone's gone.'

Now Shenanigan, Phenomena, and Erf sat in the lab, going over the case and munching thoughtfully on Shenanigan's third secret stash of biscuits. Well, Phenomena and Erf were going over the case. Shenanigan was considering turning on a Bunsen burner and setting fire to her hair, just for something to do. They had been quibbling (a good word that means arguing over something small and silly) over timings for half an hour. Shenanigan could not think of anything more boring than going through everything they'd learned all over again. The girls had never been to a real school, so she didn't know that the feeling she had was similar to the one you get while preparing for a test.

Finally, Phenomena and Erf turned to their small table of evidence: a vial containing the chunk of coffee bean, the brown-tinged swab from the hole in the wall, and the copy of *The Body in the Library*, which Phenomena had dusted for prints and found to be clean of all but Gumshoe's.

'We've made no progress on the coffee, but I do have some news about the hole in the wall,' said Phenomena, taking a swig of her Solution Solution. 'I tested the swab, and my hypothesis was correct. It's blood.'

'Which means?' asked Shenanigan.

'We don't know.'

'Oh good,' said Shenanigan, rolling a stray beaker along the floor. 'I was worried we were wasting our time.' She could be treasure-hunting right now. Seeing Aunt Inheritance in the library had inspired her to have another go at reading Cantrip's play, which made less sense to her the more she went over it.

'*Mark well the well-marked meaning of our days*' felt like a clue. And there were lots of words that could mean two things, like how *fortune* could mean 'luck' or 'a huge amount of money', and *buried the hatchet* could mean 'forgive' but in this case meant 'murdered with an axe'.

'Let's look at our suspects list,' said Erf hurriedly, sensing the tension.

Aunt Inheritance (sorry, Erf)
Daisy (SUSPICIOUS)
~~Uncle Maelstrom~~
Flora/Fauna – probably not Fauna as she is very nice
~~Man with Impressive Moustache~~ Uncle Ferrier – fell
   through a trapdoor

Candour - was looking after Aunt Dither
Atrocious - UGH - says she was on the
   phone - check
Pique - ALSO UGH - says he was on the
   phone - check
~~Cook~~
That Lady in the ~~Pelican Hat~~ African grey parrot Hat
   (Aunt Dither) - was sedated in her room

'I double-checked Atrocious and Pique's alibis,' said
Erf. 'Four different people complained about them
taking ages on the phone, and could provide timings,
so they check out.'

'Excellent work, Erf,' said Phenomena approvingly.

What about 'lest we lose our heads'? Shenanigan
wondered. That was an eerie coincidence. Cantrip
couldn't have known what would happen to Gumshoe,
could she? She stared at the page, willing the words
to behave. Was the *family tree* referring to her actual
Family, or an actual tree? And what about those *rich
in kindness* and *rich in kind*? Was Shenanigan going to
have to try being nicer if she wanted the treasure? That
didn't seem fair.

'Shenanigan? Are you even paying attention?'

'What? Oh. I'm telling you, it's Daisy,' sniffed Shenanigan, who had definitely not been paying attention. 'She was being very weird in the library, and she's conspiring with Flora. You heard her as well as I did – all that sobbing and "Oh no, what have I done, there's blood on my hands" and stuff.'

'That's absolutely not what she said!' protested Phenomena. 'And all she took from the library was an atlas. Even if she is our killer, what would she want with an atlas?'

'Maybe she's planning her escape?' Shenanigan kicked at the leg of the bench. 'I don't know.'

'I agree she's high on the list, but we need more information. All of this is what's known as circumstantial evidence.'

Shenanigan's head swam. She wasn't very good at analysing poetry, and she was beginning to realize she wasn't very good at detective work, either. All this talk of evidence and motives left her feeling scratchy and irritable. Erf was a much better partner for Phenomena. Erf could think in straight lines.

Shenanigan wished she could just climb on to the roof and sit for a bit. Maybe talk to Suleiman, though if she tried to explain everything that had happened one flash at a time she'd be Aunt Schadenfreude's age by the time she finished.

She didn't care about all these 'how's or 'why's – only the 'who's. She felt like an arrow in a bow. She needed to be pointed at a target, and let fly.

19

PAMPLEMOUSSE'S
BEST SHOT

The sun rose bloody at five in the morning, and the crows in the chimney laughed Shenanigan awake. It had been another night of scuffles and snores, of tossing and turning. Scraping, rattling sounds had continued through the small hours, as if someone was filing their nails on brick. It had taken Shenanigan a while to realize it was her relatives, up and treasure-hunting in the middle of the night.

She pulled on the first clothes she could find and ran out on to the lawn, where people were already gathering to watch the Scrabble duel. Having finished her book of ghost stories, Cook had requested flour and butter to be brought to Aunt Schadenfreude's study so she could make dough and watch over her friend at the same time. The fresh croissants had been set out with mugs of thick hot chocolate. Some people were still in their dressing gowns, and they were treating the scene a little like a picnic. Other than Inheritance – who had not only refused to attend the duel herself but had categorically forbidden Erf from doing so – only Fauna and Felicity seemed worried.

'Oh dear. I do hope the murderer doesn't turn up,' said Fauna. 'Or perhaps it will rain, and the duel will have to be called off.'

'I don't think it's like a cricket match, Fauna,' Flora said, patting her arm.

Felicity glowered into the rising sun. 'This is stupid. He's going to get himself killed.'

She turned her glare on Pamplemousse as he paced up and down the Scrabble court, occasionally stretching to limber himself up, and muttering long words under his breath.

Light slunk up the face of the House, and as the first rays hit the ground-floor windows, Pamplemousse clapped his hands.

'The hour is here and there is no sign of my opponent! *Ma Famille*, we are dealing with a coward!' He calmly took a sip of hot chocolate, swept back his frock coat and sat on the side of the court facing the House, one leg crossed over the other in an image of genteel patience.

'I shall give them five more minutes,' he declared.

If you have ever played Scrabble, then you will know that it is a board game where players take turns to set out letter tiles on a board to spell words. The tiles are assigned points. The longer and more complex the word you set out, the more points you are awarded, with bonus points if the tiles are placed on certain squares. The person with the most points at the end wins. It is not usually lethal.

The kind of Scrabble the Swifts play is not like regular Scrabble. While some rich people like to have life-size chess boards in their front gardens, the Swifts had always been more fond of word games, and their Scrabble court was the only one of its kind – the size of a tennis court, with the squares beautifully picked out in stone and coloured glass. *Embellished* is a word that can mean 'gorgeously detailed and decorated', like the tiles, but it can also mean 'with added, exaggerated details'. The Swifts had embellished the rules as much as the board itself. They started with fourteen letters rather than the usual seven, and *any* words in *any* language were permitted, including expletives – which are words

Shenanigan learned from Cook, but would never say in front of Aunt Schadenfreude.

Despite the beauty of the scene, though, Shenanigan couldn't shake off the feeling that Felicity was right and there was real danger in the air. It was obvious Pamplemousse wasn't expecting anyone to turn up. He lounged on his bench, dipping bites of croissant into his chocolate and nibbling daintily. But whenever Shenanigan looked away from the House, the back of her neck prickled, as if someone was watching.

They were a long five minutes. Dawn crept up to the first-floor windows and set them ablaze. They all shielded their eyes at the sudden brilliance, and Pamplemousse, with great theatricality, shook back his sleeve and checked his watch.

'Well!' he crowed. 'It seems the person who would push an old woman down the stairs is not interested in facing an opponent of wit and stature.' He stood, and began to dust off his frock coat, weapons clinking. 'Are you not among us, little *lapin*? Come on out! I shall be gentle. I shall even let you go first!' He gestured grandly to the stack of Scrabble tiles standing beside the court.

The Swifts craned their necks, surreptitiously

brushing away flakes of pastry. The back of Shenanigan's neck prickled again. Pamplemousse scoffed.

'Then I suppose that is that,' he said. 'Now we know we are dealing with a cowardly little—'

An arrow thudded into the ground by Pamplemousse's left foot.

For a moment, nobody moved. Pamplemousse stood frozen, staring at the arrow that still quivered in the lawn. Gingerly, he pulled it out. Several centimetres of the shaft were dark and muddy. It had sunk deep.

'What's that?' whispered Fauna.

Wrapped round the arrow was a small slip of paper. Pamplemousse unrolled it. He cleared his throat.

'*I am here,*' he read. '*You can pick my tiles.*'

He looked around uncertainly. His moustache twitched.

'But how . . .?'

Another arrow shot into the earth, landing barely a centimetre from the first. It bore another strip of paper.

'*I shall need a volunteer from the audience,*' read Pamplemousse.

Understandably, no one stepped forward. Well, Shenanigan tried, but Felicity yanked her back.

'Ah . . . Mademoiselle Fauna? If you would?'

Grey-faced, Fauna stepped forward, but her sister placed a hand on her arm.

'It's okay,' said Flora. 'I'll do it.'

She went to take the seat facing the House, but another arrow whistled past her head. Fauna let out a little scream. With shaking hands, Flora unravelled the attached note.

'*Other side,*' she read.

'They can see us,' whispered Felicity. She shivered.

Flora settled on the bench with her back to the House. Pamplemousse looked a little green around the gills, but sat down facing her. Wordlessly, the two took turns picking wooden letter tiles, each the size of a chopping board, from the stack next to the court.

Shenanigan scanned the House to see if any of the windows were open. The arrow must have been shot from somewhere high. Archers on the top of a castle always had the advantage over those on the ground.

Flora finished setting out her letter tiles on her side of the board, where Pamplemousse and the assembled spectators couldn't see. She sat back, fidgeting slightly.

Pamplemousse cleared his throat. 'I did say you could go first,' he said.

Another arrow landed, this time a millimetre from Flora. She flinched, and Fauna started forward – only to reel back as a fresh arrow struck the ground in front of her outstretched foot. The message from the murderer was clear: only Flora was allowed to move. With trembling hands, Flora removed the paper from her arrow.

'GRIFFONAGE,' she read. She began to place the tiles on the board.

Pamplemousse may have been many things – a fool, a dandy, a cartoon of a man – but he was certainly good at Scrabble. For a long time, there was no sound but the *click* of tiles being set down and *thwack* of arrows arriving, which made Shenanigan jump less and less each time one soared over her head.

In vain, she squinted repeatedly towards the House. She scanned for sly shadows, dim figures, anyone skulking, a flicker of movement with ill intent. But it was impossible to make out anything through the light bouncing off the windows.

Pamplemousse managed to set GALUMPHING on a double-letter-score tile.

Thwack! The arrow countered with UNOBSERVED.

Pamplemousse began to sweat. RAZZLE, he spelled. FRAZZLED, it countered.

'He's looking a bit frazzled himself,' murmured Phenomena, eyes fixed on the game. 'Ah! He could have played MITOCHONDRIA there.'

'If he loses, do you really think he'll be killed?' whispered Shenanigan. Pamplemousse had very clearly called for Scrabble to the death.

Phenomena didn't answer, fixated on the game.

The sunlight crept to the second floor. It would be peeking in at Aunt Schadenfreude's window now, lighting her up where she lay on the desk like a medieval saint. Not for the first time, Shenanigan half wished her aunt was here to bang her stick and put a stop to this.

Then a cloud passed across the sun. In the brief second when the light dimmed, Shenanigan saw a figure silhouetted on the roof of the House, next to the chimney above her room. She caught her breath, and the cloud passed. The sunlight hit the roof and turned the figure's eyes into two huge round points of light. She saw the shape of the murderer, and the murderer saw the shape of her.

Shenanigan lurched forward, but before she had taken two steps, an arrow whistled down, tearing a chunk out of her trousers and pinning her leg to the ground. The crowd gasped, and Fauna grabbed Shenanigan, hauling her back behind her.

'I can see them!' shouted Shenanigan. 'They're on the roof! Let me go!'

Fauna shook her head wordlessly, her fingers finding the hole by Shenanigan's shin. There was blood. The arrow had barely grazed her leg – she'd had worse falling out of trees – but Fauna looked terrified. Her eyes met Shenanigan's and for a moment, a moment that cracked open something in Shenanigan's chest, she reminded Shenanigan of her mother.

Things were going badly for Pamplemousse. He was sweating buckets now, and kept lifting up his powdered wig to mop his brow. Phenomena kept track of the points in her notebook, and chewed on the end of her ponytail as she marked down the score.

TREPIDATION, put Pamplemousse, filling almost all of what little space remained on the court. They all waited for the arrow to arc down from on high, carrying the final move.

Thwack! It landed in the middle of the court, scattering the centre tiles. Flora calmly unrolled the piece of paper.

'ABSQUATULATE,' she read. The word fitted neatly with Pamplemousse's BUOYANCY, ending right over the final triple-word score.

Uncomprehending, Pamplemousse stared at the board. Then he leapt up, knocking back his remaining tiles with such force that Ferrier had to dodge out of the way. There were high spots of colour in Pamplemousse's cheeks.

'You . . . you cheat! You have not won!' he cried, stabbing a finger towards the roof of the House. 'ABSQUATULATE is not a word!'

'I should hope it is,' called a small man near the back of the crowd. 'It's my blooming name!'

Pamplemousse began to kick the tiles off the court, puffing in fear and exertion. Flora sat down hard on the bench. There was an awful, expectant silence. The rest of the Family looked at each other, unsure. No one wanted to be the first to try to leave, in case they were fired upon.

Pamplemousse had scuffed all the tiles into gibberish. He drew his sword with one hand, his ancient palm pistol with the other. His eyes were wide and staring. He fired wildly into the trees, the lawn, the clouds, and when his pistol was empty he

pulled a dagger from his boot. But there was nothing he could do.

He looked towards the roof. They all heard the distant whistling. In his last moments, Pamplemousse must have seen, flying towards him, his opponent's final move.

'*Merde*,' he whispered.

The arrow struck him in the chest like a full stop.

Shock and horror slackened Fauna's grip. Shenanigan tore free, and was off towards the House before Pamplemousse hit the ground. Phenomena shouted her name, but no further arrows fell, and Shenanigan crossed the lawn unpunctured. She burst indoors, was momentarily blinded by the glooming dark of the hall after the bright morning outside, and took the staircase on all fours for speed.

If you had asked her what she was planning to do if she caught the person who shot Pamplemousse, she would not have been able to tell you. She was barely thinking at all. Her body had become a machine, her legs pistons, her lungs bellows, all driven by one thought that barely was a thought, more a foot on the accelerator of Shenanigan's brain – catch them! *Catch them!*

She ran to her room, threw open the skylight, and pulled herself on to the roof. It was cool, and the stones were still damp with morning dew. For a moment, a tall shape loomed in her vision – but it was only the chimney against which the archer had been leaning, still in shadow.

Shenanigan sprang forward, expecting to see a figure with the huge, blazing eyes of an insect.

She saw nothing. The roof was empty.

Below on the lawn, she could hear shouting, and doors being slammed open and shut all over the House. Looking over the little stone parapet at the edge of the roof, she could see figures swarming over the body of Pamplemousse like ants around a crumb of cake. Blood was settling into the grooves of the Scrabble court, surrounding Pamplemousse in a red grid.

Someone was calling her name. Shenanigan ignored them, and leaned against the warm brick. She was exhausted. This part of the roof formed a little courtyard flanked by chimneys, which was why Shenanigan had picked it as one of her best secret places. With a lurch, she realized that, unless they had felt like shimmying up three floors of drainpipe, the archer must have wriggled up through the skylight as she herself had done so many times before. The murderer had been in *her* room. They had picked their way across the mess on *her* floor, climbed on *her* bed. She felt sick with rage.

They had left something behind, though. Propped on the parapet, in the snug little corner where a large chimney met the wall, was Shenanigan's backpack, the one she had prepared for her escape once she had found the treasure. Placed neatly on the top, where she would be sure to see them, were her own binoculars.

There was a roaring in Shenanigan's ears as she looked out over the parapet, and her shin throbbed dully. Those who had witnessed the fatal Scrabble game recounted the event to newcomers with great enthusiasm. She watched their hands move in wild and silent gestures, pulling back and releasing an imaginary bowstring, and pointing to the roof – where perhaps she was visible, a small figure lurking in the murderer's shadow.

Someone had covered Pamplemousse with a sheet. It draped clumsily over the arrow that no one had bothered to remove, making it look as if he was lying in a very small circus tent. Candour hurried across the lawn, his big square doctor's bag in hand. He took a peek under the sheet and shook his head. Flora still had not moved from her seat, but Fauna had helpfully picked up all the arrows around her and handed them to Candour. Then two burly cousins loaded Pamplemousse on to a makeshift stretcher and carried him away.

'Shenanigan!'

Shenanigan came back to herself with a start. Erf looked as if they had been yelling at her for some time.

'Are you alright? I was watching from the dining room, 'cause Gran said I couldn't go out, but she's run off, and I just thought – the *body*!'

Shenanigan snapped to attention. *Right.* This time there was an actual dead body to investigate, not just an unconscious one, or a bloodied hole in the carpet. Phenomena would want a look.

Shenanigan thought fast.

'Okay. Candour will be taking Pamplemousse to the freezer with Gumshoe. Phenomena will have followed me – she's just not a fast runner – so we'll scoop her up and then I can keep Candour distracted with my leg while you two investigate.'

'Alright. We can – Oh no.'

Erf looked suddenly stricken and dropped back into Shenanigan's room, diving under her bed. Shenanigan felt her stomach plummet into her shoes.

When Erf reappeared, dust was greying their hair and their hands were empty.

'John the Cat's gone,' they said wretchedly. 'Shenanigan, the murderer had to have come through here. What if they hurt him?'

Panic and rage locked Shenanigan's limbs. 'You go with Phenomena. I have to find him.'

'You don't. You're the one with the bad leg – you have to get Phenomena into the freezer. I'll find John the Cat, I promise. We'll meet at the top of the grand staircase when we're done.' Erf's face was grave and set. 'Go!'

Shenanigan ran down towards the kitchens as fast as she could hobble, meeting Phenomena just as her sister reached the first floor and spinning her back the way she came. She coughed 'Body', and because Phenomena was both very clever and very used to Shenanigan she understood immediately.

They paused by the stairs to the kitchen. The burly cousins who had carried Pamplemousse's body passed them on their way out, licking ice lollies. Shenanigan focused hard on the pain in her leg. She didn't lie, but she did act. The trick to acting was to find a bit of truth and pull it round you like a raincoat until it covered your whole body. In this case, the truth was that her leg hurt. She staggered down the stairs, groaning dramatically.

'My word!' Candour's hands were full of the arrows Fauna had given him; he looked around frantically for somewhere to put them, gave up, and finally just tossed them into the furnace. 'Shenanigan, you're bleeding!'

'It hurts . . . a little. But it's nothing compared . . . to poor Pamplemousse . . .'

Shenanigan put a hand to her forehead and risked a surreptitious glance into the freezer. She could just make out the dim white shape of Pamplemousse's sheet and, deeper inside, one of Gumshoe's scuffed shoes. If the killer kept this up, the Family was going to run out of room in there.

Pamplemousse's weapons had been removed from his body and piled on the kitchen table. Shenanigan spotted some throwing stars, a beautiful stiletto dagger, and the palm pistol he'd shot at the ceiling. Her fingers itched to swipe it, but instead she threw herself into a kitchen chair with another theatrical groan. Candour dragged over his doctor's bag and crouched in front of Shenanigan, who waved Phenomena in over his shoulder while he was pulling on a fresh pair of surgical gloves.

More quietly than Shenanigan would have given her

credit for, Phenomena crept down the stairs towards the freezer.

'What happened?' asked Candour.

'I was shot with an arrow – that's all. During the Scrabble game.'

From Shenanigan's vantage point, she could see her sister's elbow, her ponytail, and a small part of Pamplemousse's sheet as Phenomena began her investigation.

'Oh, "that's all", she says. Though with the way things are going, I suppose it could have been much worse.' Candour sighed. He pushed his glasses up his nose, turning her leg this way and that. 'This whole business . . . first Auntie, then Gumshoe, then Pamplemousse, and now you, a mere child, caught in the crossfire. What has happened to this Family?' He shook his head, looking so much like a sad Labrador that Shenanigan almost patted him on the head.

Up close, exhaustion was written all over him. He had dark smudges beneath his eyes, and his hair stuck up in little tufts. He took a small bottle out of his bag. There were many more inside, clinking softly, and Shenanigan bet Phenomena would love to rifle through them – from what Shenanigan could see, she was currently rifling through Pamplemousse's pockets.

'I'm going to clean this now,' said Candour, 'and it's going to sting a bit. Hey, Shenanigan, what do you call a skeleton that goes to the doctor?'

'I don't—'

Her leg stung fiercely, and she stifled a yell.

'Late,' said Candour, dabbing at her shin with a cotton ball. 'Sorry. Honestly, after this weekend, it's a wonder Daisy still wants to marry me. I told her all about us, you know. "The Swifts are an old and noble Family," I said. "You'll be marrying into a grand legacy," I said. And what greets her? A rundown House, a chilly welcome, and murder. Just hold that for me a second – thank you.' He took a pair of tweezers and gently removed some grit she'd managed to get in the wound.

'The Swifts used to do great things. World-changing things,' he said wistfully. He took gauze and tape out of his bag and began bandaging her leg. 'We've been inventors, poets, soldiers, translators, courtiers, politicians . . . Now we just squabble among ourselves. If I was Patriarch, I'd—' He scratched idly at his hand, chuckling. 'Oh, never mind. Could you imagine?'

'I think you'd be a good Patriarch,' said Shenanigan.

'Maybe Aunt Schadenfreude will ask you when she wakes up.'

'Oh no.'

'People would like you more, I think. Flora said Aunt Schadenfreude's not very popular, which makes sense, 'cause she can be mean sometimes.'

'She *was* rude to Daisy, wasn't she?' allowed Candour. 'But I expect that was a misunderstanding.'

There was a soft shuffling sound from the freezer. Phenomena, unable to reach whatever she was after, was dragging over a crate of frozen meatballs on which to stand.

'Candour . . . how long have you known Daisy?' Shenanigan asked. She asked it loudly, to cover the noise.

'Three months, one week, and three days.' A dreamy expression crossed Candour's face at the mention of his favourite subject, and he smiled a goofy smile.

'Three *months*? And you're getting married already?'

'Time doesn't matter when you're in love,' said Candour. 'When you know, you know.'

'Yes, but . . .' She struggled internally. On the one hand, Candour should probably, definitely, know that his fiancée was up to something. On the other, if she,

Shenanigan, told him and he didn't believe her, he would probably, definitely, tip Daisy off.

Behind Candour, Phenomena stuck her head round the door and gave Shenanigan an enthusiastic thumbs-up.

'Stay there – I'll get you an ice pack for that leg,' said Candour, turning towards the freezer. Phenomena's face briefly registered alarm before she ducked back into the freezer and out of sight.

Shenanigan thought fast.

'Wait! Candour . . . if Daisy was keeping something from you, would you want to know about it?'

Candour turned round. He looked puzzled.

'Daisy tells me everything. She's always trusted me completely. It's one of the things I love most about her.'

'It's just . . . Aunt Schadenfreude not letting her marry you . . . that's a motive, isn't it? For, erm . . . murder?'

It took Candour a second to react and, when he did, he surprised Shenanigan by laughing.

'You think Daisy . . .? She could never, and besides, that's not even a very *good* motive. Daisy knows nothing will stop me marrying her! Our love is too precious! Even if I was excommunicated, cut off, disavowed!' Again his glasses slipped down his nose, and he pushed them back up, sheepish. 'Not that I think it'll come to that. When Aunt Schadenfreude wakes up, she'll change her mind. *Daisy Swift*. It sounds so lovely. And she is lovely, Shenanigan, isn't she?'

'Oh. Yes,' said Shenanigan. 'She has . . . lovely eyes. And she smells nice.'

Candour patted his pockets. 'Exactly. Now, what was I . . . Ah yes, ice pack!' He headed towards the freezer.

'No!' shouted Shenanigan. 'I . . . um, I don't need one, thank you.'

'Don't be silly. The ice will help with the swelling. You just cool off there for a second.'

Shenanigan held her breath, waiting for Candour to yell, or march Phenomena out of the freezer with her hands up, like a spy. But he didn't. He just came out with a bag of frozen sweetcorn in his hand, whistling. And closed the door behind him.

Shenanigan kept her face still to hide her dismay. She knew from yesterday's catastrophic dinner that it was impossible to open the freezer from the inside, which meant that Phenomena was stuck in there, shivering between the bodies. Shenanigan couldn't get her out without Candour noticing, and Candour didn't look ready to stop fussing any time soon. She pressed the bag of frozen sweetcorn to her bad leg and refused to panic.

'Candour, I've just thought – since Daisy's had such a bad few days, why don't you take her some breakfast in bed?'

Candour lit up. 'You know, that's a capital idea! This –' he gestured to the freezer and the multiple bodies inside – 'is hardly important. I should see to my fiancée. D'you mind giving me a hand? You make the coffee, and I'll do the toast.'

Figuring Phenomena would be fine for a few minutes, Shenanigan went to fetch the coffee from the cupboard.

'Oh, not that stuff!' called Candour as he explored the bread bin. 'I brought Daisy's. It's fancy, but it's her favourite.' He waved a hand towards the counter, and Shenanigan locked eyes with a picture of an animal – sort of like a lemur, sort of like a raccoon – that stared at her from a bag of coffee beans.

A civet.

Shenanigan had almost forgotten what Flora had said about the coffee bean they'd found near Aunt Schadenfreude. In fact, after seeing Flora and Daisy conspiring, Shenanigan had begun to write off the clue as not a clue at all, but a misdirection. Now, staring at the civet – Erf was right: it *was* adorable – the coincidence was impossible to ignore. Daisy drank the same kind of coffee the murderer did.

So Shenanigan ground the beans, filled a jug with cream, and prepared a bowl of sugar – all for a person who, an hour ago, had quite possibly put an arrow through her Uncle Pamplemousse.

Two minutes passed. Then another three. Then another seven. All the while, Shenanigan was conscious of her sister a few metres away getting colder and colder while the coffee brewed. They placed everything neatly on a tray for Candour to take upstairs.

'I think I've got it from here,' he said, loaded down with the breakfast tray. With his white gloves still on, he looked like a handsome butler. 'Thank you for all your help, and go easy on that leg! No more . . . SHIN-anigans.' And he ducked out of the room before Shenanigan could throw a tea towel at his head.

Finally, mercifully, Phenomena having now been in the cold for sixteen minutes, Shenanigan threw herself on the handle and heaved open the heavy door to the freezer.

'Phenomena?' she called. 'Phenomena!'

There was a rustling in the corner and a small

avalanche of frozen vegetables. Nestled between the carrots and parsnips was a lightly frosted Phenomena, and, though her lips were pale and she was shivering, she grinned weakly at Shenanigan.

'L-look,' she chattered. She held out a fist. Shenanigan had to prise her fingers open because they were so stiff with cold. 'I t-took it . . . off the arrow,' she said.

It was a small slip of paper, the same kind that had been wrapped round each shaft.

'Handwriting,' Phenomena said triumphantly. 'F-finally . . . a p-proper clue.'

Shenanigan unravelled the strip of paper. Written on it, in tidy cursive, were two words:

Au revoir.

Pamplemousse's left hand had slipped from under the sheet. Shenanigan noted his well-kept nails and felt sorry for him. She had heard that hair and fingernails kept growing after death, and thought that he might find that upsetting. She'd wanted to peek under the sheet and get a proper look at a real dead body, but Phenomena's teeth had been chattering quite ferociously, so with a sigh she'd left it alone and dragged her frozen sister into the kitchen to thaw.

'What did he look like?' asked Shenanigan, sorry to have missed out.

'L-like Pamplemousse, b-but dead.'

The warmth of the furnace had melted Phenomena considerably. She sipped hot chocolate and stared intently at the slip of paper and the bag of coffee Shenanigan had shown her.

'It's a good thing you got that,' said Shenanigan, nodding to the paper. 'Candour chucked the rest in the fire.'

'Yes, and now they're warming me up as they burn.'

'It's poetic, or something,' said Shenanigan, helping herself to a jar of jam.

'"*Au revoir*." Goodbye.' Phenomena frowned. 'That's a bit smug. Of course, this sample of handwriting is useless without our suspects' to compare it to.'

'Well, that'll be next,' said Shenanigan stickily. The clues had put her back in high spirits.

'And Daisy drinks civet coffee.' Phenomena frowned. 'You realize that this still counts as circumstantial evidence.'

'I don't, because I *still* don't know what that means.'

'It means that in a court of law, people could say that Daisy liking the same type of coffee as the murderer and having cryptic conversations in the dark and running about secretly are all strange circumstances, but not actual proof. It wouldn't be enough to convict her.'

'This isn't a court of law, though – it's our House,' Shenanigan pointed out. She waved her spoon for emphasis, and a gobbet of jam splattered the note. 'She's hiding something,' she continued, as Phenomena groaned and hurriedly wiped the paper with a sleeve. 'You know I can always tell. Call it . . . call it detective's intuition. Call it a hunch.'

Phenomena wrinkled her nose in distaste. 'A hunch is just your brain subconsciously taking in data and coming to a conclusion without you really being aware of it.'

'There you go, then,' said Shenanigan. 'My brain knows something's off with Daisy, but my mind's not sure what.'

Phenomena sighed. 'Here. I took this too.'

She passed over the arrow she had taken from Pamplemousse's body. It looked old, and it didn't have a proper arrowhead. It resembled a thin wooden stake, sharpened to a point and tipped with steel. Several centimetres of it were stained red.

While Shenanigan had been building the Siegemaster

5000, she'd done a lot of research on siege warfare. She'd learned, among other things, that the invention of the crossbow had been a huge leap forward for the killing-each-other-more-effectively industry, allowing soldiers to fire further, with greater force, and for greater damage. The long, thin, sharp thing in her hand wasn't technically an arrow at all but a crossbow bolt.

This meant something. The shape of it tickled the back of her mind.

'This is an antique,' she said slowly. 'From at least the 1700s, I'm pretty sure.' Aunt Schadenfreude had always said Shenanigan's obsession with weaponry had no practical application. 'Why would anyone bring an ancient crossbow with them? They're heavy. We have pistols now.'

'They could have found it in the House,' suggested Phenomena.

An idea hit Shenanigan between the eyes. She grabbed Phenomena's arm with a sticky hand.

'Occam's razor,' she whispered. 'Phenomena, we need to get Erf, and then we need to go back to the library.'

'Why?'

'I have a hunch.'

A Bolt of Inspiration

When Erf met them at the top of the stairs, it was with two armfuls of cat, four thin scratches on their neck, and one worried expression.

'I found him on top of a cupboard, hissing like mad. His fur was all on end.'

John the Cat's eyes, usually half closed and sleepy, were wide and staring. His ears flicked to and fro, as if he was listening for something.

'He's limping a little bit, but nothing feels broken. I think he was very brave.'

Shenanigan reached out to touch John the Cat's back leg. This was a daft thing to do, because John the Cat yowled and immediately leapt out of Erf's arms, leaving another four long scratches on their arm.

'John the Cat, stop!' cried Shenanigan.

'It's alright.' Erf winced as they rolled the sleeve of their jumper out of the way. 'He can't help it – it's his nature. But we have to find whoever hurt him. Murder's one thing, but you can't go around kicking cats.'

The library was unlocked but understandably deserted, which might have had something to do with the massive brown stain on the carpet. An optimistic someone had taken the cords from the red curtains, knotted them together, and strung them across the door like it was a staff-only section in a museum. The investigators ducked underneath. Phenomena closed the door, and Shenanigan grabbed the nearest (safe) large hardbacks she could find, stacking them into a staircase of books until she was eye-level with the hole in the wall.

'Look,' she said to Phenomena.

Wobbling a bit on top of *Pisa: A History*, she pulled the crossbow bolt out of her belt and slid it into the hole. It fitted perfectly. Phenomena gestured for her to get off the pile of books, and hopped up herself, squinting.

'Do you have any string?'

Shenanigan, of course, did. Phenomena tied the end to the crossbow bolt.

'Right,' she murmured. 'The bolt had to have travelled in a straight line. That's physics. Shenanigan, take the other end of this string, and walk until I tell you to stop.'

Shenanigan did as she was told and went to the opposite wall. Her sister began muttering to herself.

'Judging by the angle of impact, taking into account the . . . Hmm.' Phenomena tapped a finger against her chin. 'Stop there. That seems right, but you need to be up a bit higher.'

Erf brought Shenanigan the wheeled ladder they used to get books off the higher shelves.

'Up a step,' called Phenomena. 'And another. Left a bit? There! If the bolt hit the wall *here*,' she tapped the wall with her fingernail, 'it was fired from *there*.'

The string stretched in a straight line from the hole in the wall, over the bloody mark on the floor, to the shelf Shenanigan rested against, which had the thrilling label of *Books for Lawyers and Probably No One Else*. There was a space between two books, and at the back of the shelf was another small, round hole. Shenanigan shoved the rest of the books aside and knocked on the back of the bookcase. It made a hollow noise.

'Erf?'

Her cousin gave her a hand, then both hands when just one wasn't sufficient. Digging their nails into the seams, the two of them eventually managed to wrench the back panel away. Behind it was a small space. It contained a wooden stand, which looked bereft, as if until recently something had been resting there. At the bottom of the space was a loose crossbow bolt.

Erf and Shenanigan looked at each other.

'Well,' said Erf. 'Now we know where Pamplemousse's killer got their weapon.'

'Look at this frayed bit of string here,' murmured Phenomena. 'This was meant as a trap, to be triggered when someone took the missing book off the shelf.'

'Okay, but it *must* have gone off. Or else there wouldn't be a hole in the wall opposite.'

They all stared into the dark space. There were cobwebs in the corners, and a thick layer of dust.

'How did the murderer even know the crossbow was here?' asked Phenomena. 'That hole is hard to spot unless you're looking for it.'

'Maybe they didn't.' Erf picked up the loose bolt, turning it in their hands. 'Maybe they set it off by accident? Or Gumshoe did.'

Phenomena began to pace. The pacing wasn't enough,

so she put the end of her ponytail in her mouth and began to chew. Shenanigan and Erf sat down on piles of books and let her think out loud.

'A theory,' Phenomena said thoughtfully. 'Shenanigan and I passed Gumshoe yesterday on the way up to Atrocious and Pique's. Shenanigan, you remember him saying that stuff about having "research" to do? The most logical place to do research is here in the library. He shouldn't have been able to get in here, *but* –' she waggled a finger – 'we know that the keys have been missing since Shenanigan left them on Aunt Schadenfreude's desk.'

'Go on.'

'When we laid Aunt Schadenfreude out after she was pushed, everything on her desk got knocked to the floor, including the keys . . .'

'And Gumshoe was crawling around on the floor,' added Shenanigan. 'He could have picked them up.'

'Right. So next morning, after he'd spoken to Atrocious and Pique, he went to the library, unlocked it, and got on with his "research". He took a book off this shelf—'

'Which wasn't *The Body in the Library*, because that's a detective novel,' put in Shenanigan.

'Yes, and this shelf is for *Books for Lawyers and Probably No One Else.* There's no fiction on here. It's all books on law and land boundaries and legal history. He took a book off this shelf, setting off the crossbow trap, and . . .'

'And what?' asked Erf. 'The bolt missed him?'

'It *can't* have missed him,' insisted Phenomena. She mimed pulling a book from the shelf. 'He would have been standing . . . Erf, get back up on the ladder a second . . . about this close. Eye-level with the crossbow, which was hidden behind that panel. He wouldn't even have seen it coming. There's no way he could duck in time.'

'Then he didn't duck,' said Erf.

They all considered this for a moment. Erf got down off the ladder.

'You did find blood in the wall,' they reminded Phenomena, looking a bit queasy. 'And you said it yourself: Gumshoe would have been eye-level with the crossbow.'

A crossbow, even one a few hundred years old, is designed to punch right through armour to get to the soft person inside. At point-blank range, it would have absolutely no trouble at all going into the head of a certain unwitting detective, out the other side, and sinking into the wall behind him.

'Ouch,' Erf said decisively.

'So,' said Shenanigan, 'Gumshoe wasn't killed by the statue at all. It was the crossbow, in the eye, in the library—'

'But, hang on, his head was crushed,' interrupted Erf. 'Which makes no sense. If we're right, Gumshoe's death *was* an accident. Why go to all the trouble of disguising the body?'

'Probably because they wanted the crossbow,' said Shenanigan. 'I mean, I would. I love crossbows. I'd probably want one even more if I meant to kill someone.'

'Whichever legal book Gumshoe picked up is missing too,' added Phenomena. 'If people turned up and found Gumshoe with a hole in his head, they'd look for what put the hole there. If the crossbow was gone, they'd realize someone else had been in the room around the time Gumshoe died. If the murderer wanted to take the crossbow *and* the book with them without raising questions, they would have to disguise Gumshoe's wound.' She chewed her ponytail. 'This isn't exactly Occam's razor.'

'More like Occam's spork,' agreed Shenanigan. Erf snickered.

'I need to look at the evidence again,' Phenomena muttered. 'Or draw a diagram or something. This is all just conjecture and hypothesis.'

'Or maybe you could just give up and call the police.' Felicity had appeared in the doorway like a responsible genie.

'There's another body downstairs,' Felicity added. 'In case you haven't noticed.'

Shenanigan sat on a pile of books. 'We noticed. We just finished looking at it.'

'Of course you did.' Shenanigan had been expecting another bout of shrieking, but Felicity's eerie calm was worse. 'Too much to hope that you'd abandon the case now there's actual danger to your lives. What are you *thinking*, Phenomena?'

Phenomena frowned. 'I'm *thinking* that no one else is doing anything! The investigative standards in this House are appalling. Clearly someone has to step in and figure things out.'

'And that someone has to be you?' scoffed Felicity.

'Well, it's not going to be you, is it? Or Shenanigan? I just *met* Erf, and they've already been more helpful than both of you combined.'

'Hang on, what?' squawked Shenanigan.

'Um . . .' said Erf.

Phenomena turned to Shenanigan with an almost pitying smile. 'Shenanigan, you're a valuable Watson, but you just don't have a head for investigation. You haven't even been giving this case your full attention. You're more concerned with your stupid treasure-hunting thing.'

Shenanigan felt as if she'd been kicked, and when she was kicked her first instinct was to kick back.

'Are you serious? I've spent all my time running around finding out stupid bits of information about clues and timings because you won't accept that it's obviously Daisy! I haven't looked for the treasure at all! I haven't even been able to explore the secret room yet!'

She realized her mistake as soon as the words were out of her mouth. Six round eyes swung in her direction like headlights.

'Ah. Right,' she said. 'So there's a secret room on the second floor that I saw Aunt Inheritance go into the night before the Reunion, and I didn't tell you about it because—'

Phenomena stared at her. 'Sorry – are you saying you had information relevant to the case, to one of our *suspects*, and you're *just now* telling us about it?'

'I didn't think it was relevant!' protested Shenanigan. 'I thought it was related to Vile's Hoard, not the murder—'

'I can't believe this,' said Felicity. 'Oh, wait, I can, because you're completely, unrepentantly—'

'*Oi.*'

Four heads swivelled to Flora, who had stuck her head round the door. Shenanigan knew it was Flora because Fauna wouldn't say 'Oi', and because her next sentence was:

'Fauna wants you lot upstairs.'

'We're busy,' snapped Felicity.

'Yeah, but she said to insist,' said Flora. 'Said it's "in the name of Family unity" or something. So this is me, insisting.'

The sisters glowered. Erf looked relieved at the distraction.

'If you don't move, I'll continue to insist, and at ever-increasing volume,' Flora added. 'Go.'

They went.

22

THE MOCK-UP

In the afternoon room, which was not so large as the morning room or the evening room, over thirty relatives were gathered. Fauna stood in their centre, clutching one of Aunt Inheritance's timetables and frowning.

'. . . So, in the absence of other ideas, I thought perhaps we could shift the Mock-Up around the schedule,' said Fauna. 'We had a talk from Pamplemousse on concealed weaponry planned for right now, only Pamplemousse is, well, dead, and Aunt Inheritance is . . . well, I don't want to say *missing*, but we can't find her.'

Shenanigan wondered if maybe the Reunions were actually just an excuse to prune the Family tree. She looked to Erf, expecting to see worry. She got an eye-roll instead.

'She's probably in the secret room you didn't tell any of us about,' they said dryly.

Phenomena and Felicity had taken positions as far from each other, and from Shenanigan, as they could possibly get. They were each making a show of not looking in the other's direction, which didn't leave much to look at but the floor or the ceiling.

'Aren't you mad at me too?' muttered Shenanigan.

Erf shrugged. 'A bit. But I don't know you well enough to be properly mad at you. Your sisters know you *really* well.' They paused. 'You know, sometimes hyena cubs will kill their siblings so they can get bigger and stronger?'

'That's horrible. What's that got to do with anything?'

'Nothing, really. I was just wondering how much Grand-Uncle Vile knew about hyenas.'

People had begun to warm up. Flora cracked her knuckles. Pique smoothed his moustache. Erf looked dubious, but when Shenanigan wrote her own name on a slip of paper, Erf wrote theirs too, and dropped it into the hat Fauna had found.

A Mock-Up is, in its simplest terms, an insult contest. The players put their names into a hat, bucket, or other receptacle, and stand in a circle. The referee (in this case, Fauna) pulls out two names, and the players begin a battle of words, a one-on-one match of wits. The first person to run out of ideas or start laughing is the loser. Anyone can play – it is, after all, a remarkably simple game – but there are a few rules.

'No swearing, no foul language, nothing *personal*,' said Fauna. 'Remember, you don't try to actually stab someone in a fencing match, and you don't try to *really* hurt anyone here. My word is final. If I say you're out, you're out.'

'It won't be the same without Pamplemousse,' said Thespian morosely. 'He always had the most creative insults.'

'He once called me a *coeur de lion*.' Aunt Dither smiled. 'I don't even know what that means.'

'It means "lionheart",' Felicity grumbled. 'I'm not even sure he was French, you know. I *speak* French. I asked him to pass the salt yesterday and he told me it was in July.'

'Well, French or not, we should dedicate this Mock-Up to his memory.' Fauna shook the hat and moved into the circle. 'Winner of each match takes on the next contestant. We'll keep going to the last Swift standing, so keep some good jibes in your back pocket! Okay – first up, Tintinnabula and Covetous!'

The two women stepped forward.

'You're a puttock,' said Tintinnabula, straight out the gate. 'A seizing, grasping, witch-fingered harridan!'

'And you're a screaming kettle. A braying trumpet of gibberish! The world's most boring banshee!'

Tintinnabula's lips twitched upward, and Covetous giggled.

'Oh, c'mon, what was that?' bawled Fauna. 'Both of you cracked up, so you're OUT! Next up, Flora and Gauche!'

It was soon clear that Flora was excellent at this game. She wiped the floor with her first three challengers, and though she almost lost her cool when Fortissimo called her a 'DUKE OF LIMBS', she sent him howling with 'flat-footed stampcrab'.

As Flora blazed through her challengers, however, Shenanigan noticed that the insults directed at her were somewhat sharper than those she was dealing out.

'You're a waste,' said Aunt Jilt. 'A wizened, stunted, windblown shrub.'

'That's fine, because you're a pestilent, meat-breathed plague-taxi.'

'You're a desperate circumstance. An idling fopdoodle with nothing to recommend her.'

'And you're a bitter, dried-up lemon rind. A purse-mouthed gnashgab.'

'Pull back a bit, you two,' warned Fauna.

'You've got a sheep's name and the sense of a goat.'

'Then we can share a pasture, because you're a miserable cow,' snapped Flora.

The crowd hollered, and Jilt, red-faced and spluttering, couldn't come up with a retort. She was jeered out of the circle.

Fauna eyed her sister disapprovingly. 'You both crossed a line there,' she warned. 'Consider this a yellow card.'

Flora nodded, but the grin on her face said she thought it had been worth it. Her next challenger was Pique.

'You are a gold-guzzling gobemouche,' she began.

'And you're a tin woman,' said Pique, 'with a ball of wire wool for a heart.'

'You six-fingered, eel-tongued filcher of happiness,' retorted Flora. 'You consort with warthogs and make an ally of every slimy thing.' The audience laughed. 'You are utterly, completely, wholeheartedly—'

Out of the corner of her eye, Shenanigan noticed the door ease open. Daisy ducked into the room, waved her hand at Flora in an urgent gesture, and ducked out again.

Flora suddenly looked very flustered.

'Perfect,' she said. Pique blinked. 'I . . . yes, I mean to say that. You're a . . . a right marvel. Just swell. Peachy, I mean. The bee's knees. The cat's pyjamas. Proper . . . good.' She blinked. 'I'm – I have to go. Excuse me!' And she hurried from the room after Daisy.

'We should follow them.'

Shenanigan jumped. Phenomena had appeared by her elbow, her glasses glinting curiously after Flora.

Shenanigan glared. 'What do you mean, "we"? *I* don't have a head for investigation, remember? *I* can't be trusted. And anyway, you said Daisy can't possibly be suspicious. There's no evidence, other than all the evidence.'

She could feel her sister's frustration. *Good.*

Pique lost to Ferrier, Ferrier lost to Erf, and Erf lost to Shenanigan when she made them laugh with 'unscrupulous badger'. It was the first uncomplicated fun Shenanigan had had all weekend, until Fauna called her next challenger.

'Felicity!'

Fauna waved the slip of paper in the air, and Felicity shuffled reluctantly into the circle.

'I'd rather not play against *her*,' she said, at exactly the same moment Shenanigan said, 'I'm not playing against her. She's a fun-vampire. She sucks the fun out of everything.'

Felicity glared. 'Yeah? Well, you just suck. You're like a mosquito. All you do is buzz around, irritating people.'

People laughed, but Fauna looked uneasy.

'Felicity, if you were a colour, it would be beige,' said Shenanigan nastily. 'If you were a food, you'd be mashed potato. If you were a book, you'd be *The History of Paint Drying, Volume 3.*'

'And if *you* were a food, you'd be week-old prawns, because you make everyone sick,' Felicity retorted. 'And, by the way, just because I don't tear around with you and Phenomena *pretending* to be a detective—'

'No, 'cause you're too busy mooning about sewing dresses and being wistful and boring—'

'Hold on,' said Phenomena, shoving her way into the circle. 'I'm not having you besmirch my investigation!'

Fauna held up a hand. 'Only two in the circle at a time, please!'

'I'd rather be boring than selfish or a liar!' snapped Felicity.

'What do you mean, *your* investigation?' demanded Shenanigan of Phenomena.

Fauna's yellow card went unnoticed. The audience, far from objecting, jeered delightedly at this flagrant disregard for the rules. The sisters barely noticed. The anger crackled between them.

Phenomena whirled on Shenanigan. 'Yes, *my* investigation! You withheld evidence! You've been slipshod and reckless, you're careless with evidence, you haven't followed the proper method of detection *at all*, and half the time you don't even remember the details of the case!'

'And you've been lying to us!' added Felicity.

'Yeah, you've been pretty *devious* and *underhanded*, Shenanigan.'

No one but her sisters knew how much that hurt, and Shenanigan was suddenly, sharply angry.

'So what?' she cried. 'Neither of you even cared about the Reunion! You weren't looking forward to it like I was! I've been working on my map for months!'

Felicity made a strangled noise. 'I'm sorry, did our aunt's attempted murder ruin your weekend plans?'

'*Shut up, Felicity!*' Phenomena and Shenanigan shouted together.

There was a flash of red as Fauna held up the disqualifying card. She might as well have been waving a red flag at three bulls. The audience wasn't laughing any more, but they had the horrified glee of bystanders watching a building demolition.

'You keep talking about Aunt Schadenfreude, but what exactly have you done to help her?' Phenomena rounded on Felicity. 'You just turn up during our investigation, insult us, tell us to give up, and then storm off!'

'Because you don't know what you're doing! Someone has to at least *try* to keep you safe!'

'Well, you're not Mum!'

Felicity flinched. 'No, I'm not. You can tell because I'm actually here, not off on the other side of the world. Unfortunately.'

Shenanigan's throat felt hot.

'Well, I wish you were,' she choked out. 'You hate this Family, and you hate us, and you hate—'

'Listen,' said Erf, pushing between them, 'this isn't helping, okay? Maybe you all should calm down—'

'And maybe you should keep your nose out,' snapped

Felicity. Erf recoiled. 'I know you're everyone's new best friend, but you're *not* our sibling, so can you just—'

'That's *enough*!'

Fauna's voice rang with authority, and the children shut up at once.

Felicity put her hand over her mouth and looked at Erf as if she wanted to shove her words back in. She was out of the door before any of them could speak.

Phenomena stared fixedly at the wall, her ears crimson. 'I don't have time for this,' she muttered. She took a leaf out of Felicity's book, and took her leave. The other participants of the Mock-Up began to drift away, chuckling as if the argument had been the height of entertainment.

Erf tapped Fauna's elbow. 'So, I'm an only child. Is this sort of thing normal?'

With impressive efficiency, Fauna ushered any stragglers out of the afternoon room, sat the remaining two children down, and acquired a pot of tea. Shenanigan busied herself with tearing her Battenberg cake into pieces so Erf could have the marzipan. She felt raw and uncomfortable.

'D'you know,' said Fauna conversationally, 'I think your sister is one of the most interesting people in this House.'

Shenanigan couldn't really taste the Battenberg. 'Phenomena? I suppose. She's very clever, and—'

'Oh, not Phenomena, though she is very interesting too. I meant Felicity.'

Fauna offered more tea to Erf, who accepted gratefully and dipped their marzipan into it.

'I spent some time talking to her yesterday. Have you ever asked her why she wants to design clothes?' Fauna didn't wait for her to answer. 'Felicity says that clothes help a person show the world who they are. She wants to help people be themselves.'

Shenanigan kicked idly at the carpet and refused to say anything.

'That's cool,' said Erf. 'It's one of the reasons I took up knitting. Couldn't find a parrotfish jumper anywhere.'

'Having a mundane name is hard, as Flora can attest,' Fauna went on. 'You saw how people spoke to my sister during the Mock-Up. Felicity is clever and kind. She likes mazes and code-breaking. She taught herself French. And the Family treat her like she'll always be boring.'

'She hates us,' mumbled Shenanigan.

Fauna seemed to consider this, her eyes steady over the rim of her teacup. 'I think some people in our Family have treated her very unfairly, and that's what she hates. Felicity just wants to be seen. As we all do.'

Fauna watched Erf mopping up crumbs with a finger. 'I've been meaning to ask. When did you start going by Erf?'

Erf blinked, and then studied their crumbs with greater intensity. 'About a year ago. I'm having trouble getting people to use the new name, though. Especially . . . especially my gran.'

Fauna nodded. 'How come?'

'Well, I haven't . . . told her, in so many words,' said Erf. 'That I want to change it. It feels so . . . big. And you know what she's like. How much she believes in the Dictionary and stuff. I'm not sure she'd think we're allowed to go about changing things.'

Fauna snorted.

'Do you know, I think that's a load of . . . Well, a load of horse feathers.' She shook her head. 'The idea that a *book* can tell you who you're going to be.'

'But so many of us match,' Erf pointed out. 'Sometimes it all feels a bit . . . inevitable.'

Shenanigan thought of the gravestones in the cellar, Aunt Inheritance's white-gloved hand on the Dictionary's glass case, Phenomena's neat list of check-marks.

Fauna chewed her lip for a moment. 'You know . . . when I was born, everybody thought I was a boy. The doctors said I was a boy. My parents bought me boy's clothes. I had to learn to talk in order to explain the situation to them, and they were terribly embarrassed by their mistake.'

'Something similar happened to me,' Erf said. 'No one asked who I was, either.' They smiled. Something bloomed between Fauna and Erf, an understanding.

'What made you choose "Erf"?' asked Fauna.

'It's an old word for a plot of land.' They hesitated, then went on, 'I picked it because anything can grow there.'

Fauna laughed delightedly. 'Oh, I love that. Yes, that suits you down to the ground. No pun intended – I'm not Candour.'

'Do you mind if I ask . . . Did it . . . Was it difficult? Getting people to listen to you?' asked Erf, fiddling with their cuffs.

'Sometimes.' Fauna sipped her tea. 'There will always

be people who think they know you better than you know yourself. But I quickly learned that they don't matter; the people who love you are the people who listen. Flora got into more than one fight on my behalf when we were younger.' She chuckled. 'She was always the angry one.'

'So you're saying . . .'

'I'm saying, if you want to change your name, change it. You have people in your corner. Right, Shenanigan?'

Shenanigan nodded and brandished her fists. Erf laughed. Their eyes were wet.

'I just don't know if Gran will let me.'

'Your gran doesn't get a say in who you are. No one in the world makes that decision but you.'

Erf and Fauna smiled at each other. The moment they were having seemed very important, and did not include Shenanigan. That was fine. That was, in fact, wonderful.

Besides, Uncle Maelstrom was peeking round the door, and looked as if he was about to call her name. She slipped away before he could tread on the moment.

'By the way, I love your jumper,' she heard Fauna say as the door closed.

Uncle Maelstrom chivvied her down the hall to

quieter and quieter parts of the House. He walked quickly, and for every one of his massive strides, Shenanigan had to take three. Eventually, she gave up all pretence of walking and broke into a jog.

'What's going on?' she asked.

'Do you have your map with you?' he whispered as they headed up the nearest set of stairs. It was weird seeing him move quietly. It made Shenanigan uneasy, and she stopped. She thought of the crumpled list of suspects in her pocket, and what Felicity had said about not automatically crossing off her uncle and Cook. She thought about Maelstrom's interest in the map and the way his eyes bounced from one doorway to another like a pinball.

'Uncle Maelstrom,' said Shenanigan, 'I consider you an ally—'

'Thank you,' he said seriously.

'– but recently you've been behaving very suspiciously, and not like the uncle I know. And, because you have behaved suspiciously, I am now suspicious. Why did you encourage me to make a map of the House? Why did you ask me not to tell anyone about it? And why were you so fidgety in the freezer yesterday?'

'I can explain—'

'Good! Then explain, 'cause I'm not going anywhere with you until you have.'

Shenanigan folded her arms, planted her feet firmly apart, and fixed Maelstrom with her best piratical gaze. Her uncle sighed.

'That's what I'm trying to do, Shenanigan. You need to come with me. It's time we told you everything.'

He turned to the blank stretch of wall beside him, the wall Shenanigan had marked on her map with a big red question mark, and gave it a series of complicated knocks and taps. There was a click and the wall swung open.

Aunt Inheritance poked her head out into the corridor, eyes wide. Her gaze darted between them and past them, and, with a sharp breath, she hauled them inside.

· 23 ·

BEST-LAID PLANS

'Were you followed?' Aunt Inheritance hissed. She looked as if she had been dragged through a hedge backwards, and the hedge had put up a fight.

'Furl your sails, Inheritance,' said Maelstrom. 'There's no one in our wake. They're all distracted.'

Shenanigan took in the room around her. She'd had such high expectations that almost anything was going to be a let-down, but this was particularly disappointing.

For a start, there wasn't any gold or bones – just a lot of paper. Long, thin tangles of it collected in the corners. Huge, broad sheets, covered in numbers and diagrams, overlapped on a table, their curled edges weighed down with empty cups and saucers. Tall stacks of books lounged against the wall. The mysterious tubes Shenanigan had seen Inheritance carrying on her first night in the House were tossed to one side, empty, and a small camp bed and picnic basket had been crammed into what little space remained. No wonder Aunt Inheritance looked so crumpled. She must have been sleeping in here, holed up like a hamster in a paper nest.

There were three other unusual things in the room. One was Felicity, who regarded Shenanigan with red-rimmed eyes. The next was Phenomena, who was making notes in her casebook and pretending her sisters didn't exist. The third was a large object in the centre of the table, covered with a white sheet. Shenanigan immediately went to peek underneath, but Aunt Inheritance let out a noise like a deranged cat and slapped her hand away.

'Ow!' Shenanigan yelped. 'Uncle Maelstrom, what's going on? And why are *you two* here?' She glowered at Phenomena and Felicity.

'I was fetched *under duress* by Aunt Inheritance,' Felicity said. 'And Uncle M found Phenomena knocking on a totally innocent patch of wall down the corridor.'

Phenomena's lips pursed, but she didn't look up from her notes.

'Never mind. I'm sure you'd have found the room eventually,' Shenanigan said with a smirk.

Uncle Maelstrom leaned over before another argument could break out, and tapped the documents on the table. 'Shenanigan. D'you recognize these?'

Shenanigan looked at the papers. They were plans of the Swift estate throughout history. On one of them, the tower and conservatory were missing, and half the rooms were the wrong shape and size. In another, the tower *was* there, but was called the 'turret' instead. The original plan didn't even have the lake, just a sketch of an enormous oak tree. It made Shenanigan feel dizzy, seeing the House she knew so well with all its insides rearranged.

'This one is the newest,' added Uncle Maelstrom. He slid over the least-yellowed sheet to Shenanigan, dated 1900. The afternoon room wasn't there, but plans for the hedge maze had just been sketched, and there was a small warren labelled SERVANTS' QUARTERS, from when the Family had servants.

She frowned. 'They're all wrong.'

Uncle Maelstrom nodded. 'It's this House that's the problem. It's near unmappable. It's like living in a giant game of musical chairs, only it's more like musical architecture.' He scrubbed a hand over his face. 'It's impossible to know which secret chambers are still secret, which have been sealed up, whether the Hoard even – Steady!'

At the mention of the Hoard, Shenanigan had sprung on to a chair so she was closer to eye-level with her uncle, and begun prodding him in the chest with a finger.

'I knew it! You've been looking for the treasure without me!' That was why he'd been so shifty about her map. 'We were supposed to be allies!'

Uncle Maelstrom bowed his head apologetically. 'Aye, and I hope you'll still consider us so.'

'How long have you been looking?'

Uncle Maelstrom cleared his throat. 'It was a hobby,' he hedged, 'for a few . . . years. One I gave up soon after you were born.'

'Mutineers walk the plank, you know.'

Aunt Inheritance tapped the table. 'Shenanigan, this is serious. Looking for Vile's Hoard isn't a game. Or, rather, it *was* a game, but now it's most definitely not.' She smoothed a hand over the papers. Focusing on the documents rather than the other people in the room seemed to help calm Inheritance; it made her twitch less, at least. 'Like your uncle, I've been researching the Hoard on and off ever since I became the Archivist. For our history, you understand. Recently, it has become an urgent task.'

'Urgent?' asked Felicity.

Inheritance coughed. 'The Family funds have become somewhat . . . depleted of late,' she said.

'We're broke,' Uncle Maelstrom summarized. 'Well, we've been broke for a while, but now we're "the House is falling down around us" broke.'

Shenanigan was gobsmacked. She'd thought all the wear and tear was a deliberate style choice.

'For the past three years, I have devoted all my spare time to the search for the Hoard,' said Inheritance. 'I tracked down rare documents, scoured libraries, and visited every Swift who would speak to me in the hope of finding a clue. The fruits of my labour are in this room.' She gestured to the wealth of paper. 'A few months ago, I finally found a lead. I called the Reunion – and, unwittingly, called down doom upon our House. Now our Matriarch is . . . ill, it is imperative we find the Hoard as soon as possible.'

'What? Why?'

'Because,' said Phenomena, staring at her case

notes, 'if the treasure is found, it legally belongs to the Matriarch, and we don't have a Matriarch right now. Lots of Family members are here looking for the Hoard, and if someone finally finds it, they might just decide to keep it for themselves.'

'And whoever pushed Aunt Schadenfreude, squashed Gumshoe, and shot Pamplemousse isn't hunting for the treasure as a fun Family activity. They're willing to kill for it.'

'Precisely.' Aunt Inheritance nodded. 'Your uncle thinks you, Shenanigan, are the key to the Hoard's location. I have my doubts, but my methods –' and she glanced to the object covered in a white cloth – 'were thoroughly scoffed at, so I've agreed to let him have first crack at it.'

'This is why your map is important, Shenanigan,' said Maelstrom. 'The House has been dug up, swapped around, and shuffled like a pack of cards so often that everything from side buildings to staircases have changed position. Look.'

He picked up a map dated 1799, and laid one dated 1900 over the top of it. The paper was thin; both versions of the House were visible, the old and the new. 'I think, if we put all these plans together, we can figure out where the Hoard is. We know what we're looking for: a space that has been untouched since Vile's day, somewhere the treasure could have sat in the dark for years. But these are all useless without your map, Shenanigan. These tell us the way things were – we need you to tell us the way things are.'

'It's my map,' said Shenanigan sullenly.

'It is,' agreed Maelstrom. 'And you were the only one who could have made it. No one in the world knows a house better than a mischievous child who grows up in it.'

Her uncle's beloved face was open and earnest. Now that he'd come clean, the little nagging dishonesties that had flickered like shadows on his face were gone. But Shenanigan remembered seeing them, and how much they had hurt.

'You *lied.*'

'I'm sorry. But really, I didn't lie,' Maelstrom pointed out. 'I simply didn't tell the truth.'

Having her own logic turned back on her was not very pleasant. Shenanigan thought it over, chewing her thumb. If she handed over her map, she was giving away the best advantage she had over her relatives. But this was Uncle Maelstrom, who had earned her loyalty every day of her life. He could easily *demand* she give him the map, or just take it out of her pocket, or shout at her, but she loved him so much because she knew in her bones he would never, ever do any of those things.

Shenanigan reached into her back pocket for the map.

It wasn't there.

Shenanigan did the frantic pat-down everyone does when they have lost their wallet, or their inhaler, or their one-of-a-kind map.

'It's gone,' she whispered.

Uncle Maelstrom's brows overhung his eyes like a low fog. 'Shenanigan . . .'

'I'm not lying,' Shenanigan insisted. 'Don't make a mark in my column, Phenomena! I'm not trying to trick you. It really is gone. I promise, it's—'

'It's alright, Skipper,' Maelstrom murmured, laying a soothing hand on top of her head. The weight was familiar and reassuring, and it was supposed to mean *It's not your fault*. But it was.

Shenanigan didn't know what to say. Sometimes she put things down and forgot where she had left them, but that was why she filled her pockets with so many useful bits, so she always had a steady supply. The map was the only thing of hers that was completely irreplaceable. She didn't even know when she had lost it.

'It's not alright,' said Inheritance tightly. 'If the killer gets hold of it, *they* will have the advantage. They won't just have a great tool for finding the Hoard. They'll have a map of all the secret passages, hidden ways, and hiding places you found. Who knows what they could do with that.'

There was a moment of quiet.

'Very well, Inheritance,' said Maelstrom heavily. 'I suppose we'll have to do this your way.'

Inheritance's gloved hands made a muffled noise as she clapped them together.

'I'm telling you it will work, Maelstrom.' There was a manic light in her eyes again.

'I don't like it,' he said glumly. 'It's like whistling in the wind. It means trouble.'

'Stop being cryptic,' said Phenomena. 'Aunt Inheritance? What's your idea?'

Inheritance had drifted to the covered object on the table.

'As I said, my search for the Hoard has been mostly fruitless,' she murmured, 'until a few months ago – when I found these.'

She held up her glasses, and pulled off the arm to show them all the tiny key. 'They were up for auction, along with an old journal belonging to Great-Great-Aunt Memento, a previous Archivist. I try to buy as many Family heirlooms as I can for our collection. In that journal, Memento wrote about this room, and what it contained, and I was shocked to learn that through it she had found *incontrovertible evidence* that the treasure not only existed, but remained undiscovered.

'I called the Reunion, as I said. I left my library, armed with my maps and research. I wanted to open this room, share my discovery with the Matriarch, and enlist the help of the Family in recovering our lost fortune so we could save our ancestral home. But Aunt Schadenfreude . . .' Inheritance's expression clouded. 'She said I was a fool, and Memento a crackpot. She said the Family would never work together, and all I was doing was inviting mayhem and selfishness. And she said that she definitely, unequivocally, didn't believe in *this*.'

She whipped the sheet off the table to reveal a strange squat object, a complex machine of brass and dark wood. What looked like an old hearing trumpet sprouted from one side, and a large, antique-looking glass bulb bulged from the top.

'This,' said Aunt Inheritance, patting the machine, 'was the subject of Memento's journal. The Ecto Electric Kin-communicator, or EEK for short.'

Shenanigan eyed the machine with distrust. There was something about it that made her teeth ache. The lightbulb on top seemed to stare at her like a dead and furious eye, and the small slot in its body was too much like a mouth, and yet she knew that if nobody else was in the room, she'd be trying her hardest to switch it on.

'What is it?' breathed Shenanigan.

'It's a machine . . . for talking to the dead,' intoned Aunt Inheritance.

'Yes,' hissed Shenanigan.

'Nope,' said Phenomena and Felicity together. Their faces were a study in opposites. Felicity was leaning as far away from the machine as possible. Phenomena was suppressing giggles.

'That's preposterous,' she hiccuped. 'You can't talk to the dead. They're *dead*.'

Aunt Inheritance huffed. 'It was made by Charlatan Swift in 1888. She and Memento conducted the seance themselves. She swore it worked.'

'Yes, and her name was *Charlatan*,' scoffed Phenomena. 'She might as well have been called Fibber Swift.'

'Memento detailed the whole encounter in her journal,' insisted Inheritance. 'She said the spirit she contacted even told her how to find the Hoard!'

'I don't suppose she wrote *that* down?' asked Felicity sceptically.

'Alas, she took that secret to her grave.'

'And I don't suppose anyone thought to ring her up afterwards? No? So let me get this straight.' Felicity folded her arms, which was her attack position. 'This is the "incontrovertible evidence" you were on about? You called the Reunion and came all the way over here because you think you can ring up a dead relative and just . . . *ask* them where the treasure is?'

'Yes,' said Aunt Inheritance.

Felicity turned to Maelstrom. 'And *you* think this is a sensible idea?'

'Of course not, that's why I wanted the map.' He frowned. 'You shouldn't interfere with spirits.'

'Right. Well, since the only sensible person in this House is unconscious, I officially give up,' said Felicity, and she threw herself back in her chair, defeated.

For Shenanigan, the day was improving rapidly.

Talking to the dead! She'd tried using a Ouija board once before, but had got a very boring ghost who wouldn't answer her questions and just kept asking 'why the wine tasted funny'. The EEK felt different. Her fingers itched to touch it. Despite its age, the brass still shone, the wood gleamed. Perhaps Aunt Inheritance had cleaned it, but somehow Shenanigan didn't think so. It could have been locked in this room for centuries, and dust would not have settled on its surface.

'How does it work?' she asked.

Inheritance had been puffed up with excitement; the question deflated her slightly.

'Well, currently, it doesn't. I can turn it on, but it just spits out rolls and rolls of gibberish.' She gestured to the tumbleweeds of tangled paper that had drifted up into the corners of the room.

'Well, of course it doesn't work,' sniffed Phenomena. 'Ghosts aren't *real*. There's no scientific evidence to support them. Besides, look – that EMF meter has been completely disconnected, this seismometer is loose, and there's a mouse skeleton blocking the gears.'

There was a brief silence.

'Well, blow me down! I can't believe you didn't notice the skeleton,' muttered Maelstrom.

Inheritance grabbed Phenomena's shoulders. 'Phenomena, are you saying you can get this up and running?'

With difficulty, Phenomena shrugged. 'Give me ten minutes and a set of pliers, and I can make it work how it's supposed to – but even I can't make it talk to ghosts.' She began to fiddle away at the back of the machine, muttering to herself all the while.

Shenanigan and Felicity shared a fond look and a smile over their sister's head – until they suddenly remembered their feud, and stared resolutely in opposite directions.

Uncle Maelstrom considered the two of them.

'Not had a falling-out, have we?' The sisters' answering silence was pointed at both ends. He sighed.

'I truly believe you three girls are the smartest people in this whole House. That's why I brought you in here. I trust you further than I could throw you and, believe me, I could throw you very far. "Let's ask the girls for help," I said to Inheritance. "Put 'em together and they could steer a galleon through a gale with their arms tied behind their backs." But for such clever people, you can be very careless.'

'But—' began Shenanigan.

'Aye, careless. A crew can bicker and fight among themselves all they like when the wind is calm. But when the pressure drops and the storm comes rolling in, they know to stow it. They trust each other with their lives.' He gathered them both in a hug that swallowed them whole. 'You're all on the same crew. Act like it.'

There was a loud click behind them, as of an old wooden panel being slotted back into place.

'Fixed it,' said Phenomena.

Inheritance turned the lamps low and sat by the machine, a white-gloved finger hovering over the ON switch. She had Memento's journal open before her. She read like a typewriter types, her eyes clicking steadily over each word until, with an internal *ding*, she moved down to the next line.

'Now,' she whispered. 'The journal says we flick the switch like so . . .'

They all felt as well as heard the machine turn on – a deep, low hum in the eyeballs and teeth, and a thickening of the air that made the hairs on their arms stand up.

'That's just an electrostatic field,' Phenomena said pointedly.

The bulb on top of the EEK flashed on, and then off

again. There was a whirr and a whisper as a fresh roll of paper slotted into place.

'Grand work, Phenomena!' Maelstrom grinned. 'What now?'

Aunt Inheritance squinted at the journal. 'Just a moment,' she said. 'Aunt Memento does rather waffle on . . . Ah! Right. We need to press this button here . . .' She flicked another switch. 'And the machine will scan for nearby spirits of our bloodline. Here in the House, there should be a fair few of them. The trumpet picks up and magnifies whispers from the spirit world . . .'

'Which is nonsense,' added Phenomena.

'And the seismometer detects vibrations on the otherworldly plane . . .'

'Preposterous!'

'And the EMF senses ghostly fluctuations in the electromagnetic field . . .'

'Rubbish! Aunt Inheritance, really!'

Their arguing was interrupted by a loud *ping!* from the machine and a flash from the bulb.

'We've made contact,' whispered Inheritance. 'We can ask questions now.' She cleared her throat. 'Is anybody there?'

The bulb flashed once. Shenanigan felt the back of her neck prickle.

'One flash means *yes*. Standard ghost protocol.' Aunt Inheritance trembled with excitement. 'Oh, I had so hoped to do this in the presence of the whole Family. The first cross-plane Reunion! We could have asked Humdrum for her famous pierogi recipe, or Vex if she really did have a romance with Queen—'

'Inheritance,' warned Maelstrom gently. 'Eyes on the horizon.'

'Yes, quite.' She took a deep breath. 'So . . . what should we ask first?'

No one had a chance to reply, because as soon as Inheritance spoke, the machine began to click rapidly, and from the small slot in its side it spat out a strip of paper bearing large, black letters:

E A R W E B

'Pardon?' Inheritance looked startled.

W A R B E E

'Hang on,' muttered Phenomena. 'I just need to fine-tune the mechanism . . .'

She used the age-old scientific method of hitting it once, hard.

B E W A R E

'Beware what?' asked Maelstrom, leaning forward.

The machine hummed and clicked. With another cheery *ping!* it spat out:

D E A T H

In a secret chamber in Swift House, five members of the Family sat round a machine that could contact the dead. The soft glow of the lamps cast their faces in dramatic shadow, gleaming off the dark wood and brass of the EEK as it spewed long ribbons of paper across the table. Aunt Inheritance fed it through her fingers, sighing.

BEWARE MURDER DEATH MURDER BEWARE DEATH MURDER VIOLENCE DEATH BEWARE

'It seems to be hysterical,' she mused. 'I wonder if all spirits are this highly strung?'

Uncle Maelstrom stroked his beard. 'Could we try to calm it down somehow?' He patted the machine gingerly. 'There, there.'

BODILY HARM, it spat.

'It's a glitch,' said Phenomena. 'That, or it's just doing what it was designed to do: throw out sinister words at random to scare a gullible audience.'

'Well, it's working,' said Felicity, shivering. 'I am a bit creeped out.'

Shenanigan scowled. She had really been looking forward to talking to a ghost. Trust Inheritance to find the least interesting one.

'Are you trying to warn us?' tried Inheritance. 'A member of our Family has been gravely injured, another killed, and—'

DEAD DEATH MURDER BEWARE DEATH BEWARE BLOOD MURDER MURDER MURDER

'We could try switching it off and on again,' suggested Maelstrom.

Shenanigan lost her patience and prodded the machine. 'Oi! How did you die?'

The machine fell silent.

'Shenanigan! That's *quite* inappropriate!' hissed Inheritance.

'Were you murdered too, or did you just have an accident? Was it the plague? Was your body covered in boils? Was your sick green? You could have died in a war, I suppose. Ooh, were you hanged? Or shot, or stabbed, or mauled by a large animal? Were you a victim of cannibalism?'

The EEK clicked and pinged.

RUDE, it typed.

'That's enough,' scolded Inheritance. 'I don't know

much about ghost etiquette, but I know you should never ask a lady her age, and this seems about the same thing.'

'*Is* it a ghost, though?' asked Felicity.

The bulb on top of the machine lit up once. **YES**.

'Alright. If it can't talk properly, we'll have to try yes or no questions instead.'

Inheritance took a deep breath, resting her fingers lightly on the table. 'We thank you for speaking with us, spirit,' she quavered. 'Do you know who we are?'

The bulb flashed once. **YES**.

'Excellent. Then you know what has happened in this House over the last few days?'

YES.

'Oh please. It's just flashing at random,' muttered Phenomena.

'Do you know who attacked Aunt Schadenfreude?' Shenanigan jumped in. This was taking far too long.

YES.

'Did the same person kill Gumshoe and Pamplemousse? Who was it?' she asked excitedly.

The machine whirred and clicked, and then began to spew out paper once again. Shenanigan seized it with trembling fingers.

MURDER DEATH MURDER BEWARE

She sat back, sighing.

'I think we've upset them. Um. We should ask something else,' said Felicity.

'What about the treasure?' Uncle Maelstrom stroked his beard. 'Does it know where Vile's Hoard is? DO YOU KNOW WHERE VILE'S HOARD IS?' he asked in a loud voice, as if dead and deaf were the same thing.

One flash from the antique bulb.

'Aha! Well, where, then?'

A click, a whir, a ping.

LOOK UNDER HOUSE

'Under the House!' exclaimed Inheritance. 'That narrows things down significantly! Oh please, spirit, *where* under the House?'

'How would it even know that?' interjected Phenomena. 'You're just looking for patterns in nonsense!'

&%?!£&! babbled the machine.

'Is it swearing at us?' cried a scandalized Felicity.

'No, it's spouting gibberish!'

Shenanigan had thought Phenomena was just being a spoilsport, but now she saw that her sister was genuinely agitated, chewing on her hair again. 'We're wasting time with this, asking a machine, when we should be using our brains! Who are we even supposed to be talking to? None of you even asked that!'

SH

'It's trying to type its name!' cried Maelstrom.

'Is it trying to spell Schadenfreude?' asked Shenanigan.

'She's not even dead yet! Besides, that's not how you spell Schadenfreude. It has a CH, like Charlatan.'

'No, it doesn't!'

SHHHHHH

'Well, its name can't be SHHHH, can it?'

'Can we please all calm—'

MURDER MURDER MURDER MURDER MURDER MURDER MURDER MURDER MURDER MURDER MURDER MURDER

An awful wailing started, a noise of horror and grief that made Felicity and Phenomena clutch each other in shock.

Shenanigan leaned over the table and grabbed at the bulb. It flashed in alarm.

'Just tell us who's doing this!' she shouted as the EEK whirred furiously.

MURDER I DON'T KNOW WHY YOU'RE ASKING ME MURDER YOU'D BE BETTER OFF ASKING THE CAT

Shenanigan thumped hard on the top of the machine, making Aunt Inheritance squeal.

'TELL US!' she shouted. 'Tell us right now, or I'll rip out all your wires and use them to string a harp, which I will then play *very badly!*'

There was a screech and a grind, and Shenanigan's blow must have broken whatever Phenomena had fixed, because the machine began to spit out,

CENTURIESHOARDMURDER CATDISHONOURRENDERER ARMOUREDHEIRSUNDERCUT CERTAINHOURSMURDERED, and more and more strings of nonsensical letters, over and over. Finally, it let out one last sad whine, and stopped.

But the wailing did not, because it wasn't coming from the machine – wasn't even coming from within the room. It was coming from elsewhere in the House, and it was loud enough to rattle the canvas of the secret room.

Shenanigan and the others leapt to their feet, skidding on Aunt Inheritance's maps. Tearing out into the corridor towards the source of the noise, they flung themselves in a tangle of legs to the grand staircase, where once again an audience gathered. Only this time there was no body, just Cook, wailing.

Maelstrom ran forward, and Cook almost collapsed on to his steadying mast of an arm.

'What is it? What's happened?'

'It was too much,' groaned Cook. 'She was too badly hurt.'

Shenanigan went cold, and she saw her fear reflected in Uncle Maelstrom's careworn face. 'Cook, is she . . .' He couldn't finish.

'Yes,' she sobbed. 'She's gone. Properly, this time. Arch-Aunt Schadenfreude is dead.'

A
REHEARSAL

It was a grey, buttoned-up morning in early May, and the Swifts were in the middle of a funeral.

Abandoned cars lined the gravel driveway like honour guards, gleaming dully in the weak sun. Every so often, a shower of rain would rush overhead to see what all the fuss was about, and the crêpe bows and ribbons the Family had hung drooped wetly in the damp.

In a way, Arch-Aunt Schadenfreude's timing couldn't have been better. She would have appreciated the efficiency of dying while everyone was already present. It saved writing invitations.

There weren't nearly enough folding chairs for all the Family, and Phenomena and Felicity had had to drag almost every seat in the House outside into the drizzle. Mourners sat on kitchen stools, chintz sofas, leather armchairs, and the chaise longue from the library. That, Shenanigan knew, Aunt Schadenfreude wouldn't have liked. In fact, she wouldn't have liked a great many things. Despite all their rehearsals, Shenanigan, Phenomena, and Felicity had not been permitted to organize the ceremony according to their aunt's instructions. Instead, strange relatives, relative strangers, had swooped in with their own ideas of how to do things the 'proper way'.

The sisters were not allowed to help carry the coffin. They had not been asked to decorate, and as a result the flowers were all wrong; the mere sight of them had made Felicity burst into tears. Someone had even mentioned the possibility of a hymn being sung, and that was the last straw for Shenanigan, who knew that little irritated her aunt more than lacklustre singing. 'The human voice is nothing but a fleshy bagpipe,' she had told Shenanigan once.

She watched the slow, twisting procession enter the graveyard from her lonely perch up in the apple tree. From there, she could have swung down and dropped into the open grave. Mourners settled into their seats beneath her. Felicity, Phenomena, Maelstrom, and Cook were in the front row. Shenanigan could see her own seat beside Phenomena, reserved by a card with her name lettered in tidy cursive. The writing looked familiar.

From time to time, people looked up towards where she sat and tutted in disapproval, but Shenanigan knew she could not come down. She was supposed to be sad. She wasn't. She was furious, and underneath that fury was an emptiness so deep and dark she was scared to look into it. If she was to go down and sit in her seat and be forced to be part of a funeral her aunt would have hated, all that anger would bubble over, and she would do something dreadful.

'I'm sure Aunt Schadenfreude wouldn't want us to be sad,' began Candour, rubbing anxiously at his hand. In Schadenfreude's absence he had ended up as celebrant as well as doctor, while Inheritance stood to his left, as pale and wrung-out as a used dishcloth.

Of course Aunt Schadenfreude wanted us to be sad, Shenanigan fumed. Oddly, the only people who understood this were Atrocious and Pique; Pique wore a black velvet suit and cape, and Atrocious was near-invisible beneath a volcanic eruption of black lace. They sobbed and wailed theatrically, clutching each other. They were very well-practised mourners.

Flora and Fauna stood at the back of the gathering and, though they were dressed identically, Shenanigan could easily tell who was who. Fauna had been crying silently and steadily for hours, her eyes red-rimmed. Flora had her arms crossed over her chest, her mouth a thin, livid line. Ten minutes into the eulogy, she rose and stalked off towards the House, hands in her pockets. No one tried to stop her. When the mourners stood to sing, Shenanigan slipped back down the tree and away from the graveyard, snatching the place card from her chair as she went.

A funeral is supposed to be a way to say goodbye. You look inside yourself and find a place to put your grief, not somewhere hidden, not the top shelf or the back of a cupboard, but maybe by a window, where it can catch the light. Shenanigan couldn't do that. So many things were wrong. Aunt Schadenfreude's gravestone had been brought out, ready for the death date to be carved. On it was carved her definition:

Schadenfreude

Noun
The enjoyment felt at the misery of others

That was especially wrong. Cook had said Aunt Schadenfreude put on her iron collar when she became Matriarch. Shenanigan wondered who her aunt had been before Aunt Gracious had picked her to take on responsibility for her entire Family. Had Schadenfreude wanted that responsibility, or had it felt like cold metal closing round her throat? For as long as Shenanigan had known her, Aunt Schadenfreude had never enjoyed anyone's misery but her own.

Shenanigan's grief was beginning to transform Aunt Schadenfreude from scowling nemesis into scowling-but-sympathetic hero. Shenanigan had sworn her revenge when her aunt was merely unconscious; now she was dead, she pledged it once more. She would not rest until she'd found the person who had done this to her aunt – to her Family – and made them pay for it.

On Vile's Monument leaned a figure in a long coat. Their head turned to follow Flora trudging across the lawn. For a second, Shenanigan's eyes played a cruel trick on the rest of her and she thought she recognized her aunt, hunched over in the rain. But then the figure turned, and even behind her large pair of dark glasses, Shenanigan recognized Daisy. When she saw Shenanigan, she lifted her hand hesitantly in a half-wave. Something about it was terribly sad, as if Daisy was on a small boat drifting out to sea, wondering whether she had gone too far to be seen from the shore.

The rain grew heavier, dripping off Vile's nose and turning the grass to mud. Daisy put her hand down. She turned and followed Flora into the House.

From the top of the grand staircase, Shenanigan watched everyone come filing back in, shaking rain from their hair and umbrellas. It felt a lot like that first day of the Reunion, though the faces were more familiar now. She sat with her legs threaded through the banisters, kicking into the air. People kept coming up to Phenomena and Felicity and shaking their hands or hugging them, to their obvious discomfort. Shenanigan bared her teeth at anyone who so much as looked at her, never mind attempted to offer condolences, and in the end her lonely lookout was ignored. Only Erf, fixed to their gran's side by Inheritance's sheer worry, watched her steadily with an expression of profound sympathy. Maelstrom and Cook were blank-faced and mute, but Candour and Fauna stood beside them, answering questions they were too tired to answer but too kind to ignore. Shenanigan could take or leave much of her Family, she had decided, but she was glad those two were here.

Candour spotted Shenanigan at her solitary post, and climbed the stairs towards her. He looked even more tired than before, but the smile he summoned for her was still crooked and bright.

'Hello, Shenanigan,' he said quietly. 'Mind if I sit?'

She didn't answer. He sat anyway.

'She was very old,' he said at last.

'She didn't die from being old, though,' said Shenanigan. Her anger throbbed dully in her throat. 'She died from being murdered.'

Candour had nothing to say to that. They sat in silence, Shenanigan rubbing her thumb along the edge of her place card.

'Who wrote these out?' she asked after a while.

'Daisy. Doesn't she have the most adorable penmanship? The little loops on her F's especially . . .'

Candour began to drone on about the delightful way Daisy dotted her I's, and Shenanigan fought not to crumple the card in her hands. That was why the handwriting looked familiar! She and Phenomena had been staring at it just the night before, on a strip of paper taken off a crossbow bolt. All of a sudden, she was sick of sneaking around.

'Phenomena and I snuck in and took the note off the crossbow bolt in Pamplemousse's body,' she stated, interrupting Candour mid-flow. She ignored his gasp of horror. 'We wanted to compare the killer's handwriting with our suspects'.' She held up the place setting. 'This writing will match the note. I'm sure of it.'

'You snuck in to see the body?' Candour's soft brown eyes were wide behind his glasses. 'Shenanigan—'

'What do you expect?' she replied. 'I can't help my name, after all,' she added bitterly, feeling a pang. Aunt Schadenfreude would never say that to her again.

Candour took the place card, staring at it as if he'd forgotten how to read. 'I didn't really get a good look at the Scrabble notes, but . . . My God, do you think the murderer forced Daisy to write for them?'

Shenanigan pressed her forehead into the banister and groaned. Candour was supposed to be clever.

'Listen to what I'm telling you,' she said through gritted teeth. 'Daisy wrote the note, because Daisy killed Pamplemousse, and Gumshoe—'

'Shenanigan.' Candour took her hand in his. 'You've been through a lot. You just lost your aunt . . .'

'This isn't about that!' said Shenanigan hotly. It was as if, when a person turned thirteen, a little switch flipped in their brains, making it impossible for them to think properly. 'I heard Daisy and Flora talking the other day. Flora was helping Daisy cover something up, and they were going on about how important it was to keep it from you. Flora said that, after the Reunion, Daisy wouldn't have to act any more. They were making plans! They're in – what's that word – cahoots!'

'Complicit. In league,' murmured Candour automatically. The smallest seed of doubt planted itself in the furrow of Candour's brow. Then he smiled again.

'I'm sure this is all a mistake. But,' he added over Shenanigan's protests, 'I'll ask her about it, if it'll make you feel better. She wouldn't lie to me. She couldn't.'

Shenanigan, who could spot lies like dribbled food on a person's chin, knew you could do it to almost anyone as long as you believed it first.

Candour stood up. He busied himself brushing imaginary dust off his knees. His hair hid his eyes, and when he spoke to her his voice was strained. 'I'll talk to her. But you should get some rest. Go somewhere quiet with your sisters. None of you should be alone right now.'

Shenanigan watched him head upstairs, unsteady on his feet and shaking his head as if to clear it. She wanted to scream. She wanted to bite. She sank her teeth into one of the wooden railings in front of her and felt it give satisfyingly. She probably looked like a caged animal, which was good, because it was how she felt.

She went downstairs. One or two people tried to pat her arm, or stroke her hair, and she snarled at them until they jumped back in alarm. She didn't know where to go. Her room still felt spoiled after the killer had been in it. The library had a bloody stain on the floor. The kitchen freezer was full of bodies. Her sisters were angry with her.

In the end, she headed to the conservatory, which was green and softly noisy with the sound of growing things. She wedged herself in a nook between two huge plants. If she half closed her eyes, she could pretend she was in the jungle and her parents were just a few metres away, bug-bitten and happy.

Something warm and furry crept into her lap.

'Hello, John the Cat,' she whispered. John the Cat kneaded her legs until he deemed them comfortable, his claws snagging her trousers in the process, and then settled in to clean his paws.

She wasn't sure how long she sat there, lulled by his purr. After a while, Erf came in. Shenanigan hissed at them. Erf went away. Erf returned with a plate of food, and Felicity in tow. Shenanigan hissed again. She pretended she was covered in spines. She pretended she was venomous.

Felicity crawled into the gap between the plants and hugged her anyway.

'I'm not crying,' said Shenanigan as Felicity blurred.

'I know,' she said. 'You can not-cry on me, if you want.' She stroked Shenanigan's hair, and began to braid it absently. Erf shuffled into what little space remained and offered their plate with the air of someone trying to lure a frightened animal out from under a porch. None of them spoke. Erf just sat on Shenanigan's left, one sharp elbow pressed into her arm, and Felicity sat on her right, her fingers twisting gently in Shenanigan's hair.

Eventually, Felicity said, 'I like your jumper.'

And Erf said, 'Thank you. It's supposed to look like a death's head moth.'

Phenomena poked her head round the door.

'Oh, we're in here.' She squeezed in with her sisters and cousin. It was a very tight fit by now. She helped herself to some cake. 'Everyone keeps telling me how sorry they are. It's tiresome. I'd rather we all stopped moping about and got on with the investigation.'

Felicity's hand tightened a little in Shenanigan's hair.

'What I keep coming back to is the crossbow,' Phenomena mused. 'It's such a difficult thing to carry about. How did we not see the killer with it?'

'Maybe now isn't the time for this, Phenomena,' said Felicity gently. 'Our aunt is dead. We just had her funeral.'

'Which means everyone's distracted. Perfect opportunity for investigating.'

Felicity and Phenomena were very different. Phenomena had a mind like a microscope, focused and clear. Of course she wanted to continue the investigation. Phenomena needed to stay busy, but Shenanigan knew that as soon as she slowed down, as soon as she could no longer distract that brilliant, busy mind from what had happened, she would crumble like dry cake. But Felicity needed to cry, and hug, and play with Shenanigan's hair, and grieve for Aunt Schadenfreude with the people who knew and loved her. Each of them was too upset to see the other properly.

Somebody had to be the first to apologize. Shenanigan rearranged some things in her head, so that she could believe saying sorry first meant you were brave rather than weak, and then she said:

'I'm sorry.'

Felicity and Phenomena looked at her as if she'd grown a second, more apologetic head.

'Are you ill?' asked Felicity.

'She may have been poisoned,' said Phenomena seriously.

'Shut up,' said Shenanigan. 'I'm trying to fix things. Felicity, I'm sorry I called you a traitor. Phenomena, I'm sorry I ruined your case. Now you two need to apologize to each other, and also to me.' She thought for a moment, then added, 'Erf, you're fine. You don't need to apologize for anything.'

Erf gave her a thumbs-up, their mouth full of cake.

'This is worth at least two marks in the *Out of Character* column,' said Phenomena, amused. 'But you're right. Felicity, I understand you have reservations, but I would like to formally ask you to join the team. You're far from useless, and we could use your help. And Shenanigan . . . I know the details of detective work don't come naturally to you. I shouldn't have lost my temper.'

Felicity threw her arms round her sisters. 'I love you both very much, and I'm sorry,' she said simply.

'Hurrah!' said Erf crumbily. 'Having siblings looks exhausting.'

'And, Erf, I'm sorry I was so rude to you at the Mock-Up. I'm really glad you're here,' said Felicity.

'Oh. Well.' Erf blinked. 'Thanks. I'm – I'm glad I'm here too.'

John the Cat leapt off Shenanigan and, with an air of satisfaction, disappeared through the cat flap.

Shenanigan took the place card out of her pocket. 'Now we're all a team again, I have to show you something. We need the lab – c'mon.'

They hurried up to the attic, but as Phenomena climbed the ladder to her room she froze. Shenanigan bumped into her, and Erf bumped into Shenanigan, and they all slid back down into Felicity, who yelped.

'Phenomena?' she asked. 'What is it?'

Her sister's spine was rigid. Shenanigan stumbled out of the way as Phenomena collapsed against the wall, took off her glasses, and put her head in her hands. She made no sound.

'Phenomena . . .?'

Slowly, Shenanigan climbed the ladder. When she saw the state of Phenomena's room, she wanted to put her head in her hands too.

Sometimes when Cook saw the state of Shenanigan's bedroom, she would say things like, 'It looks like a bomb went off in here!' or, 'My word, it's like a hurricane swept through!'

She was exaggerating, because what Cook meant to say was that Shenanigan's room was very untidy. Phenomena's room, however, did look like a hurricane had hit it. There was so much broken glass everywhere that the floorboards sparkled like morning frost. Only the narrow neck of a test tube here and there indicated that it had all once been Phenomena's cabinet of beakers and vials. Equipment had been hurled to the floor. Books had been pulled from the shelves and shredded. The posters hung in tatters. The board and its list of suspects had been doused in some of her chemicals, and steamed. The only thing in the room that looked relatively undamaged was Phenomena's microscope, which was capable of surviving an actual hurricane and had merely been tipped off its bench. Shenanigan heard Felicity come up the ladder behind her, then heard her soft gasp.

In the centre of the room was Phenomena's Junior Forensics Kit, the dog's face warped and melted. Beside it was a charred cotton swab, a cinder that was once a coffee bean, a half-burnt copy of *The Body in the Library*, and a small pile of ashes that presumably used to be a handwriting sample. Shenanigan pawed through the ashes, and found one tiny corner that remained unburnt, an *oir* just visible. That was all they had left.

Something rolled towards her – Phenomena's flask, half full of her Solution Solution. Shenanigan picked it up. Horribly, there was a part of her – the part that liked to snap pencils in half and draw on wallpaper – that exulted in the wreckage, that wanted to hurl the flask at the wall and splatter green goo everywhere. She pushed down the urge.

From the ruins, Felicity fished out Phenomena's earmuffs and slung them round her neck, and then she and Erf rolled Phenomena's microscope on to one of the burst cushions and dragged it down the ladder. Phenomena took her hands from her face and curled them round the microscope.

'The evidence was all laid out on the desk,' Phenomena said eventually. 'They didn't need to search for it. They could have just walked in and picked it up. They smashed everything because they wanted to.'

'I'm so sorry, Phenomena,' Erf said miserably.

'Daisy and Flora came back to the House together during the funeral, while everyone else was outside,' said Shenanigan.

Phenomena nodded, too dazed to respond.

'They tried to burn the handwriting sample,' said Shenanigan, 'but they didn't get all of it.'

She took out the tiny scrap of paper and held it next to her place setting. Phenomena's eyes widened.

'Whose handwriting is—'

'Daisy's. It's Daisy's. That's what I was going to show you.'

Phenomena put her glasses back on and squinted at the paper, eyebrows pinched.

'I can't be one hundred per cent sure, with so little to work with, but that splodge on the *i*, like they stabbed the pen into the paper – it's certainly similar . . .'

'It's identical,' insisted Shenanigan. 'Don't tell me you don't believe me, either.'

'You might be right,' said Phenomena numbly. 'You might actually be right. Although we still need to prove it.' The prospect of scientific rigour brought a little life back into Phenomena's eyes. 'And we have a secondary issue. How did they know we had this evidence in the first place? What pushed them to take action now?'

Shenanigan hadn't thought of that.

'Something must have tipped them off,' Phenomena muttered. 'Maybe they went in to retrieve the note? That seems pretty tenuous.'

Shenanigan handed her sister the bottle of Solution Solution she had salvaged from the mess. Phenomena smiled and unscrewed the cap.

Shenanigan braced herself for the scent of fish and broccoli, but instead she smelled something else – bitter and sweet at the same time. Like Bakewell tart.

Shenanigan knocked the bottle from Phenomena's hands just before it touched her lips. Green goo splattered in an arc up the wall. Erf jerked backwards, and Felicity yelled in shock. Shenanigan grabbed Phenomena's face in her hands.

'You didn't drink any, did you?'

'Whaffrong?' Phenomena asked, squished and bewildered. Shenanigan let her go.

'Phenomena,' she said wildly, 'it smelled like almonds.'

They stared at the bottle. What felt like a lifetime ago, Phenomena had asked Shenanigan to check a beaker for her. She had made cyanide. She had then bottled it, and labelled it neatly, as she did all the chemicals in her lab, and put it away. It would have been easy for anyone who came in to find the cyanide and add it to her sister's flask. Phenomena had no sense of smell. If Shenanigan hadn't been there to play her usual role as canary, Phenomena would be dead.

Cook was fond of another saying: 'Misfortunes come in threes.' Clearly, she had miscounted. There had been many misfortunes over the past few days, and they were still coming thick and fast, clicking into place one after the other like beads threaded on a string.

The next misfortune came in the form of smoke, rising to the top of the House, making three out of four noses twitch. There was no discussion, just a curt 'Go!' from Phenomena, and the other three left her in the wreckage as they ran to check out the latest catastrophe.

On the floor below, the secret room was ablaze. The fire, fed by all that paper, was incandescent – a word that can mean 'bright,' but also 'furious'. It licked into the corridor, where Aunt Inheritance, noticeably singed, was only kept from the blaze by Maelstrom's outstretched arm. There was a lump forming on the side of her head, and she was glassy-eyed.

'The maps!' she cried. 'The machine! Our *history*! Maelstrom, let me go!'

With the adrenalin-fuelled strength that sometimes allows mothers to lift cars off their children, she tore out of Maelstrom's grasp and tried to dash into the inferno for the EEK.

'Gran!' Erf flung themself forward before Maelstrom could react, and snatched at Inheritance's cardigan. Their heels dug into the carpet as they were dragged towards the door. 'Gran, stop! It's just paper!'

Aunt Inheritance jerked. Her eyes cleared the second she saw Erf. She shrieked, 'Smoke inhalation!' and, with that same burst of adrenalin, picked up her grandchild, tucked them beneath her arm like a rugby ball, and sprinted away from the fire as fast as her legs could carry her.

Maelstrom heaved the door to the secret room closed, coughing. The fire had chewed the canvas to shreds, swallowing the painted pattern of the wallpaper and finally revealing to the world the door frame behind.

'It should burn itself out,' he said.

'Should?' asked Felicity doubtfully.

'I don't know. When I got here, Inheritance was unconscious, and there was something broken on the floor . . .'

Shenanigan looked down. A large shard of one of Phenomena's beakers lay by the door frame. Most of the label was missing, but Phenomena had helpfully added a sticker of a cartoon flame with a speech bubble saying, *I'm flammable!*

Smoke seeped round the edges of the door frame. Errant sparks blew from under the door, as if the fire was a beast behind it, snuffling.

Maelstrom used an expletive that Shenanigan suspected even Cook didn't know.

'We need to get a bucket chain going,' he said. 'Felicity, get as many people and as many vessels of water as they can carry. I'm going to block the edges of the door. That way—'

Crack.

But then another bead slid down the string of events, and this one fell into place with a sharp noise, like Aunt Schadenfreude's stick hitting the banister. Shenanigan was running towards the sound before it had finished disturbing the air.

Shenanigan was not the first to reach the scene in Aunt Schadenfreude's study. People were already walking away, groaning 'not again', as if someone had started up an unwelcome game of charades rather than tried to commit murder.

Flora was sitting upright in Schadenfreude's red armchair. There was a neat hole in her chest, just below her collarbone, and she had her finger pressed against it like the Dutch boy from the story, plugging the dam with his finger to stop the flood. At first, Shenanigan thought there wasn't much blood – but then she saw Cook's red-stained apron, and Flora's black dress, and realized much of it had soaked invisibly into the chair on which Flora was sitting. Cook turned when Shenanigan came in, as if to shoo her away, but her hands were too busy tearing strips of gauze. Behind Flora, a bookcase had been swung back to reveal a dark stone passageway with steps leading down. There were two suitcases waiting just inside.

Shenanigan was almost knocked over as Fauna flew into the room. She grabbed her sister's hand, slick with blood.

'Flora! Can you hear me?'

'Mmm?'

Flora's face was grey but her eyelids fluttered. Something slipped from her fingers and fell to the floor with a dull *clink*.

'What have you done now?' Fauna laughed, but it was a laugh that could snap in half at a touch. 'Someone's gone and put a hole in you.'

When Flora didn't respond, Fauna turned to Cook.

'Whatever it was, it's gone straight through,' said Cook. 'That's better than the alternative. Renée, did you find Candour?'

'I'm sorry, no,' panted Renée, stumbling into the room. 'Fortissimo is still looking.'

From the depths of the House, they heard Fortissimo's booming voice calling for the doctor like a cannon going off.

'Right,' said Fauna. She turned to Cook. 'What can I do?'

'You can help me stop the bleeding. Put pressure here. I need to get a few things from the cupboard.'

Fauna pressed her hands to her sister's shoulder. Flora groaned.

'Oh, I'm sorry!' gasped Fauna. 'Does that hurt?'

There was a gurgling sound that might have been a laugh. 'Too . . . nice . . .'

'You always say that. But we can't all be stubborn, cranky misanthropes like you.' Fauna's voice was steady, but there were tears in her eyes. 'Anyway, I have to look after you. If I didn't, who would haggle at markets? Who would chase off debt collectors, and tell the neighbours to keep it down? You see, I am being selfish, really.'

Flora grinned weakly.

Cook returned with a syringe. 'I'm going to put her under now.'

While Cook and Fauna worked, Shenanigan bent to pick up whatever Flora had dropped on the floor. They were the keys to Cook's motorbike. Shenanigan looked from them to the open passageway behind Flora, and recalled Daisy in her stockinged feet, plucking an atlas from the shelf.

She ducked beneath Cook and Fauna's arms, and put her face next to Flora's.

'Flora,' she said. 'Flora, who shot you?'

'Shenanigan, now is not the time,' snapped Cook.

'I can't ask later if she's dead!' Shenanigan snapped right back. 'Flora, come on.'

Her cousin's eyelids fluttered. The injection was taking effect.

'Find . . . Daisy . . .' she rasped.

Into this scene of dramatic tension entered Aunt Jilt, who rapped cheerfully on the door frame.

'Coo-ee,' she said. 'Cook, could we borrow you for a moment?'

Cook looked up from where she was cutting away the shoulder of Flora's blood-soaked dress.

'My hands are rather full, I'm afraid.'

Pique stuck his head round the door. 'It's urgent,' he said.

'More urgent than this?'

'Rather.'

Cook sighed. 'Fauna, how's your sewing?'

'It's fine, but—'

'Good. Renée, come here and give Fauna a hand.' She issued hushed instructions to the two press-ganged nurses, and they were all listening so intently that they didn't hear the next bead click into place.

There was something off about Pique's face. It was as if he was holding in a laugh. The back of Shenanigan's neck prickled. She followed Cook along to the evening room, where a large number of people were gathered, chatting politely.

'Ah, good! You're here,' said Atrocious. 'Take a seat, Cook. Have some tea.'

Cook glanced down at her bloodstained apron. 'I think I should prefer to stand, thank you,' she said politely. 'For the sake of the furniture.'

Aunt Jilt poured her a cup.

'Now, it pains me to say this –' Pique perched on the couch, and made an apologetic face – 'but I'm afraid we must formally accuse you of murder.'

There should have been chaos at this. There should have been gasps, and protests, and Cook should have picked Pique up bodily and thrown him out the window. Instead, Cook sipped her tea.

'Indeed?'

'Yes. A dreadful business. But, as you can see, we've tried to make the whole process as painless as possible. Madeira cake?'

'Thank you.' Cook took the proffered slice. As she chewed, she looked around the room, assessing the odds. There were twenty or so people squashed in. Their gold name badges were polished to a shine and, for the first time, Shenanigan noticed Cook had not been given one. All their faces were carefully blank, and they were eating Madeira cake as if they were required to by law.

'What evidence, may I ask, do you have against me?'

'Evidence?' Pique frowned. 'Well. We all sort of agreed that you made the most *sense*. As the murderer, I mean.'

'We voted,' added Aunt Jilt.

There was a hat on the table, the same one that had been used in the Mock-Up, surrounded by little piles of paper.

Cook studied the largest pile. 'Goodness,' she said. 'Look how many votes I got. There's five for Inheritance – I'm sure she'll be terribly offended – four for Maelstrom, one for Candour, seven for Daisy . . .'

'We haven't ruled out the possibility that she was involved,' explained Aunt Jilt.

'I suppose I should be flattered.' Cook put her teacup and saucer down on the table. Her hand did not shake.

There was a smear of Flora's blood on the handle of the cup. 'Any particular reason why Daisy and I were chosen?'

'Well, isn't it obvious?' chuckled Pique. 'You're not Family.'

Cook's polite smile froze on her face. Until that moment, Shenanigan had thought this might all be a bad joke. It wasn't. Her Family had drawn a circle. Inside the circle was anyone with the last name of Swift. Outside the circle was everyone else.

'Cook *is* Family,' Shenanigan protested when Cook wouldn't, or couldn't, answer.

'Cook isn't even her real name,' said Ferrier. 'It's Windsor, isn't it? Wilhelmina Windsor, or something.'

'Winifred,' corrected Cook. She looked perfectly calm, but her hand clenched into a fist. 'And Windsor hasn't been my last name for a long time.'

'Still.'

'Schadenfreude knew who I was when she took me in,' Cook said. 'I've been in this House for twenty years. I have been Cook for twenty years—'

'Ah, and that's the problem, isn't it?' said Atrocious sweetly. 'We've all read detective novels. When it comes to murder, it's always the help.'

Cook's jaw tightened, and the muscles in her arms tensed. Atrocious leaned back slightly.

'It is the height of rudeness,' Cook enunciated clearly, 'to call anyone "the help".'

'You're all being stupid!' interrupted Shenanigan. 'Cook lives with us, and loves us – she loved Aunt Schadenfreude! She loves me and Felicity and Phenomena and Maelstrom. Evidence!' she cried desperately, when all she got were pitying looks. 'You have to have evidence!'

'Alright,' said Pique. He pulled out a photo album.

Cook jerked. 'Where did you get that?' she demanded hoarsely. 'You've been into my room? You went through my things?'

'You work in this House, you live under this roof, you are employed by this Family – it's not really *your* room, is it?'

'For the last time,' Cook said through gritted teeth, '*I am not an employee.*'

Pique ignored her. He opened the album to an image of Cook, decades younger, in a large, grassy field. She was holding a bow and a trophy, and grinning.

'Isn't this a picture of you, training for the Olympics in archery?'

'Yes,' said Cook. 'Though I preferred the shot-put.'

Pique turned the page. 'Yes, I can see here. You must be very strong.'

'I am.'

'Strong enough to lift a marble bust, I daresay.'

'Oh, absolutely.'

'So you're skilled enough to shoot Pamplemousse, strong enough to club Gumshoe, and close enough to the Family to know about the Hoard,' said Pique triumphantly. 'What happened? Did you get greedy? Decide being given a job and a place to stay wasn't enough? Thought you'd bump off old Schadenfreude and take the treasure for yourself?'

'Ooh! I bet if we check Aunt Schadenfreude's will, a large amount of her money goes to Cook,' piped up Covetous. 'That's usually how it goes. In books, I mean.'

'You're right,' said Vendetta. 'Gumshoe got too close to the truth, so she had to kill him to cover her tracks.'

'And Pamplemousse?' asked Cook. 'Why am I supposed to have killed him?'

Pique shrugged. 'We'll work that part out later. What's important now is deciding what to do with you.'

Phenomena and Felicity had been right, Shenanigan realized. This was what came from going with your gut – a roomful of people pointing fingers. All Pique had was a story, but that was all anyone needed. The eyes turned on Cook were hostile and, on more than one face, Shenanigan saw something uglier beginning to emerge. She began to feel afraid. If Phenomena had been there, she could have poked holes in Pique's theory. If Fauna had been there, she would have calmed everyone down. If Maelstrom had been there, he could have stood tall like a lighthouse in a storm and dared anyone to lay a hand on Cook. But Maelstrom was fighting a different fire, Fauna was helping save Flora's life, Phenomena was squinting for clues, and Aunt Schadenfreude was dead. There was no one to help.

Cook's spine remained straight, and her eyes still flashed, but in the pockets of her apron, Shenanigan could see her hands were balled into fists.

'Right,' said Aunt Jilt cheerfully. 'Let's have another cup of tea, and decide what we're going to do next. We don't have a Matriarch at the moment, and goodness knows where our Archivist is, so I suppose we should open it up to the floor. Does anyone have any suggestions?'

'Lock her in the coal bin!' shouted one person.

'Bury her alive!' shouted another.

'Put her in the freezer with Pamplemousse and Gumshoe!' called a third.

'Hold on, hold on. Let's do this properly. Does anyone have a pen and paper?'

One was passed to the front, and Aunt Jilt began to take suggestions down, muttering as she did so. 'Coal . . . bin . . . bury . . . alive . . . freezer . . .'

'Dunk her in the lake and see if she floats!'

'That's witches, but I'll write it down . . .'

'I say we cook her,' said Atrocious calmly. She shrugged one elegant shoulder. 'It seems fitting.'

The Swifts began to debate the merits of cooking Cook. The tin bath and a bonfire were suggested. Shenanigan shouted in protest until she was picked up, carried to the back of the room, kicking and screaming, and held there while Cook sat very still and did not look at anyone.

It was very calm. It was very reasonable. People often reasonably discuss such unreasonable things.

Night was on the approach, and the windows had darkened to a mirror-shine. In the antique glass, Shenanigan saw the faces of her Family, blurred and distorted, laid over the trees and hedge maze outside. Then a flash of something white, like two pearls, two more beads clicking on to the string. Two hands in the darkness, raised, and a pale face between them – Candour.

He was wearing his white surgical gloves. Shenanigan's heart leapt. She thought maybe he was coming to help Flora, but no – he was walking away, into the grounds. Behind him floated a delicate shape, ghost-grey – Daisy. She was holding something in her arms, pointed at Candour. The last of the day's light glinted feebly off the metal stock of the crossbow, the facets of her ring. She turned to look over her shoulder, into the House.

Even through the chaos and the dark and the twisted glass, Shenanigan was sure their eyes met. Then Daisy pressed Candour into the maze.

Plans were never Shenanigan's strong suit, and there wasn't time to come up with one anyway, so she went for an old classic. She sagged in the arms of her captors, making herself a dead weight. It was a trick she used to use to avoid baths and it had stopped working on Cook years ago, but none of her relatives were as wise as Cook, or as strong. As soon as their grip loosened, Shenanigan wrenched herself free and sprinted from the room.

28 UNMASKED

Shouts nipped at Shenanigan's heels as she ran. By the time she reached the grand staircase, any pursuing footsteps had faltered into silence, but she didn't slow down. She took the banister at a reckless speed, launched off the polished wood like a ski-jump, and landed hard on her shoulder. This didn't slow her, either, but the locked front door did. Shenanigan had to rattle the handle stupidly for a few seconds before her brain, huffing and puffing, caught up. She sprinted through the billiards room, where, incredibly, Aunt Dither and a few older people were playing poker and ignoring the commotion upstairs, past the telephone nook, into the conservatory, and out through the cat flap, scraping her knees only a little in the process.

The maze was to her left, in the distance.

The sky had still not given up the last of the light, but it was dishonest light, trickster light. It bent the world around Shenanigan into the unfamiliar, reached down with its long fingers to scramble the order of things. Her eyes were worse than useless. Shadows bubbled and popped and burst into new forms, the trees shifted, the ground folded and unfolded under her feet. Once she entered the hedge maze, the strip of dim sky above was her only pathway. It felt as if she was running upside down.

Shenanigan knew her way through the maze by heart, or rather by feet. They knew what to do, and even if she closed her eyes they would carry her to the centre. Candour and Daisy weren't so lucky. She could hear them on the other side of the hedge-wall, Daisy breathing hard and Candour moving so carefully he was almost silent. Felicity had once told Shenanigan that any maze was solvable as long as you kept turning left, that no matter how many wrong turns you made, you'd eventually come right. Daisy must have heard of this method too, because she never paused, never hesitated. Again and again, her route brought her so close to Shenanigan that they were separated only by a single hedge before their paths steered them apart.

But Daisy simply had too big a lead. When Shenanigan reached the centre of the maze, a grim tableau awaited her: Daisy, stiff as the marble statue beside her, pointing the crossbow at Candour's heart.

'Daisy!'

Daisy swung round. There were tear tracks down her cheeks. She had the crossbow, and she had the advantage, but she still looked as lost as she had at the funeral.

'Oh *no*. Get out of here,' she said, her voice frayed. 'You don't want to see this.'

'Then don't do it!'

'Daisy.' Candour's eyes darted to Shenanigan and back, huge and black in the dark. 'It's alright. We can fix this. You don't have to do anything drastic.'

Daisy giggled. There was an edge to it. 'Climactic.'

'Desperate.' Candour ventured a smile. 'I know you would never hurt me. You love me.'

Daisy shook her head. Her grip tightened on the crossbow.

'No,' she said. 'I don't.'

Shenanigan leapt. She crashed into Daisy with all the force she could muster, and the bolt went wide. Daisy looked at the bow in her hands, now useless, and then at Shenanigan, her mouth open as if she was screaming or drowning silently – and then Candour grabbed the crossbow from her and cracked it into the side of her head.

Daisy drooped. Then gracefully, like a petal falling, she hit the ground.

Candour stared at the crossbow in his hands, as if he wasn't sure what it was, then at Shenanigan, as if he wasn't sure what *she* was, either. He dropped the crossbow and dropped to his knees. He peeled off one of his gloves and felt for a pulse.

'She's just unconscious,' he said, sitting back on his heels. A stray bit of hair had fallen over Daisy's forehead. He brushed it back tenderly. 'Poor Daisy,' he murmured. 'Why would she . . .' He swallowed, as if something was caught in his throat. 'Thank you, Shenanigan. I think you might have just saved my life.'

Shenanigan sat down hard. She and Candour stared at Daisy.

'You were right,' he said. 'You were right all along. I'm so, so sorry.'

Shenanigan would have liked to rub this in a bit, but it would have to wait.

'We need to go. Everyone else thinks it was Cook.'

Candour nodded absently. 'Yes, right. We should go and tell them. Get this mess cleared up.' He made no attempt to move.

'They're talking about cooking her,' Shenanigan added.

Candour snorted. 'Sorry. That's a *little* funny.'

Shenanigan looked between Candour and Daisy. She had been right. She had been *right*. She had insisted it was Daisy all along, despite what Phenomena said, or Felicity, or even Erf. Yet now, looking at Daisy's still form on the wet grass, Shenanigan didn't feel triumphant. She felt . . . wrong.

'I don't understand why Daisy would do all this,' she said slowly.

'You said it yourself,' said Candour unhappily. 'On the stairs. She was after my money. Maybe even the Family's money, if she could find the Hoard.' He shook his head. 'I had no idea she was capable of this. You were the only one who saw through her, Shenanigan.'

Phenomena wasn't there, but Shenanigan heard her sister's voice in her head all the same. She was saying that imagination wasn't investigation. A hunch wasn't evidence.

'She and Flora were working together?' She meant it as a statement. It came out as a question.

Candour's left hand, still in its white glove, scratched absently at a mark on his right one. 'They were. I came upon them at just the wrong moment. They were in the study, arguing over how to split the treasure once they found it. Daisy had the crossbow, and she just . . .' He mimed aiming an imaginary bolt at an imaginary heart. 'Another one I couldn't save.'

Shenanigan frowned. She mentally compared the hole in Flora to the much larger hole the crossbow bolt had made in the wall.

'Flora's alive. She must have been very lucky, to take a crossbow bolt at that range.'

She couldn't make out Candour's expression in the dark, but she saw his hand disappear into his pocket.

'Lucky. Yes. Thank goodness,' he said. 'Gosh, I'd best get up there. She'll need a doctor.'

Something *was* wrong. The feeling of wrongness started in the back of Shenanigan's neck, which prickled, and ran down her arms and legs, raising hair as it went. The moon cast just enough light for her to see four long, dark scratches on the back of Candour's right hand.

She knew instantly where they had come from.

They had come from climbing down through a skylight into a very messy bedroom, and accidentally disturbing a very large guard cat.

She looked at Candour, and he looked at her, and the jig, as they say, was up.

Tucked in the palm of Candour's hand was a small disc. A tiny barrel stretched down his middle and index fingers. It was one of Pamplemousse's palm pistols, and it was pointed at Shenanigan's forehead.

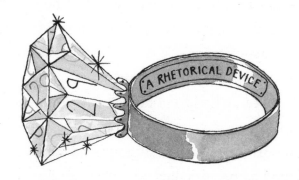

As she looked down the barrel of the tiny gun, and all the mistakes and wrong turns she'd made began to flash before her eyes, Shenanigan had one grimly resigned thought:

I suppose I will have to learn something from this.

Candour wiggled his hand, the barrel of the tiny gun just visible behind two outstretched fingers.

'Isn't this *wizard*?' he said. 'It's an antique. Took it off Pamplemousse before we put him in the deep freeze. I didn't think he'd miss it.'

The machinery of Shenanigan's mind was grinding gradually to life.

'Because you killed him.'

'Well, he did challenge me to a duel. What kind of Swift would I be if I didn't accept?'

'And you shot Flora. With that.'

'It's not as lethal as a crossbow, but it does enough damage at short range.'

'And you killed Aunt Schadenfreude.'

He winced. 'Ah. That one was a terrible accident, Shenanigan.'

Shenanigan remembered the pulled-up carpet, the stick that had been wrenched out of her aunt's hands. 'No, it wasn't,' she said.

'No, it wasn't,' he agreed.

Shenanigan prided herself on being able to spot lies, but she'd missed the biggest one of all. It was right there, nestling at the corner of Candour's mouth, hiding in that crooked smile she'd liked so much. She hadn't spotted it because it was there all the time.

There were so many questions she should ask. Phenomena, no doubt, had a list. But Shenanigan's questions all jostled towards her mouth at the same time, and the one that slipped out first was:

'What does your name mean?'

Candour stared at her incredulously.

'That's what you want to know? I'm pointing a gun at you and *that's* what you want to know?'

Shenanigan shrugged.

'Unbelievable,' he sighed. But he drew himself up, pointed at his chest with his gun-free hand, and recited:

Candour (noun)
i. openness; honesty and truthfulness
ii. open-mindedness, fairness, justice
iii. moral integrity, purity
iv. brilliance, brightness

Shenanigan squinted at him, trying to make the name fit. It didn't. Candour tapped his foot impatiently, waiting for her next question. When it didn't come, he sat down with his back against the statue, as if he was settling in for a chat with his favourite niece.

'I think it's a good name,' he said conversationally. 'Authoritative. Did you know, there's a list of Patriarchs and Matriarchs in one of Inheritance's books? It lists what the Swifts accomplished under each one's leadership. The old entries go on for pages and pages. The most recent ones barely rate a paragraph.'

Shenanigan did not answer. She was busy trying to reconcile *moral integrity* with a person who'd killed at least two people.

'Don't get me wrong,' Candour went on, 'having a last name of Swift still means something, in certain circles. It got me into university. It got me my first hospital position. It got me the attention of Daisy DeMille and all the others like her. But we aren't what we used to be.' He shook his head. 'This Family had *power*. It had money. It had respect. If there was any justice, I wouldn't have to scam heiresses to make a decent living.'

Shenanigan glanced at the diamond ring glinting on Daisy's finger. It was huge and garish, and it didn't match the subtly fashionable clothes she wore. Felicity would have noticed that. Shenanigan hadn't thought it was important.

Candour caught her look. 'I spent hours picking that out for Daisy,' he said proudly. 'I had to borrow her money, of course, but she has such perfect handwriting! Easy to forge. The funniest thing about this whole weekend has been watching you lot with Daisy. She's loaded, but half the Family treated her like *I* was doing *her* a favour by marrying her. Even though Schadenfreude called me a leech! To my face! In front of everyone!'

His genial expression flickered. Underneath his square glasses and neat hair was a very angry person.

Shenanigan eyed the gun in Candour's hand, and did one of the things she was best at: she annoyed him.

'I get it now.' She nodded as if it all made sense. 'This *is* just about money. You killed Aunt Schadenfreude because she wouldn't let you marry Daisy and take her fortune.'

'*No!*' Candour pushed off the statue and began to pace. 'No. This is what Aunt Schadenfreude couldn't understand. It's not *just about money*, Shenanigan! If I just wanted the money, I'd have married Daisy without Auntie's blessing and lived off her funds in comfort for the rest of my life. No.'

He struggled to get himself back under control.

'Auntie's been making noises about retiring almost since the day she was appointed. She hated the job, clearly, but she did her duty. For years I've known that when she announced her successor, it had to be me. I'm the obvious choice. I've *worked* to be the obvious choice, to be a credit to the Family name! I'm young, I'm intelligent, I'm full of ideas, I secured an engagement to the most eligible bachelorette in the United States – what more did the old hag *want*?'

He wasn't hiding his anger now – it came lashing out of him like a whip.

'I tried to talk to her that first night. Went to her study during dinner and made my case. Daisy's nice enough, I said, but what's important is that once we marry, her money and connections become mine. "If you name me Patriarch," I said, "I'll use those resources to make us a force to be reckoned with. I'll tear down this House and rip the treasure out of its foundations."'

'If you had Daisy's fortune, why would you need the Hoard?'

Candour growled. 'You're not listening. The Hoard isn't just money, Shenanigan. It's our *birthright*.'

Something about the way he said it made Shenanigan feel nauseous. Cantrip had called the Hoard an *ill fortune ill begot*, and she was beginning to see why. It was bad luck, born from bloodshed.

In the dark, Candour's eyes were bright and manic.

'Grand-Uncle Vile had the right approach, you know. With me in charge, with Daisy's fortune and ours combined, we could invest, we could expand. We could become an empire, rather than a rag-tag collection of relatives. We—'

Suddenly, like a switch flipping, Candour smiled. A person could be fooled into thinking his rage had gone;

it hadn't. Shenanigan could see it, banked like hot coals in the centre of him.

'Anyway, Auntie wasn't having it. Seems she had heard some unpleasant stories about me. Didn't like the way I was "using" Daisy. She said I was just like Vile – like it was a bad thing! Suddenly, everything I'd been building towards was slipping away, because one old woman was stubborn. I did lose my temper then. "I can see you're reluctant," I said, "but maybe all you need is a little push." ' He made a shoving motion with his hands, and smiled affably.

'Your jokes aren't very funny,' said Shenanigan. 'And I don't really care why you did it, or how. You killed my aunt, and Pamplemousse, and I'm not sure about Gumshoe, but—'

'Oh, that was hilarious. It actually *was* an accident – he did it all by himself. I'd seen him skulking about, *narrating*, and wanted to make sure he wasn't cleverer than he looked. He was muttering about research, so I followed him into the library just in time to see the *private eye* pick up a book and become a *private eyeless.*'

Shenanigan did not laugh.

'The book was called *The Lore and Law of the Family Swift*, by the way. It made for an interesting read.

Since I couldn't finish Auntie off, what with your Cook playing bodyguard, I started looking for the Hoard myself.'

Just then, Daisy stirred. Candour reached down to lift one of her eyelids, and Shenanigan noticed the scratches on his hand had cracked open. Blood ran down his wrist, soaking into the white cuff of his shirt.

'They look nasty.'

Candour scowled. 'Your cat's feral,' he muttered. 'Takes after his owner.'

Now Shenanigan laughed. 'I hope those get infected. I hope you get gangrene, and your fingers turn black and fall off. I hope you contract rabies, and foam at the mouth, and develop hydrophobia, which is a terrible fear of water, and become feverish and dehydrated. Rabies is incurable, you know.'

Candour stared at her for a long moment.

'You're quite horrible, aren't you?' he said finally. 'There's something very cruel in you, I think. Something very devious and underhanded.'

Shenanigan shrugged. 'Maybe. But you're the one who's a murderer.'

'So was Vile. But let me ask you something. If Vile was so terrible, why is his monument still standing?'

Shenanigan didn't know what to say to that, so she rose, brushing torn grass from her lap. Candour's gun followed her.

'Daisy will never marry you now. Aunt Schadenfreude can't make you Patriarch, because she's dead. Phenomena wasn't poisoned, the fire you set was put out, and as soon as Flora recovers she'll tell everyone you shot her. You're stuck. You lose.'

Candour didn't reply. It was fully dark now, and his expression was lost to shadow. His hand remained pointed at her face, unwavering. He could be despairing. He could be furious. It was quite possible that in a second or two he would twitch his finger and it would all be over.

Candour laughed. He had a nice laugh, the kind you would overhear at a party after someone told a silly joke. It was precisely that niceness that made it so horrible to hear in the dark, attached to a man, attached to an arm, attached to a hand pointing a gun at her head.

'Well!' he said. 'That's alright. I've picked up bits as I went along, but as I was having a flick through *The Lore and Law of the Family Swift*, I came up with a plan B. It turns out that if both the Matriarch *and* Archivist die before a new Matriarch or Patriarch has been selected, the title goes to the Swift with the *most suitable name.*' He pointed at himself. '*Honesty, truthfulness, moral purity*, et cetera . . . I mean, I think I'm a shoo-in, but I'm not taking any chances.'

He reached into his pocket, and held up Shenanigan's map. 'If I'd had this earlier, it would have saved me so much time! It was sticking out of your pocket when you were in the kitchen staring at that bag of civet coffee like you'd cracked the case. I had no idea there were so many secret hiding places in the House! Plenty of places to stash a surprise.'

Shenanigan was silent. She felt like, if she said anything at all, he'd laugh again. If she heard that laugh once more, she'd fly at him teeth first, and that would ruin her plan of not getting shot.

'Climb up that statue for me and listen to the House.'

Shenanigan pulled herself up on to the shoulders of the statue. If she craned her neck, she could just see down the black swoop of the grounds leading up to the House, where gold light from the windows leaked colour on to the lawn. It seemed a world away. She felt a stab of fear for Cook, being liberally seasoned right now.

'What do you hear?' prompted Candour.

With her head poked over the top of the maze, sounds that had been muffled by the hedges now drifted to Shenanigan on the breeze. There was music, oddly, and voices raised, but not in anger. It sounded like singing. *Why would they be singing?*

'I didn't trash everything in Phenomena's lab. Once I saw all those beakers and vials, the solution – ha! – presented itself. I imagine everyone in that House is feeling rather giddy right now.' Shenanigan could hear Candour's smile. 'They don't know why, though.'

The breeze chilled the sweat on the back of Shenanigan's neck. 'What did you do?'

Candour's white teeth gleamed in the dark.

Laughing gas was once fairly popular among doctors, but the invention of proper anaesthetic made it almost as unfashionable as chloroform and leeches. It was imprecise, and fairly dangerous. Have you ever laughed so hard your sides hurt? Until you can't breathe or speak, and you feel weak and helpless, but you can't stop? Well, that's what was about to happen to the Swifts. They wouldn't stop laughing until they stopped for good. They would laugh themselves to death.

Before that, there would also be a fair amount of wheezing, coughing, tightness of the chest, bluish extremities, hallucinations, and a sprinkling of heart attacks, but 'laughing themselves to death' sounded a lot cleaner, and so that is what Candour told Shenanigan would happen.

'They'll laugh themselves to death?'

'Yep!'

'They'll run away!'

'No, they won't. They're having too much fun! By the time they realize they're in danger, they'll be too weak to move, never mind break a door down. I've locked them all in, you see. And once everyone is dead, well, I'll be the sole survivor of a terrible tragedy. There are plenty of other Swifts around, but I doubt anyone else will want the job of Patriarch. I can take this House apart, brick by brick, until I find my treasure.'

Shenanigan stared at the dark hulk of the House, the tower pointing to the sky like a rhinoceros's horn.

'How can you restore the Family to glory if everyone is dead?'

His smile was patronizing. 'Shenanigan, don't be silly. What happens to the people in a family doesn't matter, as long as the name endures.'

You've got it the wrong way round, she thought.

'What if I helped you find the Hoard?'

Candour snorted. 'You don't know where it is.'

'A ghost gave me a clue. Hand me the map.'

Candour stared hard at her. Shenanigan wondered if he knew the same trick she did about spotting lies. He knew the trick to telling them, after all. He studied her eyebrows, her ears, the corner of her mouth, looking for somewhere a lie might hide. But, of course, Shenanigan didn't lie. He handed her the map, and Shenanigan scanned the familiar paper for anything that might fit the EEK's clue. 'UNDER HOUSE' covered a lot of space.

'I think I have an idea. But I won't tell you,' she said. Candour waved his palm pistol at Shenanigan, and she corrected herself. 'I won't tell you here. I'll show you.'

Candour gestured for her to move, but Shenanigan paused, looking down at Daisy still crumpled on the ground. The cut on the side of her head seemed to have stopped bleeding, at least.

'Oh, she'll be fine,' Candour said, following her gaze. 'Trust me, I'm a doctor.'

They wound back through the hedge maze. In truth, Shenanigan had no plan. She felt the gun pointed at her back as if in accusation. With every turn, she tried to trick herself into coming up with an idea that would solve everything.

Left.

She could dart away, run back to the House, and warn everyone.

Right.

But she had no guarantee her Family would listen to her.

Left.

She could take the gun from Candour somehow, and force him back to the House.

Left.

The gun was in his hand. It would be very difficult to part him from it.

Right.

She could cut his hand off?

Left. Right. Left.

They soon emerged from the maze, but as they crossed the lawn Shenanigan felt as if she was still trapped by towering walls and dead ends, searching for an escape. *Left. Right. Right. Left.*

'So, where are we off to?' Candour asked jovially.

'The ghost said to "LOOK UNDER HOUSE", so the treasure must be in the cellar,' said Shenanigan. 'I have an idea where, but if I tell you, you might shoot me.'

Candour laughed. 'The cellar! I was going to start at the top and work down, so this saves me loads of time. You're very clever, you know. Are you sure you wouldn't like to join me? You'd make a great accomplice – goodness knows you've got the name for it!'

Shenanigan didn't answer.

'Really! It's not fair that your parents get to travel all over the globe while you're stuck at home, playing dress-up with your sisters. You could be a real adventurer! Sail the seas! See the world!'

Shenanigan felt a pang. She *would* like to see the world. A part of her, maybe the part that gave her her name, seriously considered Candour's offer. But only for a moment.

She led him past the lighted windows of the House, peering inside as slyly as she could. No one was giggling yet, but they were still singing. Aunt Dither and the poker players were taking turns sliding down the banister. Aunt Jilt had a bottle of champagne in each hand. Uncle Ferrier swayed to gramophone music with a cushion as a dance partner. The tin bathtub sat in the middle of the hall, half filled with water, the other half filled with Cook. Her hands were bound, and she had an apple in her mouth. Everyone seemed to have forgotten about her.

'We're going to have to sneak inside,' Shenanigan said, 'to get to the cellar.'

Candour snatched Shenanigan's map and consulted it briefly. 'Nice try, but there's an outer door. We'll use that.'

He prodded her past the line of windows to the rear of the House and a weathered door set at an angle into the wall. He jingled Aunt Schadenfreude's keys at her. Shenanigan hated him.

Candour unlocked the door, and they looked down into the roiling dark. Shenanigan wondered if she could dive in before Candour could – but no, he must have seen her getting ready to spring, because he seized her by the arm and marched her down the steps.

Only days had passed since Shenanigan had last been in the cellar, but it felt as if at least three birthdays had come and gone since. That is the difficult part of growing up. It doesnt happen within the clear boundaries or landmarks set for it. Growing up happens whenever it wants to, in fits and starts and all over the place. Parts of Shenanigan had grown up a little since the last time she was in the cellar, but all at different rates, and she felt lopsided and clumsy. Before, she had seen the cellar as an adventure. Now, she was grown up enough to be afraid.

Candour handed Shenanigan a small torch, and gave a low whistle as she shone it about. Darkness scurried back behind the shelves. The cellar was vast, and without Felicity's help Shenanigan only had the vaguest idea where she was going. She made turns at random, trusting her feet as she had in the hedge maze, looking for an opportunity to dart off. But Candour had hold of her arm, and he wasn't as easily fooled as her other relatives. When she sagged in his grasp, his other hand poked her in the forehead, and she felt the barrel of the gun just between the bend of his fingers.

'This pistol is only big enough to fire a very small bullet,' he said. 'Luckily, you are a very small person. Don't try that again.'

Above her head, she heard the murmurs of her Family singing and arguing, the creak and thump of stamping feet on the floorboards. The noise that had soaked into the House so uncomfortably over the past few days was now oddly comforting, a reminder of life.

Shenanigan led Candour past D's and G's and P's and Q's, round and round the R's and O's, through the Z's squeezed against the wall by the E's. Candour kept pace, though she could feel his irritation in his grip on her arm, and somewhere around the F's he stopped.

'Listen,' he said.

As she strained her ears, Shenanigan heard a few scattered giggles.

'You can take as long as you want to lead me where we're going – I really don't mind,' said Candour. 'But they don't have that much time left.'

She heard the first real chuckle a few moments later. She hoped it was just her imagination, but then another drifted down through the dark, and then another. The singing above her head had gone off-key. She walked faster, almost dragging Candour behind her. But he soon halted her again, directing her gaze to a tall shelf. 'Look!' he said. 'There's me!'

Shenanigan pointed her torch and, sure enough, there was his stone, sandwiched between Cameo and Cannonade:

Candour

Noun
i. Openness;
honesty and truthfulness

Shenanigan didn't bother to read the rest. *Maybe the Naming was all rubbish, after all,* she thought. Some people acted the way they were expected to, and some didn't. Flora and Fauna's names didn't mean anything, really, other than that they were a matching set, yet they were as different in personality as two people could be. Aunt Schadenfreude hadn't enjoyed seeing her Family suffer. And while Atrocious was atrocious and Phenomena loved science, here was Candour: liar, murderer, thief, and all-round terrible person. He was someone who, if there was such a thing as destiny, should have been named Scoundrel or Scum.

But words had many meanings, and some of them contradicted each other. She read the rest of the gravestone. *Brilliance, brightness.* Candour, like *candle*. Candour, like *incandescent*, which meant 'bright', but also 'furious'. Candour was charming, and he flashed his teeth and told his jokes, and all that light and brightness blinded people to what was underneath, which was something white-hot and burning.

There are many meanings to a name, and many definitions to a word, and all the words and meanings link into each other like strands of a web. If you could pick which strand to follow, which version of yourself to become, Candour had picked the very worst.

Giggles bubbled through the floorboards above. Here and there a chuckle or a snort would fizz and dissolve. Shenanigan pushed on through the cellar, no longer even really looking where she was going. She thought back to the night she and her sisters had cracked her stone in half and, although it had been an accident, she was suddenly and viciously glad it had happened. Whether Shenanigan was the way she was through nature, as Aunt Schadenfreude had said, or nurture, as Phenomena supposed, or some combination of the two, it didn't matter. Shenanigan was who she was. It was nice to know that, even if – she thought of the gun at her back – it wasn't for very much longer.

When she looked up, she was standing in the H's.

'Here,' she said. She stood back. Candour swung his torch about, frowning.

' "Here"? I don't see a "Here".'

'No, there.' Shenanigan pointed at one of the stones, low on the shelf, and older than the others.

House

Noun

i. A place of abode, a dwellynge
ii. A family, royal or of noble lineage

'"LOOK UNDER HOUSE",' she said.

'We have a relative called House?'

'No. But the House is a member of the Family all the same. And houses die.' She rubbed a thumb against the crumbling wall of the cellar. 'You wouldn't get it.'

Candour looked as if he wanted to argue, but he had more pressing concerns. 'There's no way a treasure the size of Vile's could fit behind there. You're lying to me.'

Shenanigan shrugged. 'That's what the ghost said,' she replied. 'Maybe it contains instructions. Something to help you find it.'

All she needed was for him to be distracted, just for a second. Candour braced himself against the gravestone. Yes, he was stronger than he looked, but the stone was much, much heavier than the bust he'd used on Gumshoe. Millimetre by millimetre, he began to slide it off the shelf. Shenanigan watched, tensed, as the balance shifted and Candour began to take the weight of the stone. It began to tip into his arms, and he stepped back . . .

Shenanigan kicked him hard in the ankle. He dropped the stone, and screamed as it landed with a crunch on his foot.

In that brief fracture of time, Shenanigan fled. Something whizzed past her ear. She heard a curse, and then another click as Candour raised the gun again, but bullets very famously do not go round corners. If Shenanigan could only get to a turning, she'd be safe.

Just as she reached a crossroads, where H branched into L on one side and W on the other, two shapes materialized out of the W branch with a torch bobbing between them. It was too late to stop, and Shenanigan ran smack into the chest of the taller one, who hissed:

'Ow! Shenanigan, you clump!'

Shenanigan would recognize her sister's annoyed voice anywhere.

'Felicity!' she cried, and turning to the second figure, 'Phenomena!'

She heard dragging steps behind her. She tried to push her sisters back round the corner, but they wouldn't move. 'Turn off the torch! What are you doing here?'

Phenomena straightened up. Shenanigan could hear her blushing. 'Felicity said you were in trouble, and I . . . Oh fine, I had a hunch,' she said in disgust. 'And I don't feel very good about it, so don't tease me or I'll—'

A hand buried itself in Shenanigan's hair, dragging her back down the corridor.

'*Run!*' she yelled through the pain. It was ten times worse than having her curls combed. She could feel individual hairs popping free of her scalp. She didn't scream – she refused to scream – but Felicity did, high and piercing, and the sound cut momentarily through the laughter from upstairs.

Then Candour pressed the hand with the gun into the side of Shenanigan's head.

'Quiet,' he spat.

Felicity stopped screaming, confused.

'Or you'll what, poke her in the eye?'

'Gun,' Shenanigan said through gritted teeth, and she heard Phenomena, who had been working on this equation since the night of Aunt Schadenfreude's fall, finally come up with the right answer.

'Pamplemousse's palm pistol,' she whispered. 'It was you.'

'Stop prattling and let me think,' Candour hissed again. 'You stupid, silly, nosy little girls.'

Shenanigan could feel him shaking, and for a smug, soaring moment she thought he was scared. Then she saw his fist, balled tight and white with tension around the livid scratches John the Cat had left, and knew it wasn't fear, but rage.

'Here's an idea. Take me hostage instead,' said Felicity, stepping forward. 'Shenanigan's the most annoying pest on Earth. Believe me, you don't want to be stuck with her.'

'SHUT UP, FELICITY!' he screamed. Felicity's torch shone full on his face, and, finally, the Candour the girls thought they knew had been burned away. Shenanigan squeezed her eyes shut.

'Please don't shoot my sister,' whispered Felicity.

Thump. Thump. Thump.

A light appeared to Felicity's left. Someone was coming.

'Who's there?' called Candour. His furious expression didn't change, but his voice instantly became friendlier, more cheerful. It was awful.

Thump. Thump. Thump.

The hairs on Shenanigan's arms prickled. She recognized that noise. She saw from the whites of her sisters' eyes that they did too. Felicity clutched Phenomena's hand.

Thump. Thump. Thump.

The light lanced through the spaces in the shelves. They began to hear another sound along with the thumping, a scrape of someone shuffling their feet.

'I said, who's there?' called Candour.

Heavy, laboured breath. From round a corner, a lantern appeared, held aloft by a white arm, a white shape, hunched and familiar, covered head to foot in a ragged white veil. With every step, its walking stick thumped on the stone floor. Shenanigan felt Candour begin to tremble.

'Show yourself!' he cried.

The figure halted, almost luminous in the dark. Slowly, it pulled the veil from its face.

Candour screamed as the ghost of Arch-Aunt Schadenfreude raised one withered arm and pointed to him in accusation. His hands fell from Shenanigan, suddenly slack with fear. He backed away, shaking his head.

'No,' he said. 'No, no—'

Aunt Schadenfreude's ghost stepped forward.

'Candour,' it wheezed.

Candour's back hit the shelf behind him. Shenanigan would never really be sure if the missing stone had unbalanced the others, and even Phenomena wouldn't be able to tell her. But whether it was destiny, coincidence, karma, or simple physics, the shelf tipped over.

There wasn't time to steady it. Shenanigan barely had time to leap out of the way as the shelves around Candour fell like dominoes, spilling rock and dust, and crushing him beneath.

THE LAST LAUGH

Dust swirled around the cellar in search of a place to rest. It settled on Shenanigan's hair, on her skin, and on her eyelashes. She coughed.

'I am quite miffed,' said Aunt Schadenfreude's ghost, 'that the three of you allowed singing at my funeral.'

Outside the radius of destruction, the ghost stood tall, her lantern shining. She shuffled through the debris towards them. She left footprints.

'The decorations left much to be desired,' she continued. 'And whose idea was it to allow that fool to speak? The whole thing was a farce from start to finish. I don't know why we bothered rehearsing at all.'

Some sort of powder drifted from her clothes. Slowly, a smile began to form on Phenomena's face.

'We shall just have to be more thorough in future. I shall draw up a list of acceptable guests and – Shenanigan, do stop that.'

Shenanigan prodded her aunt once more to be sure. She was solid. The tips of her fingers came away white.

'Is this . . . flour?' she asked.

The very alive, very floury Aunt Schadenfreude took a handkerchief from the pocket of her dress and began wiping at her face.

'It's the best I could do on such short notice,' she said stiffly. Underneath the flour, familiar wrinkles started to show. 'And you can't deny that it was effective.'

Felicity flung herself at Aunt Schadenfreude and buried her face in her shoulder, narrowly missing the steel collar. Aunt Schadenfreude patted Felicity's head, leaving white streaks in her hair. 'There, there,' she said, not unkindly.

Shenanigan and Phenomena were not fond of hugs as a rule, but they too folded themselves into Aunt Schadenfreude's side. The dust and flour made them sneeze, but underneath it all she still smelled like their aunt – lilies and boot polish.

Aunt Schadenfreude awkwardly put her arms round them. 'I am sorry, girls,' she said quietly.

'Mmmf mmy ffm ymf mmffoo mih?' mumbled Felicity.

'Pardon?'

Felicity stepped back, angrily wiping away tears. 'Then why did you do it?' she asked.

A guffaw cracked the moment in two. In the cacophony of the collapse, they had all forgotten what was happening upstairs. Laughing gas was filling the House like helium filling a balloon, and soon the Swifts would all float away to a place where the living could not follow.

'What on earth has got into everyone up there?' asked Aunt Schadenfreude.

'Nitrous oxide,' said Shenanigan. 'We have to hurry.'

'Shenanigan, hold on—'

'Candour! Laughing gas! Murder!' she shouted, which communicated the situation nicely.

Shenanigan's map was on the floor, next to the pile of rubble that used to be Candour. One arm stuck out of the debris like a flag. Shenanigan snatched up her map, and jerked back as, to her dismay, a finger on the arm twitched. A muffled groan issued from beneath the rock.

'He's alive!' cried Felicity.

'How unfortunate,' sighed Aunt Schadenfreude. 'I'll make sure he stays put until someone can retrieve him.'

Felicity hesitated. 'Will you be alright?'

'Of course. He won't kill me twice.' Aunt Schadenfreude sliced her stick through the air with surprising dexterity, and all three girls vowed to stay on her good side in future.

Back through the underground labyrinth they ran, Felicity leading the way with the knack of a trained rat. They burst from the door under the grand staircase and into the hall, filthy and red-eyed, hair on end. When the other Swifts saw the state of them, they laughed uproariously, although in fairness they couldn't help it.

The entire room shook. Bodies lay sprawled on the stairs, chairs, and floor, quivering. Some had threaded limbs through the banisters to try to keep themselves upright. Plates lay smashed, drinks spilled, ornaments upended. Everyone was giggling, chuckling, guffawing, tittering, legs kicking helplessly at the air. It was hard to tell mirth from pain. Someone tried to pull themselves to their feet using the curtains and instead ripped them, pole and all, to the floor, which only made them laugh harder.

'What's wrong with everyone?' Felicity asked, then clapped her hand over her mouth as she, too, started to giggle.

Phenomena tore at the hem of her lab coat. She dunked the strips of cloth in a nearby vase of flowers and then handed them, dripping with water, to her sisters. She tied her own tightly round her mouth and nose.

'This won't filter out the gas completely, but it will help,' she said. 'We need to get some ventilation in here, and quickly.'

'What?'

'Open the doors and windows!'

'Candour told me he locked all the doors,' said Shenanigan.

'And the downstairs windows are too heavy to open. Cook usually has to do it,' said Felicity.

Shenanigan had been waiting for this moment her entire life. She picked up a heavy iron candlestick from the table and hurled it at the nearest window. It crashed through the pane, and cool fresh air drifted into the room.

'Break *everything*,' she said.

Shenanigan ran towards the stairs, but Felicity caught her arm.

'Wait! Where are you going?'

Shenanigan took her sister's hand and gently prised her fingers from her jumper. 'I'm pretty tired of people doing that,' she said. 'The gas has to be coming from somewhere, so I'm going to find it.'

'No, you're n—'

'*Felicity.*' She stared hard at her sister, willing her to understand. 'Uncle Maelstrom said it himself: no one knows the House better than me. Can you please, *for once*, just trust me?'

Felicity looked at her steadily. Then she let go. 'You're right,' she said. 'You're the only one small enough and smart enough and brave enough.'

She looked as if she was going to cry again, and Shenanigan wished she wouldn't. Her sister cried more than anyone she knew, and it couldn't be good for her. But Felicity simply nodded, picked up the fallen curtain pole, and aimed it like a lance at the nearest window.

Shenanigan fled with the sound of breaking glass behind her.

Have you ever been tickled past the point of endurance? It can be very unpleasant. It isn't the tickling itself that is so unpleasant, of course, but all the laughing and wriggling, the pains in your sides, the light-headedness, the stars that dance across your vision. It's a kind of gentle torture if it goes on for too long.

Shenanigan began to giggle before she'd even got out of the hall. She took a deep breath to steady herself, but that only made things worse. Phenomena's make-shift mask was far from ideal. Shenanigan couldn't smell anything suspicious, but she could feel the laughing gas beginning to tickle her from the inside. Harry Houdini could hold his breath for three minutes; Shenanigan could barely manage one. The gas would get her eventually. She had to move fast.

She checked under the grand staircase. She checked beneath the visors of the suits of armour, and in the mouth of the stuffed leopard. She checked the space in the library where the crossbow used to be. She spread out her map, overwhelmed by all the tiny marks and symbols she had drawn, all the possible hiding places.

She didn't have time.

She paused on the stairs, shaking with silent fits of laughter. The cut on her shin had opened again, and she felt blood dripping down her leg.

Shenanigan had grown up a great deal in the past few days, and still more in the past few hours, but in the past few minutes things had really taken a leap forward. She had had an emotional growth spurt. Halfway up the stairs, sweating and giggling, listening to the howls and screams of her Family below, Shenanigan had a thought. It was the first of its kind, and it arrived in her mind fully formed, as grown-up as the grey suit of a banking executive.

She couldn't do it.

This thought was so new and unwelcome, so shocking to receive for the first time, that Shenanigan's arms and legs began to give up before she did. She sat down hard at the top of the grand staircase, right where Candour had given Aunt Schadenfreude that first push.

Shenanigan had once jumped from the roof of the House. She had squeezed her mattress through her skylight, shoved it over the parapet, and then leapt to land square in the middle of it. She'd been testing to see if it would be a good means of escape, should she ever be imprisoned. Cook had never shouted at her so much in her life.

'Did it not occur to you that you could *die*?' she'd yelled.

It had not. It had never crossed Shenanigan's mind that she could be hurt beyond repair, and, until this very second, she had never really understood that she could fail, either. From now on, Shenanigan would have to learn how to be afraid. And, most importantly of all, how to be afraid, and keep going anyway.

Alright, think, thought Shenanigan. *If it was me, where would I hide a canister of lethal laughing gas?*

The truth was she didn't know. There was a difference between being devious and underhanded and being a cold-blooded murderer, and that realization might have been comforting to Shenanigan had it not meant that her good bits were going to get her Family killed.

If I was Candour, then . . . she thought desperately. *If I was Candour, and I'd had this map, where would I hide it?*

She turned her map over and frantically scanned her guide to suspicious paintings, the list of hidden holes and apertures covered by bad art. No time to check them all. She had to narrow it down.

If I was Candour . . .

'Look at me. I'm Candour,' she said to herself, her voice muffled by the mask. 'I love money and lying and bad jokes. I'm the kind of person that draws moustaches on paintings, and thinks puns are the height of comedy, and is constantly trying to make people laugh . . . Oh!'

Shenanigan ran. She let herself laugh. She was laughing as she reached the second floor, laughing as she passed the charred outline of the secret room, laughing as she followed the hiss of gas to the painting of the *Sour-faced Duchess*. She was sporting a new black moustache.

'You look a little *drawn*,' Shenanigan tried to joke, but she couldn't get the words past her own teeth. She wrenched the painting back.

The canister was almost as large as her, but light as anything, and it spat like an angry snake when she picked it up and threw herself down the laundry chute behind *Nun Picking Her Nose*. Her laughter echoed through the innards of the House. She burst out of the chute's mouth at the bottom of the grand staircase, flopped into a run, and sprang through a broken window into the garden. She dropped the canister on the wet grass and kicked it away from her, taking deep lungfuls of fresh, serious air. Then she collapsed.

The stars swam above her. The quaking in her muscles gradually stopped. A loud crash announced that someone had managed to get the front door open, and then she heard her relatives, still giggling, dragging themselves out on to the lawn, gasping for breath. Dew soaked into her dress and hair. She was cold. She was very glad to be feeling cold. She was very glad to be feeling anything at all.

While everyone was heaving on the lawn like beached fish, Aunt Schadenfreude appeared. She requested that someone please release Cook, as she needed her assistance to drag the real murderer out of the cellar. Everyone was still far too weak to show much surprise at the sight of her back from the dead, and though Tintinnabula screamed half-heartedly, it soon trailed off into coughing. Uncle Ferrier, still retching miserably, lurched over to untie Cook, but she snapped the cord tying her wrists with a brief flex of her powerful arms, took a large bite of the apple in her mouth, and followed Schadenfreude back down to the cellar.

Phenomena and Felicity plopped down next to Shenanigan. They didn't say anything, but Felicity pulled Shenanigan's head into her lap and Phenomena patted her shoulder. Shenanigan flapped a limp hand at Erf, who was held so tightly by a still-singed Aunt

Inheritance that they could barely get their own hand free for a thumbs-up. For once, however, they were hugging their gran back just as tightly.

They all waited. Eventually, Cook appeared in one of the broken windows.

'Right, you lot. You may come back in now. It's quite safe.'

The Family dragged themselves up with a groan and limped back inside. The hall was a disaster. Glass crunched beneath their feet like gravel.

Cook tutted at the mess. 'Can't be helped, I suppose.' She eyed the windows. 'Since it's a little draughty in here, Aunt Schadenfreude has decided to receive you all in her study. Come along, chop-chop.'

Upstairs, the secret passageway was closed, the fire was lit, and the blood-soaked chair was gone. Cook had even found time to bring up paper cups and an enormous pot of hot chocolate. There was some shamefaced-ness from the Swifts – after all, barely an hour ago they had been plotting to boil Cook alive. Cook made sure to look every person in the eye as she handed them their chocolate. Shenanigan could tell she was enjoying herself.

With limited seating options, most of the Swifts sat cross-legged on the floor, looking up at Aunt Schadenfreude, who had installed herself in another wing-backed leather chair. Her collar gleamed by the light of the fire. Aunt Inheritance, worn and creased, perched beside her on a stool. Across from them sat Flora, with a shawl wrapped about her bandaged shoulder, and Fauna at her side. The twins were glaring identical daggers at the other person nearby: Candour, bruised and furious, tied to the desk. One arm was in a sling. One leg had been crudely splinted. Shenanigan gave him a cheery wave.

'Well. With some notable exceptions,' Aunt Schadenfreude's eyes rested briefly on the three girls, 'you've all made right twits of yourselves.'

There were a few faint rumblings of protest. Aunt Schadenfreude cut them off with a look.

'We are waiting on a few others, but I suppose we had best begin. I'd like to see this resolved quickly, as I have been mightily inconvenienced over the past few days, and I should like to go to bed.'

Denouement

'Firstly, it was Candour who pushed me down the stairs. I can see this comes as a shock to many of you, at which I can only express my disappointment at your poor judgement of character. After I announced my retirement, Candour came to my study with a wonderful song and dance about how his marriage could save the Family, if only I named him Patriarch and blessed his marriage to Daisy DeMille. There was a lot of disturbing talk about finding the Hoard and *"restoring our Family to glory".'* Scorn dripped from her voice. 'When he was finished, I informed him of what I'd learned over the years: that he was in serious debt, that he had left several well-meaning heiresses in the lurch after robbing them of their money, and that he was currently in the process of doing the same to Miss DeMille. Is that correct, Candour?'

Candour shook his head vigorously. 'It's not true!' he cried. 'Please, everyone, you have to believe me—'

'Oh well. I suppose it was too charitable of me to think you might live up to your name at this, the denouement,' sighed Aunt Schadenfreude. 'I, however, have enough *honesty and truthfulness* for the both of us. I told him where he could shove his backwards ideals, and left the room. I didn't realize he'd followed me until he grabbed my walking stick.'

Aunt Schadenfreude paused to sip her hot chocolate.

'I was too unconscious to be a reliable witness for the next part of the story,' she said. 'Telling this tale will be a little like playing pass the parcel, each person taking off another layer of wrapping paper until we get to the truth beneath. I now pass the story to you, Inheritance.'

Inheritance adjusted her glasses. 'Yes, well . . . the history of our great Family is my lifelong passion . . .'

Inheritance told everyone of her hunt for pieces of Swift history, of the maps and blueprints, papers and letters she had amassed. How, when she had stumbled upon the lost diary of Aunt Memento, she called the

Reunion with the hope that the EEK would help finally recover Vile's Hoard and save the House.

'I wanted to tell you all right away,' said Inheritance. 'But Schadenfreude warned me to keep my discovery quiet. She *incorrectly* –' she raised her voice slightly –'assumed that the EEK was unreliable, but *correctly* assumed that someone would try to use any information it revealed about the Hoard for their own ends. I couldn't believe any one of us would act against the Family's best interests.' She ripped off the pinky finger of one glove in agitation. 'I was a fool. And what was even more foolish was asking Gumshoe to look into what had happened to Aunt Schadenfreude. I thought, with the name—'

'I believe Shenanigan, Erf, and I were next,' interrupted Phenomena. Her fingers twitched with the desire for a board, or a piece of chalk, or something with which to gesture. 'Despite Gumshoe's appalling destruction of the crime scene—'

'Be nice, Phenomena – he is dead,' murmured Cook.

'I won't pretend he was a good detective just because he's *dead*,' huffed Phenomena. 'Anyway, despite him, we began our investigation logically. Our shortlist of suspects was made up of everyone who missed dinner that first night, and shortened further by establishing everyone's alibis. We initially dismissed Candour because Aunt Dither said he had given her a sedative to help her cope with her deipnophobia, and stayed on watch with her afterwards.'

'He did,' insisted Dither, her parrot hat wobbling with conviction. 'We played chess and then, when the others turned up, we switched to scabby queen to accommodate the extra players.'

'The . . . others?' asked Phenomena.

'Of course! Pharaoh Ramses III, my brother Findal, and Mary Shelley.'

There was a brief silence.

'They're all dead people, Aunt Dither.'

'Really? Well, dead or not, that Ramses owes me fifty pounds.'

'I suppose it must have been a rather strong sedative,' said Phenomena weakly. 'I think it's safe to assume that Aunt Dither's statement was not reliable.' She gathered herself. 'Er. Yes. Our first real clue was a partial bean of *kopi luwak*, or civet coffee, found at the crime scene . . .'

Phenomena's part of the story took them through their chat with Flora and Fauna, their chance encounter with Gumshoe, and their interrogation of Atrocious and Pique, which had given them the idea that the Hoard and the attempted murder might be connected.

'Following the conversation, I had several questions,' said Phenomena, pacing back and forth with her hands tucked behind her back. 'What was our would-be-killer's motive? Who stood to gain the most from Aunt Schadenfreude's death? I don't mind saying that, at the time, my main suspect would have been you, Aunt Inheritance. But that was before we overheard a suspicious conversation between—'

At that moment, the door to the study opened, and Uncle Maelstrom entered, supporting the last missing member of the group.

'– Flora and Daisy,' finished Phenomena.

When Daisy saw Flora, she gave a cry and ran to her, clasping her good hand.

'I'm alright,' said Flora. 'I'm *alright*.' Her eyes flickered over Daisy, as if she was checking every visible millimetre for damage. Daisy looked awful. Her hair was in disarray, and she had a bag of ice pressed to the side of her head. Shenanigan remembered the sickening crack the stock of the crossbow had made when it connected with her skull.

At the sight of her, some of the charm leaked back into Candour's face. 'Daisy,' he breathed, 'you must help me. Tell them I didn't—'

'*Don't you dare!*' The glare Flora turned on Candour could have melted steel. She tried to struggle upright, but Fauna and Daisy pressed her firmly back into her chair.

'I *don't* think so,' said Daisy to Flora, exasperated. 'You can sit right there until you've proved you can keep all your blood inside you. Right, Fauna?'

Flora slumped, scowling, between her wardens – but her hand remained in Daisy's.

'Miss DeMille,' said Aunt Schadenfreude crisply, looking Daisy over with faintly pursed lips. 'If you are feeling up to it, we should like to hear your side of things now.'

Daisy turned to face the room. Her spine straightened. Shenanigan was reminded again of that steel core running through her centre.

'In some ways, I guess this is an old song,' she said. 'Sing along if you know the words.

'I met Candour a few months ago. He swept me off my feet. He was sweet, funny, charming, kind, adventurous – he wanted to see the world, like I do, and help others. We went on vacation together. He met my family. He proposed.'

Thespian nodded. 'A whirlwind romance.'

'A perfect match,' added Renée.

'You were the golden couple of the society pages,' said Covetous. 'But then . . .?'

'But then I discovered money had been going missing.' Daisy twisted the ring on her finger. 'Candour said he'd "borrowed" it to buy my engagement ring.'

'He said he was just having a little financial trouble, perhaps?' suggested Pique.

'But still wanted to buy you something worthy of your beauty?' added Atrocious.

'Yes, and I believed him, and we put it behind us.' Daisy's eyes glittered. 'But the money kept disappearing. My signature turned up on cheques I'd never signed. I knew he was drawing money out of my bank account, but it wasn't like I couldn't spare it and, anyway, I loved him.'

'You're right,' said Aunt Inheritance. 'This *is* an old song.'

Daisy looked up. When she spoke again, her voice was hard. 'Let me tell you something about my family. Our name isn't as established as yours. My parents came from nothing, and some people never forget that. This awful old dowager once said to me that "new money is paper, old money is gold", and it took me a while to understand what she meant. She meant that my family could have more money than the Federal Reserve, but because there isn't a coat of arms somewhere with *DeMille* on it – or even *Mills*, which was our name before we changed it – we don't *matter.*'

Flora squeezed Daisy's hand.

'Like I said,' she said, breathing deeply, 'it's an old song, but I didn't learn it till it was too late. When Aunt Schadenfreude called Candour a leech that first night, it was like a pail of cold water. I knew I had to confront him about the missing money.'

Daisy didn't look at Candour. She fixed her eyes on the far wall.

'He just laughed. He told me he'd gained access to my accounts within a month of meeting me, and had been siphoning money ever since. I said I wanted to break off the engagement, but he said that if I exposed him, my family would never recover from the scandal. We'd be laughing stocks. It would confirm everything people thought about us. He said the only way to save face was a sham marriage and a divorce in a year or two, once he'd got all the cash he needed.'

The Swifts nodded. It was the story Shenanigan herself had been telling about Daisy and Candour the whole time – that one of them was marrying the other for their money. She'd just got it the wrong way round.

Daisy shook her head, disgusted. 'You all probably think I'm stupid.'

Aunt Schadenfreude shook her head. 'No,' said she and Flora together. Candour looked as if he wanted to say something, but Aunt Schadenfreude's stick slipped and caught him on the broken leg.

'Candour made up something about migraines to explain why I wasn't coming down for dinner,' Daisy continued, 'but after Cook brought me my tray I snuck out. I was still in shock, I was just wandering. I ran into Flora by accident. She took one look at my face – I'd been crying, I was a total mess – and told me to tell her everything. She promised to help me.'

'You didn't think to come to us?' Aunt Schadenfreude turned a disapproving stare on Flora.

'Obviously not,' snapped Flora. 'You gave us no reason to trust you.'

'I swore her to secrecy,' Daisy put in. 'I couldn't risk word of this getting out. We wanted to contact my lawyer – Atrocious was hogging the phone, we couldn't get to it right away – and find a way to quietly dissolve the engagement without my family's name getting dragged through the mud. Afterwards, I ran back to my room, in case Candour noticed I was gone.'

'And you never suspected him of pushing Aunt Schadenfreude?' asked Phenomena.

Daisy shook her head. 'I didn't think he was capable of that. I didn't even know he'd been to see her that night.'

'*I* suspected,' said Flora. Her good shoulder lifted in a shrug. 'But then, I suspected most of you, because you're heinous. It didn't matter. Once the cars and the phone were sabotaged, we had no way of getting a message out. I remembered the hidden passage in your study, Aunt Schade, from when Fauna and I stayed here. Daisy and I were going to borrow a road atlas, steal Cook's bike – sorry, Cook, we nicked your keys and one of Maelstrom's compasses – slip out through the passage and drive till we found the nearest phone.'

'But then tonight I was packing for our escape, and I knocked over Candour's bag,' added Daisy. 'The crossbow was inside.'

'And by that time he'd somehow found out about us working together. He found me in the study. He had this tiny gun . . .'

Aunt Schadenfreude pulled the palm pistol from her pocket and placed it on the table by her elbow.

'Yeah,' said Flora. 'That one.'

Shenanigan stared at the palm pistol. She had been the one to tell Candour about Flora and Daisy. Her map had led him to the study. Daisy and Flora could have got away unharmed, but instead Daisy had found Flora slumped in a chair, bleeding and seemingly dead. No wonder she had turned the crossbow on Candour.

Aunt Schadenfreude tapped her stick thoughtfully. 'I think it's best if we call for an interval at this stage,' she said. 'More refreshments are needed. If you wish to use the toilet, go now.'

It really was like the interval in the middle of a play. People chatted among themselves as Cook came round again with more cocoa for the deserving. Candour did not get cocoa. Candour got filthy looks, mostly. He bore this with unnerving calm, smiling absently at the wall, as if he had a second gun hidden up his sleeve, invisible and loaded. It made Shenanigan uneasy.

They resumed their tale at the death of Gumshoe. Erf had to relate this bit over loud, despairing noises from Aunt Inheritance, who'd assumed her grandchild had been sitting quietly in a corner out of harm's way the entire weekend.

'The statue trap didn't kill Gumshoe – *Gran, please* – the crossbow trap did,' said Erf. 'Gumshoe arrived late to the Reunion, so he didn't hear Aunt Schadenfreude's speech about how dangerous – *I'm alright, I promise* – the library is. He found Aunt Schadenfreude's keys, and assumed it was fine to go in and start rifling through the books.'

'It was *The Lore and Law of the Family Swift* that got him,' added Shenanigan. 'Candour was following him, and saw the crossbow go off. He just took advantage of the convenient weaponry, and disguised the cause of death.'

Phenomena rubbed her temples. 'No wonder I've found this case so difficult to crack,' she muttered, glaring at Candour. 'You hardly planned *anything*. Everything you do is reactive. You're like nitrogen. On your own, pretty harmless, but introduce you to an unstable situation and . . .' She made an explosive sound. 'You make everything worse.'

The story was passed back to Phenomena, who recounted their retrieval of the crossbow bolt from Pamplemousse's body and the note with the killer's handwriting. When she mentioned that the place cards at Schadenfreude's funeral had been done in the same writing, Flora groaned.

'I never saw – I didn't even *look* at my card, or I'd have recognized the writing from the Scrabble moves. Wait – were you going to *frame Daisy*?' Flora struggled to her feet again, glaring hatchets at Candour, but Daisy and Fauna each put a hand on her good shoulder and sat her down.

'Everyone knows doctors have appalling penmanship,' noted Phenomena. 'And he'd already been forging Daisy's cheques for months.'

'Daisy would have been the easiest suspect to sell to the Family,' added Cook. Shenanigan remembered with shame the speed of her own suspicion. 'What a good thing *most of you* decided it was me.'

As Jilt and her cohorts shuffled their feet and coughed uncomfortably, Maelstrom, clearly feeling left out, recounted the seance they had conducted with the EEK. When he mentioned the ghost's message that the treasure was 'UNDER HOUSE', several people surreptitiously made a note. One or two eyed the door.

'It wasn't a ghost,' insisted Phenomena. Cook looked smug. 'It was a random fluctuation of electromagnetic energy or – or we subconsciously influenced it, or something!'

'Speaking of dead people –' Felicity glared at Aunt Schadenfreude – 'what did we bury?'

This pause was more uncomfortable than the first.

'Ah, yes.' Aunt Schadenfreude sipped her chocolate.

'You buried a suit of armour, actually. I woke up after Pamplemousse's unfortunate demise. Cook was by my side. The two of us hatched a plan: she would smuggle me out of my study via the secret passage, we would fake my death, and I would wait in the cellar until the time was right to reveal the truth. I borrowed a trick from Shakespeare and was going to surprise Candour by appearing as a ghost at dinner tonight.'

'And you thought this plan required just the two of you?' asked Maelstrom, his voice soft and hurt.

'I rather wanted to derive some joy from Candour's suffering. If only there was a word for that.'

'Ah, I see. The girls and I were *grieving*, Schadenfreude,' said Maelstrom.

Aunt Schadenfreude shifted. 'I . . . underestimated the impact my death would have. We have rehearsed it so often.'

Maelstrom gave her a look that promised future discussion.

'Shenanigan,' he prompted, 'it's your turn.'

A few hours ago, Shenanigan would have relished being the centre of attention, the grand finale to a long and complicated mystery. But now all she wanted to do was sleep. Still, she gathered herself up, and stretched.

'Alright,' she said. 'So, while you were all busy wrongly accusing Cook, and Aunt Schadenfreude was hiding in the cellar, and Flora was bleeding everywhere, I saw Daisy leading Candour into the hedge maze . . .'

When Shenanigan had finished her part of the story, there was a sigh of relief.

'GOOD SHOW, SHENANIGAN!' said Fortissimo.

'Yes, you were so very brave!' said Dither.

'You could have been a bit quicker off the mark,' said Pique.

'So, who's going to call the police?' asked Felicity.

There was a dead silence. Aunt Schadenfreude blinked. 'Police? Nobody is calling the police.'

It said a lot about Felicity that, despite all the outrage she'd expressed in the past few days, she still had some left over.

'But . . . but Candour *murdered* someone!'

Candour, who had almost faded into the carpet, finally spoke.

'Technically,' he said, a smile in his voice, 'I didn't murder anyone. I just took a crossbow, borrowed a book, and . . . rearranged Gumshoe's head a bit. Auntie's obviously fine, as is dear Flora. I'm not even guilty of property damage – I've no idea who stole all your steering wheels, or broke the phone.'

'Oh,' said Daisy, 'I'm pretty sure that was Gumshoe. I saw him tossing things in the lake on the first night.'

Phenomena sighed, and Shenanigan rolled her eyes. Trap everyone in the House to stop the killer from escaping, and buy himself time to solve the case? That seemed like a Gumshoe move.

'He still tried to poison me!' said Phenomena.

'And kicked John the Cat!' added Erf.

'He *murdered Pamplemousse*!' cried Felicity. 'In front of all of us!'

Candour grinned lazily. 'Aunt Inheritance?'

The Archivist sighed. 'There is no Family law against *attempted* murder,' she said grudgingly. 'In the past, it was considered useful training, so one could get used to outsmarting assassins. As for Pamplemousse,' she continued over Felicity's indignant shout, 'he challenged Candour to a duel to the death. Candour won. Under the duelling code set out by Litigious Swift in 1737, Candour committed no crime by killing Pamplemousse. It's all set out quite clearly in *The Lore and Law of the Family Swift.*'

'So . . . he isn't going to be punished?' asked Shenanigan.

She looked at Felicity, whose expression was the same as it had been after Felicity had released the moths from her wardrobe roughly seven hundred years ago. Then she looked at Aunt Schadenfreude, stiff-necked and impassive.

'Yes, he will,' the Matriarch said. 'He will be excommunicated. He will be stripped of his name. No one in the Family shall ever contact him again, or provide him any aid or assistance. Flora, Daisy – if either of you should wish to hire a bounty hunter to enact further justice for the injury you have suffered, that is within your right.'

'I'll think about it,' said Flora grimly.

'In short –' Aunt Schadenfreude's tone was icy, and Candour quailed under the gaze she now turned on him – 'Candour Swift will no longer exist. Inheritance will expunge your name from our records. All documentation proving your existence will be shredded. Every one of your assets – your money, your home, your medical degree – will be seized, redistributed, or destroyed. You will have nothing. You will be no one.' Her lips quirked. 'Not even a ghost.'

'But I didn't do anything *wrong*,' said Candour, his voice shaking. 'You can't – you can't do that.'

'I can,' said Aunt Schadenfreude. 'I have already started.'

And she reached out and tore the gold name badge from his jacket.

Candour began to shout. They weren't even words. They were howls, incoherent screams of rage. He thrashed in his ropes, rocking the desk, until a paperweight fell and hit his broken leg. He shrieked once in pain, and then lay back, panting.

'This is an injustice,' he hissed. 'I know some of you agree with me. And there are others. I won't be made to disappear. I—'

'Cover him in a blanket and toss him in the freezer with his handiwork. At breakfast tomorrow, I shall pick my successor,' said Aunt Schadenfreude, ignoring him thoroughly. 'Dismissed.'

34. KIN AND KIND

Shenanigan woke before dawn with Phenomena's elbow in her face and Felicity's knee in the small of her back. She sat up. She had been thinking in her sleep, and all the tossing and turning had loosened the braid Felicity had plaited into her hair. The moon lit her sister's room like a black-and-white film, all deep shadows and shades of grey.

It was the work of a moment to pickpocket Phenomena's lab coat and take her casebook. Shenanigan crouched in a handy scrap of moonlight and flipped past the neat notes and diagrams of the case to a page at the back, where Phenomena had drawn the table titled *Nominative Determinism in the Case of Shenanigan Swift*. She totted up the marks in the *In Character* and

Out of Character columns. There were an equal number of marks in each.

Shenanigan, it has been mentioned before, was a doing-something person. Looking at the page, at the summary of herself, she made a decision. She wasn't sure if what she was about to do was *In Character* or *Out of Character*, right or wrong, but she felt it was something she needed to do.

The door to the Coral Bedroom, when she reached it, was open, the room empty. She found Daisy sitting on the top stair of the grand staircase in her dressing gown and a yellow silk hair wrap, clutching a cup of coffee.

Shenanigan perched beside her. She wasn't too sure of her welcome.

'I'm drinking one of your clues,' Daisy said, by way of greeting. '*Kopi luwak*. I figured if I paid for it, I might as well drink it.' She winked conspiratorially at Shenanigan, and lowered her voice to a stage whisper. 'Don't tell Flora, but I don't get the fuss. It tastes just like regular store-brand coffee to me.'

After everything that had happened, Daisy was being nice to her. It was unbearable.

'I'm sorry I thought it was you,' blurted Shenanigan. There was more she wanted to say. She had considered pledging a life debt, or offering her service as squire or something, but she was pinned in place by Daisy's softly startled look.

'You're a *kid*,' Daisy said, as if that explained everything.

They both stared down into the hall. Much of the broken glass had already been swept away, and all seemed perfectly normal until Shenanigan spotted a nailed wooden board where a window should have been. The Family had been wounded, and the House along with it. Shenanigan was about to wound them further.

'What do *you* want, Daisy?' asked Shenanigan. 'Nobody asked.'

Daisy sipped her coffee.

'Is it revenge?'

Daisy shook her head. 'There's a saying – "he who seeks vengeance should dig two graves".'

Shenanigan thought. 'Well, that doesn't make any sense. Unless you need to get revenge on two people, I suppose.'

Daisy, when she laughed for real, snorted a bit.

'Justice, then,' Shenanigan pressed. 'I don't know. I just thought that, even though you didn't get shot or poisoned or pushed down the stairs, you still got hurt.'

She chewed absently at her thumb. 'I came to tell you that I can get a message out, if you still want help.'

'How?' Daisy asked.

Shenanigan led Daisy through the still-sleeping House, up to the skylight in her room and on to the roof. The sky was going grey at the edges, ageing into morning. She fished out her torch.

'Won't you get in trouble?' asked Daisy.

Shenanigan grinned. 'Oh yes. But I'm used to it.'

She sat for a second, trying to figure out how she could possibly sum up everything that had happened. Then she remembered the first piece of Morse code her Uncle Maelstrom had ever taught her. It was what ships used when they were in trouble and there was no time to explain the situation. It was what people used when they needed help, and all the words in the world wouldn't work as well as three simple letters.

Shenanigan flashed her torch.

$\cdots - - \cdots$

S O S

★

The sound of giggling yanked Shenanigan out of sleep for the second time that morning and, for a split second, she thought she was back in the cellar, listening to her Family laugh themselves to death. But as her eyes focused she saw Felicity and Fauna at the dressing table, rifling through her sister's make-up.

'How about this one?' said Felicity, holding up a small tube.

'I've never really liked lipstick,' Fauna admitted. 'Flora, do you want to try?'

Fauna had a towel wrapped round her head, and was wearing a long, patterned dressing gown. Flora sat on the end of the bed, throwing coffee beans with her good arm and catching them in her mouth.

'Hmm. Maybe?' she said. She took the tube and squinted at the label. 'On second thought, no. I'm not wearing anything with a name like Pink Passion.'

Shenanigan started. Flora's hair was gone. Not all of it, but most of it, and what was left had been cut into a short, sharp bob. She looked as if she should be in a cabaret somewhere. She wore all black.

'I think *I'm* more of an eyeshadow person,' said Fauna decidedly. She picked up a pot of emerald green and turned it in her fingers. She had painted her nails.

'Ooh!' squealed Felicity, 'I made a dress in just that colour!'

'What are you all doing?' mumbled Shenanigan.

Fauna beamed at her. 'We're having a makeover!'

'Right now?'

'No time like the present. Ugh, Purple Prose? Who names these?' muttered Flora, rummaging through Felicity's box of make-up.

Shenanigan's gaze flicked from one twin to the other. 'I thought you liked to look the same?'

Fauna smiled. 'Things are changing. For the better, I think.'

'Yesterday was . . .' Flora made a gesture with her good hand, which Shenanigan took to mean *catastrophic and generally very bad*.

'Flora nearly died,' said Fauna. 'I saw her and it was like looking into my own face.' She shuddered, and applied some powder to her eyelid. 'I realized that if she died . . . I'd spend the rest of my life looking into a mirror and seeing my dead sister.'

'And I realized that it was holding us back,' said Flora. 'The more alike we looked, the harder we clung together, the harder it was to let the rest of the world in.'

'Besides, Flora and Fauna aren't words that mean the same thing, are they? They complement each other,' added Fauna.

'So we decided: no more matching. No more compromising and trying to avoid things the other doesn't like. Life is short.'

'And now so is your hair,' said Fauna. 'Which leads nicely into *my* big reveal. Ready?' She stood up, one eyelid green with eyeshadow. 'Okay . . . and . . . ta-dah!' She whipped the towel from her head, revealing her newly scarlet hair, still damp from the shower. She beamed.

Felicity clapped. Flora tried to clap, winced, and settled for giving a thumbs-up instead. 'Oh, you look *excellent*,' she said. 'I definitely couldn't pull that off. Aha!' She pulled a small black tube out of Felicity's make-up box. 'Signature Scarlet. Fliss, how about this one?'

'Go for it,' said Felicity, who had been half swallowed by her massive wardrobe. A dazed moth fluttered out and landed on the mirror.

Flora swiped her lips with a deep red, and eyed herself critically. 'Hmm. Not bad.'

'I couldn't pull it off,' said Fauna.

The twins looked into the mirror. The crease in Flora's forehead was still there, and the laughter lines at the corner of Fauna's mouth. But Shenanigan couldn't believe she'd ever got them confused. They'd maybe looked the same, but that was just to hide the fact that they were very different people. Now Flora was sharp and dark with a slash of red lipstick, and Fauna soft and bright with hair like a beacon. The only thing that matched was their smiles.

Shenanigan left them trying on clothes and wandered down to breakfast. On the way, she passed the door to the once-secret room, now just a charred hole in the wall. Inside, Phenomena was glaring at the EEK and making notes on a clipboard. Her white lab coat was smudged with soot, but the machine was just as clean and shiny as ever.

'I *will* find out how you work, you wretched thing,' Shenanigan heard her mutter.

Shenanigan slid down the banister and marched through the hall, passing the stairs to the kitchen as Cook and Daisy emerged with a platter of bacon and a tureen of scrambled eggs. Daisy looked a lot better, and had just said something that was making Cook laugh uproariously. Shenanigan took advantage and stole a rasher of bacon while she was distracted.

At the first unboarded window, she looked out. Uncle Maelstrom stood on the edge of the lake beside Pique, Renée, and Ferrier, each holding fishing rods. Pique began to reel in his line, dredging a round shape out of the water – a steering wheel. He added it to the growing pile behind them. Maelstrom clapped him on the back so hard he nearly tipped into the lake.

In the library, Aunt Inheritance was frowning at a very shaky Erf. Shenanigan paused by the door, in case they needed back-up.

'It doesn't fit me, Gran,' they said. 'Everything about it feels wrong.'

'But, dear,' Aunt Inheritance said, 'the Dictionary gave you that name. It knows all. It . . .' But then she hesitated. Inheritance looked at Erf and the way their hands fidgeted in the cuffs of their jumper, though their gaze was steady. '. . . It doesn't know everything. And neither do I. But I'd like to learn.'

She began fumbling through her pockets, and brought out a plaster.

'Erf, dear,' she said, and Erf's eyes widened at the use of their real name, 'do you have your name badge?'

Erf dug the little bar of gold out of their trouser pocket. Aunt Inheritance stuck the plaster over the name, then looked around for a pen, finally locating one in her hair.

'There,' Inheritance said, writing three letters on the name tag. 'Until we get you a proper one made.'

Erf's grin could have felled someone at fifty paces. Inheritance took off her white gloves and wrapped her arms round her grandchild.

Shenanigan left Erf to do the crying and hugging, making a mental note to find them later. They could take a little trip to the cellar and get rid of Erf's old gravestone. Phenomena probably still had something explosive stashed away somewhere. They'd need matches, a rope, and a skateboard.

After today the House would be empty again. There would be a great exhale of people, and all the Swifts would fly back out into the world, for better or worse. Shenanigan was relieved. Family was exhausting, and complicated, and everyone was their own person, which meant you had just as much chance of getting along with them as you did with any stranger off the street. Just sharing blood wasn't enough to make someone *proper* family. She'd take Cook over most of her blood relatives any day.

As she ate her breakfast, she considered their guests. Uncle Ferrier could go, she decided. And Aunt Jilt. And Atrocious and Pique. Shenanigan had already put a long, jagged scratch down the side of Atrocious's car and hidden an egg under Pique's back seat, and she was confident that she could keep her grudge well fed until the next Reunion.

But then there was Erf, her new best cousin. And then there was Fauna, and Flora – and Dither and Fortissimo weren't so bad, really, and she probably would have grown fond of Pamplemousse if he'd lived longer. Maybe that was what Cantrip had been trying to say: *Be rich in kindness, and be rich in kind . . . each Reunion riches shall ye find.* She hadn't been talking about money. The point of the Reunion wasn't really to find the Hoard – it was just an excuse to bring everyone together as a family and find the worth in each other.

At the end of the meal, when the plates had been cleared away, Aunt Schadenfreude pulled back her chair with a screech.

'Right,' she said. 'We're all here. I'm sure you're waiting to hear who will take over from me as head of the Family. Well, I'm not going to beat about the bush. There was only one choice, for me.

'Over the last few days, I've heard of this person's courage, dignity, and sensitivity. Their kindness, as well, was an important factor. Many of you think I lack it. No one could say that about her.' Schadenfreude's hand drifted to her collar. 'If she will accept the title – though goodness knows why she would – then Fauna Swift is to be our new Matriarch.'

Fauna clapped a hand over her mouth. The applause was too loud for her to do anything but nod. She made her way to Aunt Schadenfreude in the green gown Felicity had made, her hair blazing, with her sister drumming on the table so hard Shenanigan worried Flora's bones might break. Beside Flora, Daisy was trying to show Erf how to whistle through their fingers.

Inheritance gently laid the Family Dictionary – liberated from its glass case for the occasion – on a lectern. Fauna placed her hand on its cover.

'Arch-Aunt Schadenfreude, Matriarch of the Swift Family, do you relinquish your title, and the powers and duties bestowed on you by the Family?' asked Aunt Inheritance solemnly.

Aunt Schadenfreude nodded. 'I do.' She sat. 'Finally.' She looked lighter. It was as if she'd been carrying something heavy for years and years, and had finally found a place to put it down.

She reached up and, with a tiny key Shenanigan had never seen before, loosened her iron collar.

Aunt Inheritance turned to Fauna.

'Fauna Swift, do you accept the position of head of the Family under the title of Matriarch?'

'I do.'

'Do you vow to uphold the honour and position of the Family, and to perform the duties that accompany this title? Do you swear to resolve disputes to the best of your ability, to protect and shelter those members of the Family who need it, to provide counsel and assistance to your kin? Do you swear also to gather us in when each decade passes, to reaffirm the ties between us, in blood and in bond?'

'I do.'

'Then, Fauna Swift, you are the new Matriarch of the Swift Family, and we trust your judgement.'

Fauna curtseyed, radiant. Cook brought out an

434

immense bouquet of flowers from the conservatory, and a kiss on the cheek from Fauna turned her scarlet. Someone called, 'Speech!'

Fauna held the flowers to her chest. 'A speech?'

'You'll have to make a lot of them,' said Aunt Schadenfreude. 'Might as well start now.'

'Alright.' Fauna paused to collect herself. Shenanigan saw her run her finger over the gold-embossed cover of the Dictionary, and smile.

'Aunt Schadenfreude is awful,' said Fauna.

Shenanigan choked on her orange juice. Fauna waited with a mischievous smile for everyone to stop squawking, though Aunt Schadenfreude herself looked unperturbed, even a bit amused. She nodded for Fauna to continue.

'It's right here, in the older section of the Dictionary.' Fauna pointed at a page, one of the early ones on parchment with long S's that looked like F's.

'Listen to this entry.'

awful (adjective):
profoundly impressive; inspiring respect

'Back when this was written, the word *awful* could mean something positive. Aunt Schadenfreude *is* awful.

She *is* profoundly impressive, and she certainly inspires respect.

'But, over time, people started using the word differently, to mean something terrible, or unpleasant. If you look at the newer section of the Dictionary, there's a fresh entry –' she flicked forward several hundred pages – 'here.'

> *awful (adjective)*
> *generally very bad*

'And so –' she closed the Dictionary with a thud – 'a few hundred years of language evolution later I've insulted my aunt. Oh dear.'

'Some would say the modern definition still applies,' said Aunt Schadenfreude archly.

A few gentle laughs. Fauna tucked her newly scarlet hair behind her ear.

'What I'm trying to say is that meanings evolve over time. Language changes, because people change. We need new words, new names for things. Like . . . like the way there wasn't a word for "telephone" until the telephone was invented. Do you see?

'The job of a Dictionary isn't to tell us what words

have to mean – it's to record us, as we are, and to change alongside us,' said Fauna. 'I think it's time for us, as a Family, to make a fresh entry. To do things because we think it's the *best* way, not because it's how we've always done them. To stop defining things, and start trying to describe them. And, if we can, to allow ourselves, and each other, to change and grow.' She smiled around at them. 'With that in mind—'

They all heard the noise, a blaring, still far off. Shenanigan's eyes met Daisy's over the porridge tureen. Atrocious pulled a pair of opera glasses from her pocket and went to the window.

She cursed. 'It's the police.'

A few people started to their feet, but Atrocious waved them back, her eyes still glued to the glasses. 'They're fiddling with the lock on the gate. Oh, one of them has bolt-cutters. They'll be here soon.'

Arch-Aunt Schadenfreude rose in a fury.

'Was I not clear?' she demanded. 'Who did this?' Her eyes swept the room.

Shenanigan took a steadying breath. She'd accepted the consequences last night. She wondered what Suleiman had said to the police to persuade them that a Morse code message from a child was grounds for an investigation. She wondered, once again, if she had done the right thing. She opened her mouth to confess.

Felicity stood up.

'It was me,' Felicity lied. 'I went to the roof, and I used Shenanigan's torch to signal for help.'

A groan rippled around the room. Shenanigan was still hovering half out of her seat, and Daisy had a look of confusion on her face, but Felicity shook her head minutely at them both – *no*.

'After I specifically told you not to?' cried Aunt Schadenfreude.

'Yes.' Felicity's chin was raised in defiance. She looked around at her Family. No one was telling her to shut up now. People were finally listening to what she had to say.

'We *aren't* better than anyone else,' Felicity said. 'You all keep talking about how special the Swifts are, how the rules don't apply to us. Candour believed that, and he did awful things, and then we turned around and only punished him for what he did to the Family, not to Daisy or any of the other people he swindled. If we let him out into the world, how long will it be before he finds someone else to cheat and manipulate and hurt? They might not be Swifts, but they'll be *someone*. Aunt Schadenfreude, you know I'm right.'

Aunt Schadenfreude looked devastated. 'I forbade this,' she said. 'Not as your aunt, but as your Matriarch. My word is – was – law.' Her fingers touched the discarded iron collar by her plate.

'Fine, then.' Felicity didn't cry. 'Do what you have to do. Kick me out, take my name badge, whatever—'

Daisy and Flora started shouting, and Inheritance started shouting, and Shenanigan climbed on the table so as to have the tactical shouting advantage, and Fauna had to bang on the lectern to be heard over the din.

'*Excuse me.* Could everyone please be quiet? And sit down.' She smiled at Felicity. 'I haven't finished my speech.'

Felicity sat. Shenanigan took her hand under the table, and squeezed it tight.

'I was *going* to say we should do things differently. Well, let's start now. Felicity, no one's kicking you out over one mistake. I don't even believe you made a mistake in the first place. You did what you thought was right – regardless of the consequences.' Fauna winked at Shenanigan, and Shenanigan knew she'd been rumbled.

'I'm dissolving the decree of the previous Matriarch – which I *can* do,' she said, raising her eyebrows at

Inheritance as if daring her to contradict her. 'Felicity, you won't be punished. Also . . .' Fauna winced. 'We are going to co-operate with the police. To an extent, at least. I don't want to see Candour back out in the world any more than Felicity does. Someone had better fetch him from the freezer. The rest of you . . . figure out what you're going to say when the police arrive.'

Fauna sat down. Aunt Schadenfreude gave her a look that would be inscrutable to most people, but that Shenanigan knew was reluctant approval. That was a relief. As Matriarch, Fauna would be living with them at the House now, after all. She wondered what role she'd play in Aunt Schadenfreude's funeral rehearsals.

In twos and threes, people left the dining room, some muttering furiously about standards and tradition, others commenting that perhaps, maybe, possibly, in extreme and trying circumstances, change *might* be quite good.

'Well,' said Atrocious, sidling up to Shenanigan, 'here come the coppers. And you thought Gumshoe was bad.' She shuddered. 'At least they can't make the place any more of a mess.'

'The House will be fine. We'll fix it when they're gone,' Shenanigan said defensively.

'You will not. A team of highly skilled contractors and

conservationists will fix it,' Atrocious corrected. 'That's what I'm paying them for.' At Shenanigan's astonished look, she laughed. 'Oh, don't look so surprised. De-Millions over there offered, but Schadenfreude wouldn't take her money. It's the principle of the thing. The House is our responsibility, so it ought to be a Swift who pays. I agreed to foot the bill for repairs and upkeep, on one condition.' She pointed, with an elegant finger, through the window and the grounds, to the splinter of Vile's Monument. '*That thing* comes down.'

Shenanigan stared hard at Atrocious. This was the last thing she'd expected. 'But . . . why?'

Atrocious shrugged. 'Why does anyone do anything?'

'I don't understand you,' said Shenanigan.

'I should hope not.' Atrocious nodded to her. 'I will be watching your career with interest, Shenanigan Swift.'

Shenanigan waited until her sister had finished a conversation with Daisy – an intense, animated affair that left Felicity beaming – before approaching.

'I'm making a promise,' she said solemnly. 'From now on, no rats in your bed. No more pranks. No more making fun of the things you like. I'm sorry I ever said you were boring. Or a traitor.'

Felicity rolled her eyes.

'If you stop doing all those things, how am I supposed to recognize you? I'll settle for no rats, thanks.' She spat on her hand and shook Shenanigan's. 'Ugh, that's disgusting.' She wiped her hand on Shenanigan's shirt.

'Have I missed something?' asked Phenomena warily, eyeing the two of them as if she was expecting a fight to break out. She had finally torn herself away from the EEK to grab what looked like a slice of toast with porridge spread on it.

'Lots,' said Felicity crisply. 'But actually, Phenomena, I've got something here I've been waiting to show you.' She pulled a notebook from her pocket. '*Voilà!*'

The last page contained the final, nonsensical words of the EEK, organized by someone with a talent for anagrams.

CAT DISHONOUR RENDERER

CENTURIES HOARD MURDER

CERTAIN HOURS MURDERED

And then, circled, was:

CANDOUR IS THE MURDERER

Phenomena stuck the end of her ponytail in her mouth.

'No,' she said flatly. 'Absolutely not. That is stup— No. There are thousands of possible letter combinations here. There's no reason to believe . . .'

Felicity hummed in amusement. 'Yes, you're right. It could have been saying –' she squinted at the page – 'ADDER HUM RESURRECTION. Or HORRID CENTAUR RESUMED. Perhaps MUSHIER CARROT ENDURED. Bit of a strange coincidence, though.'

'Yes, coincidence,' said Phenomena, but she looked unsure.

'And,' added Shenanigan, delighted, 'it *did* say we'd be better off asking the cat who the murderer was, and John the Cat was an important witness. He even scratched Candour.'

Phenomena looked as if her entire world had been picked up, turned upside down, and shaken for loose change.

Felicity smiled. 'Well, this has been fun, but Daisy told me she's thinking of moving to Paris, and I'm welcome to visit. And since it might only take her a few weeks to find an apartment, I'd better start packing now.'

Shenanigan watched her sister skip off to her room. Felicity would thrive in Paris. Her French was impeccable, or so Shenanigan supposed, as she herself had never bothered to learn a word of it.

There was a clatter as Cook knocked over the coffee pot, and Inheritance shrieked, grabbing the Dictionary out of its dark, paper-staining path. Then Inheritance screamed again, almost dropping the Dictionary into Schadenfreude's chair with an exclamation of horror.

'My gloves! I'm not wearing my gloves! Oh, the natural oils in my skin are sure to mar the paper and . . .'

She ran from the room.

Shenanigan approached the Dictionary. The EEK had been right about John the Cat. It had told them the identity of the murderer – in a roundabout way, at least. But what about the third message, the one about the Hoard?

For all Phenomena's antipathy toward hunches, Shenanigan wanted to follow this one. She had been thinking about Cantrip's prologue, about what endures. Opening the Dictionary – without gloves, because despite everything, she was still Shenanigan – she flipped through. Words flew past in scrawled handwriting, in crooked print, in neat typeface; on vellum, on parchment, on paper. She flipped past *gimbal* and *fractious* and *flibbertigibbet*, *karst* and *mellifluent* and *porcine*, until she found what she was looking for. It was old – one of the original entries. From, say, Grand-Uncle Vile's time.

house (noun)
i. a place of abode, a dwellynge
ii. family, royal or of noble lineage

The EEK had said to LOOK UNDER HOUSE. That could mean LOOK UNDER *THE* HOUSE, in the foundations. It could mean LOOK UNDER 'HOUSE', beneath the gravestone in the cellar. Or it could mean a third thing.

Shenanigan tore out the page and held it up to the window.

Light streamed through the thin paper. Buried among the type, winding their way through the definitions, were faint lines, the ghosts of rooms.

It was a map of the whole Swift estate, and in the middle of the page, right under *(noun)*, was an X.

Mark well the well-marked meaning of our days, Cantrip had said.

LOOK UNDER HOUSE, the ghost had said.

Cantrip Randrup-Swift, said the signature scrawled faintly on the page.

It really was silly to think that, with so many Swifts hunting for the Hoard for so many years, no one had ever found it. Grand-Uncle Vile didn't seem to have been very clever, after all. But his sister was. More importantly, she had loved her Family.

Shenanigan took out her own map, and started walking. There was no tower back in Vile's day, no conservatory. There were stabes, and an arboretum, and a folly, all of which had long since been demolished or rotted away, replaced by new embellishments. A hedge maze. A Scrabble court. Things changed, because things always do. The great oak tree that had flourished when three siblings were young had been cut down, reduced to a stump.

Shenanigan walked through the ghost of the House-that-was, and out of the House-that-is, into the grounds. The noise of sirens grew louder. Shenanigan followed the map until her feet hit wooden boards, and then she stopped.

There also hadn't been a lake in Vile's day. Cantrip had put it there. She had cut down the oak to make

room for it, hacking down the Family tree as brother
had hacked down brother.

But as you seek your pocketful of crowns,
Recall the poor man floats, the rich one drowns.

Cantrip had seen what wealth could do to her Family.
Of course she wouldn't want the treasure found – greed
could tear them apart, as it had before. But as long as
the Hoard remained lost, the lure of it of it would draw
the Swifts together, decade after decade, to search.

Cantrip had hidden the treasure in a fitting place:
somewhere the more gold you tried to carry, the more
it would weigh you down.

Shenanigan took off her shoes and socks, rolled up
her trouser legs, and let her feet dangle off the edge of the
pier. The police were crunching their way up the drive,
moving slowly past the other cars. The outside world
would be here soon, and Shenanigan didn't know what it
would bring. She stared into the lake. She could tell Aunt
Schadenfreude what she'd found, or Aunt Inheritance,
who would be over the moon at their recovered history.
She could tell Fauna, who was so kind and selfless that
she would probably donate it to good causes.

Or . . .

Harry Houdini had been able to hold his breath for over three minutes. With practice, Shenanigan was sure she could match that. No one would think it was strange if she took up swimming; she wouldn't have to tell anyone what she was really doing, not even Uncle Maelstrom. She could dive down and take the treasure for herself, piece by piece, and hoard it until she was old enough to steal it away. A real pirate at last.

The Shenanigan from a few days ago would have done exactly that – but things change. This Shenanigan, this several-days-older, morally gangly Shenanigan, wasn't so sure. And if she could become so different in only a few days, what would the Shenanigan of next month decide? Or next year?

Uncle Maelstrom and the others were putting away their fishing rods. The police were at the front door. Shenanigan tore the page into little pieces and scattered them on the lake. Then she picked up her shoes and socks, and headed back to the House. She didn't have to make her decision right now.

She would wait, and see who she grew into.

ACKNOWLEDGEMENTS

This is my first book, and my thanks go out to all the people who are as joyful and relieved as I am that it is out in the world:

To the WriteNow team at Penguin Random House UK, for running the scheme that changed my life.

To everyone at Puffin, for their hard work and enthusiasm.

To my long-suffering editor Ben Horslen, for being my mentor throughout this process. I handed Ben five chapters and a shrug of an outline, and he patiently guided me through every draft and every moment of self-doubt – until I'd made a book, where there never was a book. Thank you, Ben.

To my agent, Zoë Plant, for being generally incredible and specifically shrewd; for working harder and smarter than anyone I know, and for being my second in every (professional, book-related) duel.

To my US editor, Julie Strauss-Gabel, for her interest, insight, and expertise, and for pushing me into making this book the best version of itself.

To Claire Powell, for drawing the Swifts and making them real.

To my family – immediate, extended, and chosen – for supporting me through my deadlines and making sure I did all the trivial things like 'sleep' and 'go outside'.

To my friends, who have had to listen to me talk about nothing but this for the past few years.

To my partner, Stuart, for everything.

And, lastly, to my many, many teachers, in and out of school, from whom I have learned much and will continue to learn until the lights go out.